Author's disclaimer

*The following is purely a wor***

*and institutions are produc***

*intended to represen***

Also by Jonathan Last and
available from Amazon

Teaching with Chopsticks:

TEFL from the Frontline

How hard could it be?

Looking to 'do something totally random and out of character', recent graduate Jonathan Last took his lack of classroom experience and wariness about children onto a plane heading for Sanbon, South Korea and into a job teaching English as a foreign language (TEFL).

His year turned out to be a fascinating, honest insight into a diverse worldwide industry of countless personalities and cultures. His sometimes fun, sometimes painful, frequently hilarious journey required him to think on his feet and learn fast – not least about himself.

The Great
Football
Conspiracy

Jonathan Last

Contact the author

Twitter *@lastjonathan*
Email *greatfootballconspiracy@gmail.com*

© Copyright 2020 Jonathan Last
The right of Jonathan Last to be identified as author of
this work has been asserted by him/her in accordance
with the Copyright, Designs and Patents Act 1988
All Rights Reserved

This book is for Jasper

'If football has taught me anything it is that you can overcome anything if, and only if, you love something enough.'
– Lionel Messi

'Just because you're paranoid doesn't mean they're not after you.'
– Joseph Heller, *Catch-22*

OCTOBER, 1863.

The grandfather clock's third chime faded to silence within the cramped attic. The Captain raised his head. And as he cast an eye over the men stood before him, he smiled.

His ten brethren faced him in two lines of four with a pair up front. Apart from the armband engraved with a letter C that their leader wore, they were all dressed identically, in green hooded cloaks with white football pitch markings sewn on the chest. The night outside was moonless, and the only light flickered from candles, which bathed the ceremony in a hypnotic glow.

The Captain was smiling because he was proud. Together they were fathering the birth of a new age, right here above The Freemasons Tavern in London.

'Brothers,' The Captain began. 'Each of you plays a key role in our society. Representatives of the left and right wing, defenders of the realm, forward thinkers... you all have your position but are part of a greater whole.'

Sombre nods greeted his words.

'We all knew this day would come. The game has moved on from battles between rival villages, organised by local breweries to create a thirst for them to satisfy. It is time to turn chaos into order, to organise the rabble.'

The Captain went on to recap the basic rules of association football. Each man present marvelled again at the simplicity of the sport, how children could play it in a park with nothing but a ball and rolled-up pullovers. But the men also knew that the professional game needs parameters: 11 playing on each team; play lasting 90 minutes; one goal meaning one point. These rules, and others, had already been established ahead of this formal documenting ceremony.

The important part came now.

The Captain waited until each man's head was bowed.

'Let us not be naïve, gentlemen. The game is sacred; therefore, it is vulnerable. It needs guardians. The world changes and so football should accordingly. But there are fundamentals which must never alter, lest the game be corrupted. In addition to the rules we are putting onto official record today we shall create two more, which together will act as an impenetrable line of defence, unbreakable under any circumstance.'

The Captain explained that they were to forge these 'defences' and then store them securely. The group was to take measures so that only one whose heart was truly pure in football would be able to find them – and use the enlightenment they contained to defeat the game's foes.

The Captain outlined the rest of his plan. And when he was done, and the men raised their heads, a single thought occupied their minds. Football is important – more important, perhaps, than life or death. They hoped that all this was merely a precaution, that the game would never find its core principles so fatally threatened.

They hoped.

A UGUST, the present.

'Blimey, this looks a bit posh.'

Frank Tuttle halted his mates Joel and Andy on the street six yards short of *Bar Onze un Côté*. The three of them were just shy of the velvet rope that would soon hold back hordes of London's trendy young drinkers, but which stood alone right now since the men were unfashionably early.

In fact, Frank, it has to be said, was unfashionable full-stop. Since on this night he was taking a rare step out of his comfort zone, he had dressed up for the occasion: his best M&S 'casuals line' shirt clumsily ironed; relaxed-fit jeans; trainers scrubbed to a bright white; beige bomber jacket tucked in.

Usually a Friday night out for Frank meant between six and ten pints of lager in his local, The Crunching Tackle on Brent Park High Road, a stone's throw from Wembley Stadium. Then the evening would conclude with a visit to Abra-kebabra takeaway, followed by Frank vomiting up a doner wrap with chilli sauce during the stumble home. But tonight was different.

Joel, his decades-old Ben Sherman hanging half in and half out, nudged Frank forward. 'Can't bottle it one-on-one with the keeper, mate,' he said, referring to the beast of a bouncer who was eyeing up the three 40-something white men warily.

Together the trio moved behind the rope and joined the non-existent queue.

'Come on, Franko,' Andy said, checking that the taped-on arm on his glasses was holding. 'You won this prize; we may as well have a butcher's.'

This wasn't quite true – Frank hadn't *won* the hundred-pound bar tab and place on the VIP guest list, he'd *earned* them. Finding himself at a loss following The Incident at the final game of the Brent Under 14s Boys League last season – which had been his last game as the team's manager – he had begun playing the FA's *Official Online Fantasy Football (OOFF)* over the summer and had been awarded the prize for a record-breaking string of results. The catch was that it was valid for tonight only – pretty tight, considering he'd only been informed over the phone this afternoon. Frank was pleased with what he'd achieved on the fantasy football game, but it felt hollow: applying his unconventional yet inspired grasp of football tactics to a simulation was nothing compared to the real thing.

Frank didn't want to admit it to his mates, but he was a bit intimidated by the swankiness of where they were to spend this week's Friday night session. He felt like he had at 16, trying to get into the pub with a fake ID. But he hitched his jeans above his gut and straightened up, so his bald patch was about level with the bouncer's pectorals.

'Frank Tuttle,' he told the man. 'I should be on a VIP list or something…?'

The bouncer frowned and consulted his papers.

'Frank? Who's that?' asked Joel.

'Yeah,' added Andy, 'your name's Colin, not Frank.'

Frank smiled awkwardly as the bouncer continued to look down his list of names.

'In,' the man said finally. 'And no trouble.'

'You pair of muppets,' Frank grinned at his mates as they all entered.

The three of them headed straight for the bar, dodging the currently empty dancefloor. A few suits stood about with their end-of-week drinks.

Andy was reacting to the bouncer's comment. '"No trouble"? Who's he think we are? Bloody hooligans?'

'Calm down, Anders,' said Joel. 'He didn't mean nothing.'

'No, but… few blokes turn up who aren't working for bloody investment banks and he thinks we're here for a tear-up. Wanker. We ought to show him and actually *have* a tear-up.'

'Crikey.' Joel turned to Frank as they reached the bar. 'Franko, you better get some liquid to put him out.'

Frank got the barmaid's attention.

'What can I get you?' she asked, after confirming his bar tab.

Frank scanned the selection. 'Er, you got nothing on tap?'

'Afraid not.' She gestured behind her. 'But we have a large selection of bottled lagers.'

Joel brazenly put his hands flat on the bar, said "Giz a look," and then leaned over. Frank, suspecting that Joel really wanted a closer look at the barmaid, mouthed *sorry* to her. She took it in her stride and smiled at Frank.

The three men went for a Korean lager named Hite and, once Frank had got over how a three-person round cost more than 20 pounds, they settled into a booth. Although they had access to the VIP area, they all felt more comfortable drinking in the regular bar for now.

Finally, they could relax and focus on their favourite topic.

'Thank God it's back tomorrow,' said Frank.

'A reason for living again,' said Joel. The three of them clinked bottles.

'Still,' said Andy after they'd all taken a swig, 'you know this season is gonna be the same as every year.'

'Bloody hell,' said Joel. 'Captain Negative on the deck.'

'He's right, though,' said Frank. 'The stuff we get annoyed about every year. Like refs favouring the bigger teams.'

'And them same big teams getting injury time until they score a winner,' said Andy.

'And diving.'

'And dodgy offside decisions.'

'All of that.'

'What about VAR?' asked Joel. 'Ain't that levelled things up a bit?'

Andy waved dismissively. 'They'll find a way of fiddling it eventually.'

'Bloody hell,' said Joel again, taking a big gulp of beer while watching a group of young women sitting down. 'Not worth having football back if it means I've got to listen to you two's moaning.'

'Well,' said Frank, 'that stuff does happen, you can't deny it, mate. But at the same time, isn't that what makes the game...' He searched for the right word.

'Frank's right, it's all part of it,' Andy conceded. 'And it gives us something to talk about in the pub. It just feels like it gets worse every year. Like it's not just an ugly side, but the ugly side is taking over.'

The statement hung in the air.

'Still though,' said Frank, 'we all go on about how things are biased against us, no matter who we support. But it's just pub talk. Right?'

Andy and Joel shrugged.

Frank tried to lighten the tone. 'What about this Family Fun Day they're doing over at Wembley tomorrow? That's something good, right? Gonna be stuff all over the stadium apparently, games and that, prizes, ex-players in a charity match and all of it.'

Joel had been watching the women's table again, but this got his attention back. 'Yeah, and right before the 3pm games kick off we're gonna finally find out what this big FA announcement they've been building up to is all about.'

'Yeah,' said Frank, 'been hearing about that all day on the radio.'

'Probably cost of tickets going up again, further pricing out the average supporter,' said Andy.

By now a DJ had appeared and was beginning his set.

The three men winced at the loud dance music. While they were acclimatising to the noise, Joel had a thought.

'Eh, Frank,' he shouted with a glance at Andy. 'Maybe this announcement thing is gonna be a call for some tactical ideas from the common man.'

Frank sensed a wind-up and smiled back wanly. 'Yeah, yeah. Good one.'

'Not so common if they're your tactics though, eh Franko?' said Andy.

'Come on Frank. What one would you tell them about? What about the "noughts and crosses" formation?'

'Or the one about playing for throw-ins. How does that work again?'

'Oh yeah, how *does* that one work?'

Frank knew they were taking the piss.

But he couldn't help himself.

'Well,' he began, shifting position, 'I came up with it after watching Stoke back when they were in the Premier League. That Rory Delap fella. So, the idea is—'

But before Frank could get into the nitty-gritty, he had to attend to his ringing mobile phone.

One look at the caller ID and his mood plummeted.

Frank swallowed hard and swiped the screen.

'Hi, Bethan.'

Andy and Joel winced in unison.

'Where the hell are you? It's really loud.'

Frank cursed inwardly. It seemed that he had *more* contact with his wife now that they weren't living under the same roof.

He made a *you-know-how-it-is* face to his mates and headed to the smoking area.

Outside in the courtyard Frank returned to his call.

'Is this better?'

'So, what, you've started going out to bars now?'

Frank struggled to control his emotions. A couple of bevvies with his pals on a Friday night, albeit in a trendier place than normal – so what?

'Just drinks with the boys. It's a funny story actually – you know I told you I've been playing that football management computer game? Well—'

'Yeah yeah.' Bethan got straight to the point. *'I'm just calling to remind you about... well, why don't you tell me?'*

Frank gritted his teeth. 'I know where I need to be tomorrow morning, Bethan.'

'And where is that? Indulge me.'

Frank sighed. 'Picking up Ian after football training.'

'Good.'

'Is that everything?' He knew that it wouldn't be.

'Frank... don't make a scene tomorrow. Okay? Please?'

The Incident. Of course, she couldn't resist bringing *that* up. Frank had to control his temper – the very thing that had got him into so much trouble in the first place.

'What you mean by "scene"?'

'Don't be obtuse, Frank. It'll be the first time you've been there since... well...'

'Since they fired me as manager.'

'Yes.'

'You know they overreacted, Bethan.'

No reply.

'I was only trying to—'

'Frank, what you did – during a game, in front of a group of 13-year-olds, not to mention all the parents – was unacceptable.'

Now it was Frank's turn to be silent. She was right. He *had* overreacted and he *had* been in the wrong. Thinking about the example he had set for his son Ian still made him feel sick with guilt.

Frank knew what he needed to do. What would make things right and put him on the path to repairing his marriage: apologise. Reach deep inside, past his pride and bitterness, and say the words *I'm sorry.*

What he actually said was, 'Yeah, well, I was just sticking up for my principles. The sacking was all political.'

Bethan was quiet for several seconds. Finally, unable to keep the disappointment out of her voice, she simply said, *'Just be there.'*

Then she hung up.

Frank stared at his phone for a long time. It was only a man asking, 'Hey mate, you got a light?' that snapped him out of it.

Frank brushed off the smoker and headed back inside.

When he returned to the booth only Andy remained.

'Alright, Frank?' he asked cautiously.

Frank slumped into his seat. 'Yeah. Just... yeah.'

Andy nodded. 'Well, Joel's gone to the bar. He's, uh, got some company now.'

Frank grinned. He craned his neck and spied his other mate, talking to three young women. They were decorated with L plates, had feather boas around them and one was wearing a tiara. Joel caught Frank's eye and gestured to him to come and join them at the bar. Frank ducked back into the booth.

'I was there a minute ago,' explained Andy, 'but I wanted to wait and see if you wanted to keep the table. So...'

Frank smiled. 'Go for it, mate. I'll join you in a bit, just gonna finish this.' He held up his half-drained bottle of Korean lager.

Andy nodded. He stood up, gave Frank's arm a supportive squeeze, and then made a beeline for Joel and the hen party.

Frank slumped down into his seat. As he downed his beer he stared into the middle distance. Not really looking, not really thinking, just processing. Trying to suppress the regret, the self-loathing.

Then something in the empty booth opposite caught his attention. It was reflecting the multi-coloured lights.

Frank put down his empty bottle and got up to investigate.

The thing that was reflecting the lights turned out to be a pocket-sized tablet computer, no bigger than a large smartphone. Swiping the screen did nothing; it was either switched off or dead. Frank looked around; no one seemed to be looking for it. The booth was otherwise empty.

Frank decided he would hand the tablet over to the bar staff. So, he put it in his jacket pocket, left the booth...

'Whoop, someone's keen.'

And went face first into a large pair of breasts.

'Oh, God, I'm sorry...' Frank recoiled, beetroot red. The face he saw when he looked up was staring at him angrily.

And then she burst out laughing.

Joel appeared and slung an arm around Frank. 'That's it, mate. General Franko on active duty.'

Frank took stock. Joel had got sick of waiting and had brought the hen party over.

'Sorry about that, love,' said Frank to the hen, with whose breasts he had inadvertently become acquainted.

'Don't worry about it,' she replied. 'Means I've already done one of my challenges for the night: get a good-looking guy to bury his head in my tits.'

'Aw, Cassandra, does that mean you won't be repeating the trick?' pouted Joel.

'Who says I can't?' shrieked Cassandra – and with that she grabbed Joel and Andy's heads and stuffed them both into her chest. Her friends all burst out laughing, as did Frank at how much Joel played up to it and how much Andy squirmed.

The hens were only too happy to follow the three men into the VIP area. Joel needed no encouragement and Andy took only a few drinks to get into the swing of things.

As for Frank, he was polite, but more interested in the shots menu. Flaming sambucas, tequila slammers, Skittle bombs, Jaeger bombs...

And so Frank Tuttle quickly forgot all about the tablet he had found, and it stayed right there in his jacket pocket into the early hours of Saturday morning.

3

THAT same evening, across London at Wembley Stadium.

It was not unusual for the FA's director of communications and partnerships, Susan Clyne, to work late the night before a big announcement. And tomorrow's was without a doubt going to be the biggest of her 13 years at the Football Association.

Tonight, she was sitting alone at a desk in the stadium's cavernous Media Centre. Susan was an imposing figure, a statuesque brunette who was all-business, from her smart pencil-skirt suit to her minimal make-up and penetrating grey eyes that missed nothing. She had reached a point in her career where no content could leave the FA without her approval, not a press release or tweet or Facebook post. Susan had her own office these days, but when working late she preferred to be back on the open-plan comms floor where she had made her name at the Association.

The glow from Susan's laptop was the only light illuminating the usually bright and buzzing workspace – on this moonless night, the hallowed Wembley pitch was only just about visible through the huge window that dominated the outer wall. Susan had sent her department home hours ago – the rows of PCs and banks of wall monitors were all off. Usually statistics and social media feeds filled the room, alongside huge screens showing national and international news. One corner was set up for making TV broadcasts. All in all, the FA's Media Centre was like something from a science fiction movie, as if the comms team were managing a park of reanimated dinosaurs rather than media platforms and press interactions.

'Everything ship-shape?'

So, she *wasn't* the only one still here, after all.

He had startled her. She hadn't seen him since their weekly one-to-one lunch earlier that day; a lunch at which she had suddenly lost her appetite.

Susan had no reason to be scared of him and yet he gave her the creeps. Maybe it was the voice, familiar to the nation but rougher off camera, a disconcerting mix of arrogance and weariness.

'Of course it is,' Susan replied.

He approached her from the shadows. Susan glanced sideways at him, smiled briefly and then started tapping the keys on her laptop loudly.

He changed course to Conference Room One, the glass wall of which bordered the main Media Centre. Susan stopped fake typing and watched him stop outside Wembley's largest and most lavish meeting room.

He spoke without looking at her. 'To think, all of the dignitaries who will populate this room tomorrow. The history that will be made – that *we* will make, you and I.'

Susan nodded. She had found herself regularly glancing at Conference Room One, too. Whenever she had thought ahead to tomorrow over the past months, in fact all the way up to when she had sat down to lunch today, she had thought that on the night before she would feel excited.

But all she actually felt right now was gnawing anxiety.

She wondered if he had noticed. He noticed *everything*.

Sure enough, as if reading her mind, he turned and asked, 'Tomorrow *is* fully on track, isn't it?'

'Yes, absolutely.' She flashed him another smile and this time made sure that it stuck.

It worked; he mumbled, 'Do excuse me, I'm giving an interview first thing,' and walked away. She watched him leave, one shoulder ever so slightly hunched – a souvenir from '90 in Naples.

Susan had known that her killer smile would do it; she'd worked in marketing her whole professional life, so she knew how to sell something. And in the hours between now and 3pm tomorrow she was going to have to be at the very top of her game.

Susan turned back to her laptop. She wasn't going home any time soon.

4

*T*HIS is it. Cool, calm, composed.

In five minutes, the team will walk down the tunnel before lining up on that famous pitch to shake hands with the opposition, pose for photos, and then get into formation for kick-off.

None of this is a big deal to Frank. He's done it all more times than he can count.

And now he's 90 minutes from winning England their second World Cup – in the same venue as their first triumph, more than 50 years ago.

'Lads,' he begins, pacing the dressing room. *All banter and horseplay stops and the millionaire athletes turn to their manager, rapt. He has their attention. He has their respect.*

'You all know I've taken teams to finals and won the lot. Blimey, it's getting a bit embarrassing now – maybe I should throw this one and give another gaffer the chance to lift a trophy.'

Laughter, confidence-building laughter. Frank is just as renowned for his man-management skills as his tactical genius. He allows himself a little chuckle, then sets his features to stone. Gives his troops the famous Frank Tuttle Stare.

'The odds are against us; we all know that. Them lot in the other changing room are most of the squad what won the last two World Cups. They got three Ballon d'Or winners and haven't conceded a goal all tournament.

'But let me tell you a story. A story about overcoming the odds in my very first managerial position, in the Brent Boys League. I had my ups and downs; I was even suspended at one point.'

This isn't banter. This is a man they respect – no, love *– putting his pride on the line to inspire his men. They hang on Frank's every word.*

'I could've thrown in the towel. But I manned up, I apologised to the league, and I apologised to my wife and my son, who was the team's star player. And after a couple of games' ban, reduced on appeal, I was back, and we annihilated that league. Records broken all over the shop. It was in the nationals and everything.

'So, if I can come back from that, from humiliation and professional disgrace, then I reckon you lot can kick a ball into a net more times than some other rabble. Am I right? AM I RIGHT?'

The team roars in agreement.

'Then let's get out there and do this. COME ON!'

Frank leads the team out into the glare of the Wembley floodlights. The sell-out crowd's applause is deafening, and Frank raises his hands to acknowledge it. He turns toward the adulation, but the light is so bright that he can't see. He keeps running, shielding his eyes and turning his head away, trying to escape the blinding glare, but as he keeps on running and blinking he still can't focus, and now the sound of the crowd is so loud that Frank has to cover his ears and he's been running for so long that this isn't even Wembley, it's somewhere else and it's so bright that things have gone dark and he realises, all too late he realises—

'Frank.'

'Wha—'

'Frank, stop screaming. The neighbours are gonna think there's been a murder.'

'Eh?'

Frank slowly came back to consciousness. He rubbed his eyes and squinted.

Someone was moving around him. 'Bethan?' he asked weakly.

'No, I'm not your wife, Frank,' came Andy's voice. 'If I was, I wouldn't have given you such a generous lie-in.'

All at once it came to Frank – where he was (Andy's sofa) and how he felt (terrible – the hangover hit him like a free kick to the face).

'Ohh,' Frank moaned, holding his head in his hands.

Andy was making a cursory effort to tidy up his bachelor pad, picking up empty beer cans, putting plates and glasses on the kitchen counter.

'Cuppa?' he asked.

'Yeah, ta,' managed Frank.

It all flooded back. He was living with Andy for a while so Bethan could Just Have Some Space.

'We were out... late?'

'Er, yeah mate. We got chucked out that posh place and ended up at a lock-in at The Tackle.'

Frank groaned and rubbed his aching temples.

'You, my friend,' Andy continued while forcing rubbish down into the bin with his bare foot, 'were having it what in the '90s was referred to as "large."'

'I *was?*'

'Let me put it this way: you put 'Vindaloo' by Fat Les on the jukebox, took your shirt off, and the rest of us cheered you on as you performed a dance routine consisting of football moves.'

'Oh Lord.'

'The spinning volley into header was especially well-received, if I recall.'

'Oh... bloody hell.'

'Don't worry, there's biscuits to go with the tea. That'll sort everything out.'

Frank raised a weary thumb while he massaged his temples.

Then he jolted up.

'*What time is it?*'

5

O N THAT particular Saturday morning in late August, the first day of the
new football season, Wembley Park tube station was extremely busy.
There was an event on at the stadium, the much-anticipated Family Fun Day,
and it was to this that everyone was heading.

Claire Butterfield was part of the crowd, and while she was indeed
heading to Wembley, it was for a day of work, not fun. And yet Claire – doing
what she did, where she did it and for whom – was every bit as happy as
anyone else who was heading to the home of English football on that sunny
summer morning.

Claire all but skipped off the tube train, dodging politely around her fellow passengers. She hummed to herself as she rode the escalator up, smiled as she went through the ticket barrier and waved hello to the Transport for London staff. They all waved back to the cheerful, pretty young blonde in the denim jacket and floral dress who brightened up their morning five days a week.

Usually Claire would now carry on down the steps outside the station and head up Olympic Way. But today, for no specific reason, she decided to stop outside the station and take a look at where she was headed.

Her favourite sight in the world.

Claire had grown up with the original Wembley and its famous twin towers, attending games with her football-mad dad. They were both lifelong Charlton Athletic fans, and one of her happiest childhood memories was of going bananas among all the other red-shirted fans at the 1998 First Division Play-off Final, when Sunderland's Michael Grey missed the decisive kick in the penalty shootout and sent the Addicks up to the Premier League. Her GCSE History project on Wembley's cultural impact had earned her an A. She could reel off stats about games played there, record-breaking finals and attendances, folklore and superstitions. For her it stood for purity and goodness, the embodiment of football's soul, the sacred arena where England had won the 1966 World Cup, where Manchester United had become the first English team to lift the European Cup in '68, where Gazza had scored his wonder goal against Scotland at Euro 96.

So Claire had been distraught when the iconic monument was torn down in 2003. During the rebuild, talk was all about delays and overspending and Wembley became a tabloid joke. She never visited its temporary replacement, the Millennium stadium in Cardiff, out of principle.

The new Wembley opened in 2007. Claire, by then 18, told herself that she no longer cared. She had new interests: music, going out, boys. She still liked football, but rarely went to games anymore, which saddened her dad.

And by then it seemed silly to hold this stadium – a mere pile of concrete and metal – in such high regard.

The following summer, after her first year at uni, her dad emailed her an advert for temporary holiday jobs with the FA. Claire applied for one, seeing it as extra drinking money and nothing more. She had convinced herself that the new Wembley was a travesty, that replacing the twin towers with a crappy arch was sacrilegious.

But all of her cynicism evaporated the first time she set eyes on the stadium as an FA employee. *They had made it even better.* The arch was a noble hand, holding the structure in place, nurturing it. Keeping all that was virtuous and magical about the game in place. Claire fell in love with Wembley all over again; she carried on temping there every holiday and after she graduated joined the FA's communications team full-time – and had been there ever since.

And today, as she squinted at it in the bright sunshine, all at once she was rapt, full of the joy of being part of an internationally respected institution.

Turning her mind back to the present, Claire finally descended the tube station's steps. It was going to be an exciting day. For months, the FA's staff had been kept as much in the dark as the public about the big announcement – even comms managers like Claire, which was highly irregular. But this afternoon the secret would finally be out. She was sure it would be something awesome.

Claire left Wembley Park Drive and began the short walk up to the stadium's Bobby Moore entrance. Among the crowd, she noticed a lot of people wearing yellow polo shirts, speaking to the public and showing them where to go – no doubt they were something to do with the Fun Day.

As the statue of England's World Cup-winning captain came into view, Claire was struck with an idea for her blog. Why not write a new, updated history of Wembley? One which was aligned to her own personal experiences: matches she had gone to, events she had seen. She could ask her dad to help; he'd like that.

25

Her blog, *Under the Arch,* had been steadily growing in popularity, as had her Twitter handle, *@wembleychick66.* It was good to have an outlet for her thoughts and feelings; sometimes she worried that she went a bit far with her claims and theories, but it was what people liked to read.

Heading up the ramp now with Sir Bobby's statue bearing down on her, Claire was filled with a familiar urge. Usually she ignored it, but today she was in an indulgent mood.

So, she stopped still, stood erect, and saluted the statue.

'Claire?'

She jumped. A figure in a security uniform was approaching.

'Perry – oh no, I can't believe you saw that.'

'That's fine, Claire. Look I have to—'

'God, I'm *so* embarrassed. Promise you won't tell anyone? Please?'

She flashed Perry a winning smile. He was alright; truth be told he was pretty hot and flirting with him was one of the highlights of her day.

But Perry didn't look alright now. Usually he was quick to flirt back. Usually he let the visage of stern authority his job demanded drop.

Usually, he wasn't confiscating Claire's staff ID from out of her hand.

'I have to escort you from the premises, Miss Butterfield. I'm sorry.'

Frank didn't stop for a morning cup of tea with his friend and temporary flatmate Andy. He was so late that he managed to get himself out the front door less than ten minutes after awakening.

Frank ran a small logistics company, Top of the League Deliveries. His sky-blue van – embossed with logo, a football-shaped package flying toward a letter box, and slogan, PACE, POWER AND ACCURACY – was parked outside Andy's block of flats and it was to this that Frank now marched, holding his jacket and still buttoning up his shirt.

Frank jumped in the van and turned the key. His hangover made each pump of blood in his head a dagger. Why had he done it? How was Ian going to feel? What was Bethan going to say?

He shifted the gearstick and pulled away while dialling his son's mobile.

It rang. No answer.

Frank left a message. 'Hi, it's me. Sorry I forgot to... I didn't forget, I mean, I just... overslept. Look, I won't be long but in case you've already left, just meet me in the usual place. Okay? Sorry. Okay, bye.'

He hung up, cursing himself.

He turned on the radio which, as usual, was tuned into *Sport Chatter*.

'*So, still no word from the FA on this big secret announcement coming today just before 3pm – when, of course, the new football season will kick off. Tim, any updates?*'

'*Afraid not, Darren. The Football Association remain tight-lipped, only saying that the announcement will be broadcast on terrestrial television, as well as on their website and screens at every English football stadium, not to mention those at Wembley itself during today's Family Fun Day. But even with my legendary charm on full offensive, I couldn't get any details from the FA. Not a badger.*'

'*Well, Tim, since your "charm" truly is offensive, that really doesn't surprise me. Anyway, coming up next, I'm going to be interviewing legendary ex-England goalkeeper and captain—*'

Frank switched off the radio. It was making his hangover worse.

He had arrived at Preston Park recreational ground – itself only a short drive from Wembley Stadium, on which so many people had their attention focused today. Frank had no idea that soon he was going to be one of those people himself.

As Frank turned his van into the car park, his heart sank.

Had he got there on time, Frank would have been met by the sights and sounds of dozens of junior footballers running around on the recreation ground's pitches.

Instead there was no one.

Then Frank noticed a man in his early 20s picking up some cones. He was pale, skinny and wore thick glasses. Despite being dressed in the team tracksuit, he looked to Frank more like someone who fixed computers than a football coach.

Still, what did Frank know about the youth of today?

'Excuse me, mate?' Frank called to the young guy as he stepped out of his van.

The tracksuited man, holding a pile of cones in each hand, turned to face the approaching Frank.

'Yes?'

'You new here?'

He put down his cones and gave Frank a timid smile. 'Gary Ward. Just started as Brent Bruisers' trainee coach for the new season.'

'Oh... right.'

Frank didn't know what else to say.

Gary broke the awkward silence. 'Um, do you have a boy in the team?'

'Yeah, Ian Tuttle. I'm Frank, his dad.'

'Frank Tuttle? *You're* Frank Tuttle? Our ex-manager?'

'Yeah... 'til last season.'

'Right, until...' Gary trailed off. Frank held his stare.

Gary busied himself with the cones again. 'I can see the family resemblance. But I'm afraid you've missed Ian.'

Gary headed towards an equipment shed and Frank followed.

'Why didn't he wait for me?'

Gary opened the shed's door and dropped the cones inside. 'I don't think he was... um, too happy when you forgot to pick him up.'

Frank felt his temper rise. 'I didn't *forget*, I just...' He composed himself. 'I overslept.'

Gary shrugged and locked up the shed. Meanwhile, Frank tried Ian's mobile again. No joy.

'I'm always telling the boy to charge that thing,' Frank muttered. To Gary, who was zipping the shed keys up in his rucksack, he said, 'Did he have the proper hump?'

Gary scanned the field for other training items then, seeing none, turned to face Frank. 'He left saying something about it being quicker to catch the bus.'

Frank sighed. 'Got the will of his mother, that one.'

'Well, I'm about done here, so...'

Frank glanced around the car park. His van was the only vehicle.

'What, you walking?'

'Yeah, the tube station's only up the road.'

'Wembley Park?'

'Yeah.'

'Come on, I'll give you a lift.'

'You sure?'

'Yeah, hop in. We'll cruise by the bus stop.'

But Ian wasn't at the bus stop.

'Don't matter,' Frank told Gary, who was sitting next to him in the passenger seat. 'We always go to this café for a brew and a fry-up after training. He must be there. Unless... unless he's *really* angry.'

Gary nodded absently. He was busy on his smartphone.

Typical of these kids, Frank thought. *Always staring at some device or other.*

'What you reckon this big FA announcement is all about, then?' Frank asked by way of conversation.

Gary didn't look up from his phone. 'Dunno. It's trending on Twitter, but no one seems to actually know what it's going to be.'

'*Trending?*'

'Yeah, you know, popular. Being talked about on social media.'

Frank nodded slowly. 'So... on Facebook?'

'Oh yeah, it's all over that, too. People reckon the FA are gonna reveal some changes to football's rules. You wouldn't believe the theories going around.'

'Rule changes? Like what?'

Gary glanced up from his phone. 'Like, a sinbin if you get a yellow card, unlimited substitutes, no more offsides, a goal being worth more points if you score from outside the area...'

Frank snorted. 'Blimey. Why can't they just leave the game alone?'

'Well, rules do change, football has to move with the times. Look at VAR. And I read somewhere that you never used to be able to have *any* substitutes.'

'Yeah, I remember my dad telling me about that.'

Again, Frank glanced from the road to Gary's phone, watching how Gary moved his thumb around the small screen: opening and closing apps, scrolling up and down, switching between multiple windows.

'Dunno how you can have your nose in one of those things all the time, your generation.'

'Oh, I *love* my phone, I couldn't live without it.' Gary cradled the device like a keeper smothering a loose ball.

No wonder the boy's got those Coke-bottle glasses, Frank thought. Frank did have a smartphone, a birthday present from Bethan, but he barely used its functions, except for looking up the football results. He certainly wasn't interested in any of those other devices the kids felt were indispensable.

Then Frank remembered. He reached into his jacket – sure enough, it was still there. He took out the mini tablet that he had found last night and handed it to Gary.

'Here you are, this'll be right up your street, mate.'

Gary held it in awe. 'Wow, this is top of the line. Compact seven-inch screen, ultra HD, super light weight...'

'It's not mine. I found it last night, gonna return it today.'

Gary was turning the device around in his hands. 'It wasn't on when you found it?'

'Nope. Give it a go if you like, power the thing up.'

Gary pushed the power button. After a couple of seconds, the screen lit up.

'How about that,' said Frank with a sideways glance.

'Full battery,' replied Gary, waiting for the tablet to cycle through its start-up routine.

Then he gasped.

'Frank, *where did you find this?*'

'FIRED? But... why?'

Perry the security guard hadn't been able to give Claire a reason. She was now heading down Olympic Way back towards Wembley Park tube station, the spring she had had in her step just minutes ago long gone. She staggered in a daze, nearly colliding with the people rushing in the opposite direction towards the stadium for the Family Fun Day and with the staff dressed in yellow polo shirts, who seemed to be everywhere.

After Perry had told her about her dismissal, the first thing Claire had done was call her boss, Susan. No answer. That was on Susan's mobile; when

Claire had tried the office, an automated message had answered, 'The FA's switchboard is not available to calls from this number.'

They've put my mobile on the barred list.

Next, she'd called her friend Laura, an FA sports psychologist. It was to her that Claire was now speaking as she came out from under the bridge and climbed the steps back up to the tube station.

'"Broke contract"? *That's* what they're saying? How am I supposed to have broken my contract?'

Laura didn't know anything more, had only heard the rumours circulating the office. She was taking Claire's call from a Wembley toilet cubicle, communication with a contract-rebel being strictly forbidden under FA regulations.

Worried about being caught, Laura whispered an apology, promised to stay in touch and hung up.

Flabbergasted, Claire could only stare at her phone.

What did I do? I've given them my whole working life.

She was great at her job, diligent to the point of obsession, full marks in appraisals, never late, never sick. So why such swift and brutal action?

Claire was compelled to keep moving but didn't want to go home, so she swerved the station and walked northwards up Bridge Road.

Soon she was at the crossroads with Forty Avenue. She looked across the street and saw a place she could go to think.

Minutes later, she was taking her first sip of weak tea and feeling a lot calmer.

Claire took stock of her surroundings. Pippa's Café wasn't her usual sort of place – she was more of a Starbucks kind of girl. But right now, she really needed a bacon roll smothered in brown sauce. The greasy spoon had an unglamorous aesthetic that was cosily British: Formica tables and cheap wooden chairs; laminated picture menus; yellowed posters of burgers and milkshakes; the smell of onions wafting in from the open kitchen.

From her corner table, Claire glanced around at the assortment of builders, elderly couples... and one teenaged lad, sitting on his own by the window.

The boy was dressed in a green and red hooped football kit and trainers (his muddy boots were in his kit bag, Claire supposed). He seemed sad; perhaps he'd just lost a match. The boy was trying to get his phone to turn on without success. Was he waiting to meet someone?

Just then, a man and a woman wearing the bright yellow polo shirts that Claire had been seeing all morning entered the café – up close she noticed that the tops had the letters RCE written on their fronts. They walked straight up to the boy and addressed him cheerfully; they seemed to be congratulating him, although Claire couldn't hear them properly over the music from the radio and the conversations around her. The lad didn't seem to know them, but after a while he got up and left with them.

It didn't feel right. Why was the boy walking off with these strangers? Should she find out what was going on?

But by the time she had made her decision and reached the café's door, she was only in time to see the three of them pull away in a van. It was yellow and had RCE embossed on it.

Frank Tuttle was looking for a parking space on the street near Pippa's Café while half listening to Gary Ward prattle on about the tablet.

'Who knows what kind of information is on it? It could be anything, their deepest secrets, things that they don't want *anyone* to know about...'

Frank found a spot, backed in and yanked up the handbrake.

Then he faced Gary, cutting off his flow.

'See over there?' Frank pointed across the street.

Gary looked. 'The café?'

'Hopefully that's where we're gonna find my boy. And once I've got him back, we're gonna march right across to Wembley Stadium and give that device back. In the meantime, try not to share that we've got it with the whole world on your social media, okay?'

Gary nodded.

Frank looked down at the tablet, which the other man was still clinging to.

Its screen read:

Confidential Football Association content within

NOT TO BE SHARED OUTSIDE OF
FA SENIOR MANAGEMENT

Tap to start Phase One

Despite himself, Frank was curious. 'What you reckon it's all about?'

Gary considered. 'Could be anything. Details of players' wages. Plans for stadium remodelling. Or maybe... just maybe...'

'What?'

'Maybe it's got today's big announcement on it.'

'And what, they keep it on one of these devices? And then leave it in some bar for any old mug to find?'

'Why not? They've got to store information somewhere. And confidential documents *can* get lost.'

Frank pondered this.

Gary was still animated. 'Just think of my ranking if I *did* tweet this... the extra followers, the favourites, the retweets.'

Frank looked sideways at the younger man, then back at the tablet. 'I'm returning it and that's that.' He thought for a moment. 'Although... suppose there's no harm in having a *quick* butcher's...'

He leant over and tapped the screen.

The display changed to a few lines of text, finishing with what looked like a cryptic crossword puzzle clue, complete with a box for the answer.

'What does *that* mean?' Gary wondered.

Frank rubbed the back of his head. 'Christ knows. Look, this thing is probably a fake anyway. Something some nerd set up to amuse himself.'

'Maybe...'

'Anyway, your tube station's just round the corner, so...'

Frank took the tablet back from Gary, who watched it all the way.

'Nice meeting you,' Frank added pointedly.

'Well,' Gary said slowly, eyes still on the tablet, 'I'd quite like to pop into this café with you, just so I know that Ian's alright.'

Frank turned off the engine and stashed the tablet in the glove box. 'Come on then, look lively.'

Pippa's Café was still packed with Saturday morning customers. Frank made a beeline for the elderly Turkish man at the till while Gary hung back.

'Can I help you, my friend?' the man asked.

'Hope so, pal. I'm looking for my son, 13 years old, about this high, light brown hair, wearing a green and red hooped football kit?'

'Sorry mate, it don't ring no bell.'

'Excuse me?'

Frank turned to see an attractive woman in her 30s approaching him.

'Er, yeah?' he asked.

'I think I saw your son. Green and red kit? Number 9?'

'Yeah, that's Ian.'

She pointed towards the door. 'He left with a man and a woman, less than five minutes ago.'

'He *what?*' Frank looked at the door then back at the young woman.

'I was sitting over there, eating my bacon roll. I noticed your son – he looked like he was waiting for someone. And then these two people came in, they chatted for a few minutes, and he left with them. They all went off in a van.'

Frank cursed inwardly. 'Who were they? Police?'

'No... they did have uniforms on, though. Sort of. These yellow polo shirts.'

Gary stepped forward. 'Hey, Frank, I saw a bunch of people in those tops outside when we were driving past.'

Claire nodded. 'They're all over Olympic Way, all the way up to the stadium.'

'Hmm,' said Frank.

Outside, Frank, Claire and Gary crossed the road to Frank's van. Introductions were made on the way.

At the van, Frank said, 'Right, we're gonna have to drive right up to that bloody stadium and make a pick-up as well as a drop-off. Do you mind coming along, love, point out if you see the ones what took him?'

'Sure, not like I have anything else to do today.'

The trio got in the van: Frank behind the wheel, Claire in the middle, Gary shotgun.

Claire was confused about something Frank had said. 'What do you mean, you're making a drop-off at Wembley?'

Frank shook his head dismissively. 'Just some FA thing I gotta return.'

'Really? Huh.' Claire narrowed her eyes.

'What?'

'I was working for the FA until... until they fired me this morning.'

Frank wasn't sure how to react to this piece of personal information. He was suddenly conscious the he was still wearing last night's clothes: he had beer stains on his shirt, there was dried mud on his jeans from where he must have fallen over while walking home hammered... he just hoped he didn't smell too bad.

Meanwhile Gary had opened the glove box and was handing the tablet to Claire. 'This is what Frank's talking about,' he said.

Claire swiped the screen to life – and gasped.

'Where... where did you get this?' Her hands were trembling.

'Blimey, you sound just like Gary here.' Frank made a sharp turn, directing the van towards Wembley. 'I found it in this bar last night. I was gonna hand it in there and then, but... well anyway, I'm doing it now.'

Claire swiped the screen in stunned silence.

'Frank here reckons it's a fake,' said Gary.

'This is definitely not a fake,' Claire said flatly. 'This contains information very, very valuable to the FA.'

Frank glanced at Gary, who gave him a *told-you-so* look. To Claire Frank said, 'Well, why don't we take a look, then? May as well. And, um, sorry, by the way. About you losing your job and that.'

'Thanks,' said Claire. 'This tablet... I've heard about it. I mean, my God, I thought it was only a rumour.' She struggled to compose herself. Took a deep breath and let it out slowly. 'If it is what I think it is, then what we're reading here is the first in a series of clues.'

'Clues?' asked Frank.

'Clues about what?' asked Gary.

Claire took another deep breath. 'It's The Campaign.'

Frank and Gary stared blankly.

'I'm sorry,' said Gary, 'the *what?*'

'The Campaign. It's a legend, a myth about the origin of football's rules.'

'The rules?' asked Gary. He and Frank exchanged a glance.

Claire nodded.

'Supposedly it's a quest that reveals the whereabouts of two additional rules, hidden somewhere in London, which date back to the founding of football and are said to be safeguards designed to protect the game. Unlike the official rules, which have been tweaked over the years, these are unbreakable under any circumstances. They're known as The Halves.'

Claire let this sink in. Gary frowned while Frank tried to focus on the road.

'Two halves,' Gary said.

'Yes.'

'As in, "a game of two halves."'

'Yes, I know how it sounds. I'm just telling you what I've heard.'

'Go on, Claire,' Frank urged.

She continued. 'Well, completing The Campaign is supposed to reveal the true meaning of football, and give whoever gets that far the power to fight against a threat to the game.'

'Threat?' asked Frank. 'Like what?'

Claire ran her hand through her hair. 'Like something that the FA feels they have to make a special announcement about – and they won't even tell their comms managers what it is beforehand.'

Then Claire gasped again.

'What?' asked Frank, nearly swerving on the road.

'My God. I know why the FA fired me.'

Claire asked Frank to stop the van for a minute so she could get her head together and explain everything to him and Gary.

Frank silently pulled up in the Premier Inn car park opposite Wembley Stadium, and now he and Gary were looking at Claire expectedly.

Claire composed herself. 'Okay. So, I work... *worked* in communications for the FA. Making sure the right things get reported about the Association, releasing information to the press, social media, and so on.'

'Okay,' said Frank.

'But as well as that, I've got a presence on social media. My Twitter handle is *@wembleychick66*...?'

Frank's face was blank.

But Gary said, 'I follow you. You were talking recently about equal pay in the women's game.'

'Right. Last night, I posted an article on my blog, *Under the Arch*, about refereeing standards in this country. How the bigger teams get all the decisions, the record of poor offside calls, VAR being just another tool of the elite, that kind of thing.'

'Sounds like the stuff fans moan about in the pub,' Frank said.

'Sure, except I had carefully researched stats to back everything up. But some of my data came from within the FA itself, stuff that... it's a matter of public record for anyone who digs deep enough, but...'

Frank took stock. 'So, you reckon you got too close to the truth and they axed you.'

'I think so.'

'And you think this announcement has something to do with biased refereeing?' asked Gary.

'Could be,' said Claire. 'The only reason this tablet would leave Wembley's grounds was if someone wanted to destroy it – or if they planned to use it. So, it does beg the question – why now? As a reaction to what?'

Gary and Frank sat there for a moment, taking all this in. Frank reached for his keys in the ignition, but hesitated.

He turned to Claire and asked, 'Alright, so what do you think this means? This first clue?'

Claire unlocked the tablet's screen. It showed what Frank and Gary had already read:

To find the two Halves,
simply follow these Capital instructions.

Phase One

Clue One

Circling legends combined

Enter number here ____

'"Capital instructions."' Claire shook her head and smiled. 'That means that there are clues, actual physical clues, around London. Most likely at football stadiums.'

'So, wait, this Campaign is written by the FA?' Gary asked.

'No. Not the FA. The Custodians. Another group who formed at the same time as football's official, public-facing association but who operate in secret and only interfere under the direst circumstances. In the terms under which football was first established, they hold even more authority than the FA – which explains why the Association has let The Custodians use one of their ultra-modern tablets to store its quest.'

'The Custodians...' repeated Frank.

'Yes. They keep an eye on the game and make sure that it remains fair and keeps its integrity.'

'Doesn't the FA already do that?' asked Gary.

'They have a Department of Fair Play, sure, but The Custodians are something else. Their members are all unknown and their leader is said to be directly descended from one of the 11 men who set football's rules over 150 years ago. The Custodians are independent, have no commercial interests and operate in total anonymity. They don't officially exist.'

Frank and Gary exchanged another glance.

Claire shrugged. 'If you believe the legends.'

'Look,' said Frank after a moment. He reached for the key in the ignition and this time held onto it. 'Whatever this business is all really about, I'm not going to sit around discussing crackpot conspiracy theories when my boy's missing. We're marching right up to the front door of that stadium and that's that.'

Frank turned the key and looked over his shoulder.

But before he could back out, his phone rang.

Frank glanced at his mobile's display. 'Huh. The number's not in my contacts.'

He showed it to Claire and Gary. Claire took a sharp intake of breath. 'That's an FA number. It's... *it's coming from inside Wembley.*'

Scowling, Frank put his phone on speaker for the benefit of his two passengers.

Before the caller had a chance to say anything, Frank got the first word in.

'Now listen here, whoever you are, what you want with my son? What, you're so embarrassed about the England team you gotta start grabbing young boys off the street? My Ian may be good and if you've had scouts watching him then... well, as his father, you better know that I represent him, I'm not having any agents getting involved. We'll just sit down you, me and the boy and...'

Claire touched Frank's arm. 'Let them talk,' she implored.

Frank stopped his tirade. For a panicky moment they all thought the caller had gone.

But then a voice spoke, heavily muffled and distorted.

'*So, this* is *Frank Tuttle?*'

'That's my name, don't wear it out.' Frank winked at Claire and Gary.

'*I only said it once.*'

'Right.' Frank cleared his throat and placed his phone on the dashboard.

'*Frank,*' the muffled phone voice was saying, '*Don't worry about Ian. He's not been—*'

'Listen, if you want this computer with all your secrets and that on it, let my son go. Or else I'm going to drop the bloody thing off round at the *Daily Mail* and call the old bill on my way.'

'*Your son isn't being held against his will, Mr Tuttle. He's quite safe and enjoying the attractions at the FA's Family Fun Day.*'

'Is he bollocks. You lot—'

'*Mr Tuttle listen to me. The tablet is real, The Campaign is real. And the threat to the game from today's announcement is very real. You must solve the clues and save football. And I promise that you will be reunited with your son along the way.*'

Frank looked down at the tablet.

This thing? he thought. *This bloody toy?*

Could he really be holding the destiny of football in his hands?

Frank stiffened. He leaned in towards the phone. 'I wanna speak to Ian.'

'*He's not with me at this moment. But... hold on a second.*'

Frank waited. Drummed his fingers impatiently on his knee. Claire and Gary looked on in suspense.

Frank's phone buzzed. He picked it up and opened a picture message.

He held it up for Claire and Gary. It was a photo of Ian, on the pitch at Wembley. Around him were stalls, rides, vendors selling snacks – a carnival scene. Ian was about to run up and kick a ball, his face set in concentration. And he was surrounded by people, cheering him on.

'*We are watching him,*' the caller said, '*and making sure he is safe while he waits to be reunited with you.*'

Frank was torn. He knew that if he wasn't going to go and get Ian, he should at least tell Ian's mother what had happened so that *she* could head to Wembley instead. But that would mean admitting to Bethan that he had failed to pick up Ian like he promised. He could ask one of his mates, but again, he was too ashamed – it would mean that stupid old Franko Tuttle had done it again.

Frank did have one idea. 'Hold up,' he said. 'These two here what I just met, Gary and Claire. They can do this quest. They seem to know their stuff; they can handle it and I'll just come and get Ian.'

'*No,*' said the voice firmly. '*You found the tablet, Frank. You must lead the team who embark upon The Campaign.*'

Frank cursed.

'Like I said, taking The Campaign is how you will get Ian back. Turning up at Wembley and causing a scene will only get you arrested. And I know that you don't want to get the police involved, despite your idle threats.'

Claire raised her eyebrows at Gary, who seemed to be suppressing a grin.

Frank remained silent.

'Complete The Campaign,' the voice said. 'The very future of football depends on it.'

The caller hung up.

Frank stared at the image of his son that was still on his mobile's screen.

Ian was 13 going on 30. He walked to school and back every day alone, took himself off up town to meet his mates at the weekend. Surely, he would be alright for a couple of hours, in a busy place, overflowing with security and with hundreds of CCTV cameras, while Frank was preoccupied with such an important task? Surely Ian – who loved football, for whom football was his whole life – would understand?

Slowly and without meeting anyone's eyes, Frank put the phone back in his pocket.

He let out a long sigh.

Then he asked Claire, 'Any idea who that was on the blower?'

She shook her head. 'No. But if they've gone to the trouble of disguising their voice, they must be from a rebel faction within the FA.'

'Or connected to these Custodians,' suggested Gary.

'So, what do you think, Frank?' Claire asked tentatively.

Frank thought for a moment. He consulted his watch.

'There's two of these... Halves, right?'

'Yes, two of them, according to the legend.'

'Look, I don't really believe any of this stuff,' said Frank. 'But... We'll go and try to find the first one. Do the clues or whatever, see if we get anywhere. And if I don't get any nearer to my son, I'm throwing this bloody device in the Thames and marching straight up to that stadium.'

'I'm going to help,' Claire said. 'And if it means rubbing the FA up the wrong way while we're at it... good.'

Frank looked to Gary but saw that he was again busy with his phone.

'What you reckon, Bill Gates? Can you tear yourself away from the social network for more than two seconds and give us a hand?'

'Eh?' said Gary looking up from his phone. 'Oh, sorry. Twitter is still going crazy about this announcement.'

'Hmm,' said Frank.

If you'd been half as concerned about my boy as you are that phone, we wouldn't be in this mess.

'But yeah, I'll help,' Gary was saying. 'In fact, after Claire mentioned that the clues might be about football stadiums, I realised where we have to go first.'

Frank raised an eyebrow.

'Not to Wembley?' asked Claire.

'No. Somewhere I see from my bedroom window every day.'

'Right then,' said Frank, finally starting the ignition up again. 'Let's get our arses in gear.'

THE IDEA for the Family Fun Day had been rattling around the FA's corridors for years. The huge debt from rebuilding Wembley Stadium meant that the Association had to figure out how to claw some money back any way they could. Holding more concerts was a given, as was making Wembley the only venue for the England national team's games. The stadium also started hosting other sports, such as American football.

But the FA were still struggling to make repayments. Using the Wembley pitch for a carnival was just one idea that its financial think tank floated – and one that was swiftly rejected. The Association could only charge visitors so much otherwise no one would turn up, and it could not justify the man hours needed to organise all the activities and the myriad of companies who would run them, not to mention having to pay these businesses upfront and the admin *that* involved. The figures would not balance, so the FA left the idea on the back shelf.

But when Susan Clyne was promoted to director of communications and partnerships and started to plan the release of the big announcement, she quickly dusted the Fun Day proposal off and fast-tracked it. She took steps to make the event economically viable, including temporarily removing all of Wembley's seats to cram in more attractions.

'I'm sorry, did you say a... fan day?' her new boss had asked her, while tucking his silk Bottega Veneta tie into his horizontal pin-striped Alexander Kabbaz shirt.

They were sitting at an outside table at *Undici a Lato*. The Italian *ritsorante* was not far from Wembley but Susan had never eaten there – it was notoriously hard to get a table, not to mention obscenely expensive. This didn't seem to matter to her boss: he had announced this morning that they would be having a lunch meeting there every Friday.

'Family *Fun* Day,' Susan repeated.

She watched his face. It seemed like his expression might be changing, but she couldn't be sure; it was like studying the hour hand on a clock.

Rather than wait it out, Susan went ahead and clarified her idea. 'The FA need this for more than purely financial reasons. You told me that we've reached an agreement that will take care of all the Wembley rebuild debt.'

'Yes, we have.'

'Great – although I still don't know the details of—'

'The details aren't pertinent at this juncture.' He dabbed his mouth with a napkin, despite them not having started eating yet.

Susan wasn't happy about being fobbed off. 'OK, but does this deal have any ramifications that may be interpreted by the public as... negative?'

She thought she saw him smile. But she couldn't be sure.

'Potentially,' he said at last.

Susan sighed inwardly, focusing on the sizable pay rise that had accompanied her promotion. 'If that's the case, then the Association needs to start regularly releasing goodwill PR. The Fun Day is a good place to start.'

Her dining companion weighed this up, while Susan worried that these lunches would end up consuming her entire Friday afternoon every week.

Finally, he spoke. 'We'll have to give them something more as well, but it's a satisfactory start. Yes – *this* is why we're working together, Susan. You understand our customers. You understand... *the people.*'

Then their *antipasti* platter arrived and with it the topic changed. Susan remembered reminding herself that she would have plenty of time to scrutinise the exact details of this miraculous, debt-eliminating deal later.

'Later' has a habit of coming sooner than we expect.

Right now, months later and on the day that millions of football fans look forward to each summer, Susan was standing in her office in the Media Centre, looking out onto the Wembley pitch. She'd been in this spot for 15 minutes now, not moving, just watching through the vast window. Thousands of men, women and children were wandering around the stadium: buying useless souvenirs; wasting money on impossible-to-win games; shovelling down sugary snacks that would give them an energy boost. Kids laughed on a slide. A boy chased a girl past a fortune teller's booth, pulling her ponytail. A father carried a youngster on his shoulders.

Late last night Susan had ended up falling asleep on her office sofa, showering and changing this morning in the executive bathroom. Since yesterday lunchtime she had eaten no specific meals, just drunk coffee after coffee, supplemented with pastries.

Now, it was time to go downstairs. To be among the people.

Down on the Wembley pitch, 13-year-old Ian Tuttle punched the sky in triumph. He'd got the ball through the highest hole – a whopping 100 points. There was no way the other boy could catch him now.

Still, Ian didn't want to gloat. He had celebrated the winning kick silently – what was the point in making the poor kid feel any worse?

Ian turned to look at his opponent as the boy put his own ball down to take his final, futile kick. He looked nervous and flustered.

Ian turned his attention to the man behind the other boy, who was presumably the father.

'You've messed it up again,' the man was saying. 'Surprise, surprise. What do I keep telling you? There's nothing more important than winning.'

The kid shifted where he stood. 'Dad... I tried my best.'

'Oh, well then, all's forgiven in that case.' The father's sarcasm turned his voice into a nasal whine. 'Go on, kick it. Mess up again. Embarrass yourself as usual.'

Despondently, his son went back to the ball. Channelled all his concentration into staring at it, as if through sheer force of will he could make it fly straight this time. And make his dad proud.

As Ian watched all this, his emotions swung between sympathy for the other kid and anger at the dad.

He marched up to the boy. 'Hey, mate.'

The other kid jumped. 'You're not supposed to be on my side of the line.'

'Just what do you think you're doing?' the dad asked angrily.

Ian ignored the adult.

'I think I know what you're doing wrong, mate.'

'What?' asked the boy, shooting a glance back at his dad.

'Excuse me young man,' the father said to Ian, 'but we don't need—'

Now Ian did look at him. But he didn't say anything or change expression. He just looked.

The dad stepped back, mumbling.

Ian turned to the boy again. 'Listen to me. Your technique's not bad. You strike it well.'

'Not well enough,' the kid said bitterly.

Ian shook his head. 'You're not doing anything wrong. But... you're a defender, right?'

'Yeah... centre back.' He said it almost guiltily.

'Right. So, I bet all you've been taught to do is kick it away. "When in doubt, hoof it out," right?'

The boy looked up. 'That's exactly what our coach says.'

'Well, this game's offensive, not defensive. It's not about power, it's about accuracy. You can pass the ball, right?'

The boy puffed out his chest. 'Course I can.'

'Okay, well,' Ian pointed towards the target, 'all you have to do is pick one of those holes and pass to it.'

'But the 100 one is so—'

'Don't go for the 100. Forget about it, that's the Hollywood pass. Why don't you try for the 50? Or even... you know what, I reckon you could get the 75.'

'You reckon?' The boy now had hope in his eyes.

'Sure. May as well give it a go, you've got nothing to lose.' Ian spoke casually, removing the pressure.

He backed away, giving his opponent some space. Watched as the boy set the ball down, stepped back and readied himself.

The boy strode forward.

Connected with the ball.

And sent it cleanly through the 75 hole.

A cheer rang out. Both boys looked around, surprised – out of nowhere, quite a crowd had gathered.

Ian walked toward the other boy but didn't stop. Didn't make a big deal out of it, just patted him on the arm and kept on walking.

He didn't give the father a second glance.

Ian left the ball-through-the-holes game and resumed wandering aimlessly around the Fun Day. He took out his phone; he knew it would be as dead as it had been the other dozen times, but he went through the pantomime of checking it, all the same.

Oh Dad, he thought.

Yes, he'd been mad at him. Otherwise he wouldn't have gone with the two weirdos in the café. Of course, he knew to not get into a van with a couple of strangers, but he'd seen loads of those yellow polo shirts milling about so was confident that they were legit. It was his anger at his dad that had made him openly disobey one of childhood's key rules.

But he wasn't mad anymore. He knew his dad tried hard and was going through a tough time with his mum, getting kicked out of the house and everything. He'd never forgotten to pick him up from anywhere before and he knew that the old man would be feeling guilty. Ian did plan to rub it in when he saw him again, but only long enough to make a point.

Ultimately, he just wanted to see his dad again.

The Fun Day was... fun, but weird on your own without the *family* part. Ian had decided that he should now get back to the café or, as a last resort, take the bus home and tell his mum what had happened. He didn't want to grass his dad up, but he was running out of options.

Just then, as he stood watching a pellet gun game, a smartly dressed woman walked up to him.

'Ian Tuttle?' she asked with a huge smile.

'Um, yes?' he replied. The woman seemed friendly – somehow *too* friendly.

She bent down to him – somewhat patronisingly, Ian thought.

'My name's Susan. How are you enjoying the Fun Day?'

Ian knew how to talk to adults: you just said what they wanted to hear. 'It's great, I'm having such a *fun day.*'

But this woman was savvy. She could tell that Ian wasn't being honest.

'Is something the matter?' she asked.

Ian scrutinised her.

She seems like someone important.

He realised that maybe this businesswoman could help him.

'Well,' he said slowly, 'I was supposed to meet my dad earlier, but I missed him. I was waiting for him and then these two people in yellow polo shirts...'

'Our Fun Facilitators. Yes, that's how I know who you are.'

'Right. They came up to me and said that a kid hadn't turned up to claim his free entry pass and so they had gone looking around outside the stadium for someone to replace him.'

'Oh, lucky you.' The woman stood up straight again; Ian saw she had realised that she didn't need to talk down to him .

'Yeah,' he said, meeting her eyes, 'it's been great, but I really should be getting back to finding my dad now.' To underline his point, Ian turned and scanned his surroundings, as if at any moment he expected to see Frank Tuttle pop up between the horserace game and the test-your-strength machine.

'Oh sure, sure.' The woman's note of understanding was so false that it annoyed Ian.

No. I don't need her help.

He turned away again, now genuinely looking, but not for his dad – he was trying to find the exit.

The woman finally got to her point. 'Ian, let me ask you something.'

Irritated, but remembering his manners, Ian turned back to her. 'Yes?'

'Have you played the new *Ultimate Soccer Challenge* on the Playstation 5?'

Ian stared at her. 'Did you say, "The new *Ultima Soc*"?'

Susan nodded.

'But, but...' Ian gasped for air. *'That's not even out yet.'*

Susan shrugged nonchalantly. 'Doesn't mean it's not been *made* yet. Doesn't mean we don't have a preview copy in our Games Room.' She indicated the far end of the stadium.

'Really?' Ian suddenly forgot about his cynical detachment. Now divorced from rational thought, he barely even realised that he was following the woman away.

'You betcha,' she was saying. 'Come on, I'll show you.'

But though trapped in the tractor beam of a new video game, Ian hadn't totally forgotten himself. 'Will there be somewhere I can charge my phone?' he asked.

'Oh sure, we'll find you somewhere.' Susan flashed another big smile. Then she switched to sincere interest. 'So, you know, this new game, I'm not really an expert, but I heard that it's supposed to be the best ever, right?'

'Oh yeah, I've been reading about it for months. They've given the gameplay a total overhaul. Also, they've taken...'

Susan nodded along, her face the picture of captivated attention.

'That is the most bonkers thing I've ever heard,' said Frank.

'Well, have you got any better ideas?' asked Gary.

Frank opened his mouth again but closed it without saying another word. He went back to focusing on the road.

Claire had been listening to the two men either side of her in this van argue all through the drive away from Wembley.

Circling legends combined.

While the other two bickered over the merit of the answer Gary had come up with to The Campaign's first clue, Claire mulled it over in silence. Working for the FA had given her an insight into football lore, but after searching through her mental database for references to circles, legends and combinations of the two, she had come up blank. Gary's idea seemed their best bet – and she noticed that, despite his scepticism, Frank had kept on course for the younger man's suggested destination.

Claire hadn't been sure the two men would believe her tale about secret Custodians dedicated to protecting football, and that the FA tablet they had found held a quest to uncover two hidden safeguards, known as Halves, whose secrets could change the fate of the game. Why should they, when she wasn't even sure that she believed it herself?

But she *was* sure that something was rotten in football, and if there was a chance to change that – well, the FA may have cast her aside but she remained devoted to the game, no matter what.

She realised that both the men were looking at her and she cleared her throat.

'I think Gary's idea about what the clue means is as good as any,' Claire said.

Gary crossed his arms in triumph. He quickly raised his eyebrows twice at Claire and she replied with a perfunctory nod. She didn't want to get too chummy. Gary seemed an okay bloke; a serious nerd, but that wasn't so uncommon in guys these days. But she'd caught him staring at her a few times and didn't want to give him the wrong idea.

She looked now at Frank, who was gripping the wheel hard and staring ahead with steely intent. She was sympathetic about how torn he was between getting his son back and helping football, and she had even started to find him quite amiable in a blunt-instrument kind of way. He was essentially harmless, as was Gary. Since she had dived into a van with these two strangers, she had to believe that. And her instincts were usually right.

It was instinct that had led her to believe that the boy Ian was in trouble back at the café and even though she didn't know him like Frank and Gary did, she too was as compelled to get Ian back as she was to complete The Campaign.

And of course, for her, there was more to all this.

Breach of contract.

That stupid blog.

Like many who worked in communications, Claire fancied herself as a bit of a writer. Churning out press releases and back-slapping puff pieces for the Football Association didn't quite fulfil her artistic needs, so she posted on her blog *Under the Arch* at least weekly. Recently her writing had got more confrontational and controversy-baiting and the blog had picked up more subscribers accordingly. Had she finally pushed it too far? Was it her use of internal FA data or her accusations about the partiality of referees that had pissed off the FA?

She had taken the offending post down via her mobile while the men were arguing, and had again tried to contact her ex-employer, still without success. So, Claire had decided that to find her answers she would need to keep on this journey until the very end. Wherever it took her.

Right now, it was taking her south down Holloway Road. Frank flicked on his left indicator and turned down Hornsey Road, which led them to a mini roundabout. Turning left on that, Frank parked on the side of the road and killed the engine.

The trio looked out of Frank's window up at Emirates Stadium, Arsenal Football Club's ground since moving from Highbury in 2006.

'Alright then,' said Frank. 'Let's give this a go.'

They all hopped out and climbed the steps.

At the top, they saw that the intimidating stadium was affixed atop a huge concrete platform – to Claire, it resembled a flat egg on a pedestal. A forecourt circled the ground, making it possible to go all the way around on foot – which was exactly what they intended to do.

They all stared up at a mural, situated just above ARSENAL and just below EMIRATES STADIUM.

'So, you're telling me,' Frank said to Gary, 'that every time you get up in the morning and open your curtains, you have to stare at Dennis Bergkamp's bum?'

Claire sniggered.

'No,' replied Gary in all seriousness. 'My flat's in a block facing the *other* side. It's Pires's greasy hair I see every day.'

'Hey, I used to quite fancy Robert Pires,' said Claire.

Frank and Gary stared at her.

Around the stadium's circumference were murals of 32 lauded ex-Gunners, standing with their arms around each other, backs to the world. Backs with numbers on them, which Gary reckoned they needed to add together.

Circling legends combined.

'There's something I've been wondering before we get started,' said Frank. 'Arsenal haven't only ever played here. How can some ancient quest know anything about a stadium that weren't even built back then?'

'The Campaign isn't the same now as it was when it was first written,' Claire explained. 'According to the legend, The Custodians update the clues over the years – including when a club moves to a new ground. Someone had to upload it all to this tablet, so that's probably the last time it was revised.'

'Let's hope we're using the latest version,' said Gary.

Frank thought about this, then shook his head.

He pointed at Gary. 'Okay. So, you go round that way—'

'Clockwise,' said Gary.

'Yes, clock-bloody-wise. Count 'em up. Me and Claire, we'll go round the other way.'

'Anti—'

'Yeah yeah, anti-clockwise. Meet you halfway round the back.'

'Got it.'

'Okay,' Claire said as Gary sped away, 'so Bergkamp 10, Wilson 1, Hapgood 3, George 11... that's 25 on the first mural.'

'Right,' said Frank.

'Come on, let's get the rest.' Claire jogged around the stadium counting the numbers out loud. She tried not to move too fast as she could hear Frank wheezing from behind her.

Counting the numbers gave her a chance to take stock of their situation again.

Are we crazy to be doing this?

The Campaign, the two Halves, the secret Custodians who came up with it all as an insurance policy against football corruption... it was one of those rumours about which all FA employees knew. If someone sent around a non-work-related email, linking to an amusing YouTube clip for instance, a colleague might reply back satirically with 'No non-work-related emails: REMEMBER THAT THE CUSTODIANS ARE WATCHING YOU.' The idea had an absurd, 1984 Big Brother vibe to it. Yet she remembered one particular instance, when she was grabbing lunch in the canteen with her friend Laura and the other girls. They were having a moan about working hours, and one of the girls made a crack about how she should chat up one of the IT guys and see if she could find 'the sacred tablet' and take The Campaign – hopefully one of the two safeguards was that FA workers mustn't exceed a 40-hour week. They'd all laughed, but Claire had caught her boss Susan shooting their table a dirty look as she went by.

Claire brought her focus back to the present; she needed to concentrate, or she would lose count.

The next Emirates mural depicted David Seaman, Ted Drake, David Rocastle and Alex James, whose numbers added up to 27. The third reached a total of 28, from two 8s, a 7 and a 5: Ian Wright, David Jack, George Armstrong and Martin Keown.

Having made it halfway round the stadium, Claire and Frank saw Gary coming from the opposite direction, one hand pushing his glasses back up his nose and the other gripping onto his bouncing rucksack. He negotiated through some Japanese tourists, who were taking photos of each other in front of the stadium, and made his way over.

'So,' Frank panted, 'what have you got so far?'

'119,' said Gary.

'Okay, and we've got...' Frank looked to Claire.

She shot Frank an incredulous look. 'But... I thought *you* were keeping track.'

Frank slapped his sweaty forehead. 'Oh, for the love of—'

'Kidding, kidding.' Claire smiled sweetly at Frank, then told Gary, 'Ours add up to 80.'

Frank gave Claire a wry grin then said to Gary, who had opened his phone's calculator app, 'Alright, so 119 plus 80...'

'Equals 199.'

Frank got the tablet out of his jacket pocket. 'Right then, let's see how she looks.'

Claire and Gary came in close as Frank typed in the three digits. The sun was out in full force and glared onto the screen; they had to move closer to the stadium so its shadow fell over them, and they almost collided with another group of tourists. Claire noticed that every one of the group was wearing a different retro Arsenal shirt, and she wondered briefly if they had ever even attended a game.

Frank tapped in '199'. After a short wait, the screen changed. It became a map of London, zoomed in on Emirates Stadium.

'I think that confirms we're looking in the right place,' Claire said.

'Yeah,' said Frank. 'Look, now it's moving to a new location.'

'That must be where the next clue is,' said Gary excitedly.

The three of them watched in suspense as the map zoomed out and then headed northeast.

It stopped. Zoomed in again.

Green filled the screen.

Frank, Gary and Claire all frowned.

'Where's that?' asked Gary.

'Middle of Epping Forest,' said Frank.

'Oh no,' said Claire.

The display then returned to the clue screen, where their answer '199' had turned red.

Incorrect.

Frank paced around, clasping the tablet tightly in his hand, cursing under his breath. Gary watched him warily, looking to Claire like he was worried Frank would squeeze too hard and break the device.

Claire, meanwhile, gazed up at the mural of Patrick Vieira, Reg Lewis, Lee Dixon and Joe Mercer that loomed above them.

What did we miss? Where did we mess up?

'Guys,' she said eventually, still looking up at the four ex-players. 'I think I know what we did wrong.'

Gary Ward didn't like to be ordered around by the likes of Frank Tuttle. Forget your tin-pot kiddies' leagues – Gary was going all the way. And when he'd made it as a professional football coach, then *he* would be the one giving the orders and the Tuttles of this world would be begging for the chance to clean his boots. But for now, he graciously accepted that if he was going to get caught up in this conspiracy business, he would have to grin and bear certain liberties.

The woman, on the other hand, was a different matter. Claire was lovely, squinting as she was right now in the sunlight beside Emirates Stadium: shiny blonde hair, nice skin, lively green eyes. He didn't mind taking orders from *her* at all.

'What's your idea, Claire?' he smiled at her.

Claire gave him a brief smile back but turned to Tuttle. Gary scowled. Clearly, he had superior football knowledge to that oaf – after all, Frank wasn't the one who had correctly identified Arsenal's ground as the location for the first clue. Gary consoled himself by remembering with amusement the 'innovative' football tactics that he'd heard about Frank using, before his well-deserved sacking.

Tuttle's never a better coach than me. Never.

Claire was now speaking while tying up her beautiful hair in a ponytail.

'I think we were on the right lines, but we took it too literally. We saw the numbers and thought that it was those that we should add up. But the clue didn't say anything about shirt numbers.'

Frank read the clue back from the tablet's screen. '"Circling legends combined." So, you reckon it's worth…?'

'A go, yeah,' Claire finished.

Gary had failed to grasp what they were getting at.

'What?' he asked. 'What's worth a go?'

While still looking at Claire, Frank said, 'It wants us to combine the legends themselves. So maybe we need to add up the number of letters in their names and use *that* as our answer.'

Claire nodded once and Frank returned the gesture.

The two of them already shared a rapport, Gary observed jealously.

He reminded himself again that there was a wider purpose for all this and exhaled slowly. 'Right then, let's do that. See you back round at the entrance.'

Off Frank and Claire went before Gary had had the chance to suggest that *he* go with Claire this time.

When they met back at the front of the stadium, they combined their two new totals – and came up with 194.

Gary entered it in – but the small difference in answer resulted in the map moving only very slightly. It was still in the forest and the number still turned red.

'Bollocks,' said Frank.

'Hold on,' said Claire. 'It says "combined" … Gary—'

'On it,' he said, tapping away on his phone.

Gary added the answer they had got combining the shirt numbers to the new one they now had of how many letters were in all the names. It came to 393.

The tablet thought about it. Then it zoomed out from the Emirates again, moved across London, this time southwest, and stopped.

'Eh?' said Tuttle, scratching his head.

61

'Oh no...' said Claire, shaking hers.

Gary said what they were all thinking. 'You... *we* must have made a mistake. Counted them wrong.'

Frank glanced at him briefly but remained silent, obviously grim about the prospect of dragging his gut around the stadium all over again.

Not only had '393' gone red, but it had made the map move to a screen of unbroken blue – the Thames River.

'Wait a sec,' said Frank. 'I've got an idea.'

'What is it?' asked Claire.

Gary had his phone out. 'Frank, why don't I just Google—'

'Hold your Googling,' Tuttle dismissed him with a wave of his hand, 'and gimme that thing again.' Frank grabbed the tablet from Gary. He swiped backwards to return to the screen that asked for the number answer. This time, he entered one digit less: 392.

The three of them watched as the map scrolled again. It only moved a fraction from their last guess – but from the location it settled on they knew they had definitely got it right this time. Confirming that the new answer had turned green was only a formality.

Claire broke into a huge smile. Gary, despite himself, found that he was grinning too.

Maybe I've underestimated Tuttle, he thought.

'Looks like we're off to the Borough of Hammersmith and Fulham,' said Frank.

As they ran down the steps towards Frank's sky-blue van, Gary asked Frank how he knew that they had gone over by one.

'Lucky guess?'

'Nah,' Frank answered, trying not to sound too out of breath. 'I realised I overshot one of mine. Did one digit too many.'

'How did you know?' asked Claire, focusing on not tripping up on the steps.

They stopped for a passing car then crossed over to the van. Frank unlocked it, then turned to the two expectant faces. 'Frank McLintock. Old-fashioned Scottish defender, hard as nails.'

'What about him?' Gary didn't want to admit that he'd never even heard of the player.

'As we were running around and I was trying to keep pace with this one,' he jerked a thumb at Claire, 'I was counting letters, but I counted *every* letter.'

Gary and Claire were confused for a moment. Then Gary got it. 'You counted the small *c* in *Mc* as a letter of its own.'

'Yep. Daft, eh?'

They piled in. Again, Claire took the van's middle seat and Gary was by the window.

'Guys,' she said as she was belting up, 'you do know what this means.'

'What?' said Frank, checking his rear-view mirror.

'The Quest is real.'

Gary looked at Frank, tried to read him. He seemed to be mulling Claire's comment over and opened his mouth as if to respond.

But then, abruptly, Frank pulled away from the curb without saying a word.

'I'll look up the best route to Craven Cottage,' said Gary whipping out his phone.

'Don't bother,' Tuttle said as he fastened his seatbelt. 'I got us here, didn't I? Drive around London delivering stuff all day, don't I? I know the best route. Why don't you just busy yourself twittering on your Facebook, we'll be there before you know it.'

Gary said nothing. He did start using his phone, but not because Frank had told him to.

Meanwhile, Claire started to quiz Frank. Gary pretended to be absorbed in his device but was listening to their conversation keenly.

'So, do you always pick your son up from training?' Claire was asking.

Frank changed gear while scratching his nose. 'He got a lift in with the neighbour's kid, but I was supposed to be there to get him. But that's only started this season; before I was taking him there and back.'

'Why the change?'

Gary froze, waiting to hear what Frank would say.

Tuttle cleared his throat. 'Well, up 'til last season I was manager of Ian's team.'

'Really?'

'Yeah, I had them first in the league.'

'So, what happened?'

Gary smiled to himself. Would Tuttle admit the truth about his sacking?

For the first time, Frank let his guard down in front of the other two. His voice was full of shame. 'Let's just say, I let my passion for the game overspill a bit.'

'But what actually happened?' Gary could resist asking no longer.

Frank opened his mouth, but then changed his mind.

'Nothing,' he said instead. 'It was... political.'

Claire furrowed her brow. She looked to Gary and he so wanted to spill the beans... but he was afraid of how Frank would react. So, he just shrugged.

Claire then mused on something else. 'So... it's an official league that your son plays in?'

'Yeah.' Frank smiled, brightening up. 'He's a nippy lad, top scorer every year.'

'So, you know what that means,' said Claire. 'We've both recently been sacked by the FA.'

Frank smiled wanly. 'Oh yeah.' Then he frowned. 'You really think they gave you the axe over something you wrote on the internet?'

Claire puffed out her cheeks and exhaled. 'I think so.'

They drove on.

'Hold your horses,' Frank said after a short while. He nodded at the road ahead.

64

'Well,' Gary said smugly, with a glance at Claire, 'I could have checked online for any road works, but—'

'It's not road works, Gaz,' said Frank.

Gary looked ahead. The side road they were travelling down contained two bright yellow vans parked on the curb, each with RCE: RESEARCH CREATING EXCELLENCE printed on their sides.

Frank idled in neutral less than 100 yards from where the two yellow vans were parked on the otherwise empty side road.

'Those are like the van Ian got into,' Claire confirmed.

Frank sprang for the door, but Claire grabbed his arm.

'Wait a second, Frank,' she said gently. 'Just drive up beside them.'

'Alright.'

He shifted into first and rolled forward.

As well as two vans, four of the yellow polo shirt-wearers were standing around. All were young, good looking and clean cut.

'Any of these the ones what took Ian?' Frank asked Claire. She shook her head.

As Frank pulled up next to the first yellow van, an RCE man approached. Frank rolled down his window.

'Hi,' the man said enthusiastically.

'Alright, mate,' said Frank.

'Can I ask you something?'

Frank gave the man a probing stare. He didn't trust anyone this chirpy and enthusiastic. 'You can try.'

'Do you like football?'

'Yeah.'

'Can I ask you a few questions about your views on the game?'

'How about I ask *you* some questions? Like, where's my son?'

The man looked bemused.

Claire read the firm's name from the side of the van out loud. 'Research Creating Excellence. You're... a PR agency?' she asked.

'And so much more,' grinned the man.

'What's your game, then? Do you lot work for the FA?' Frank asked.

The RCE man's disposition remained as bright as his garish top. 'If you'll just take a moment to answer some survey questions...'

'Is this something to do with this announcement thing today?'

'Then you will be able...'

'Do you know who's got my son?'

'To receive some fantastic offers on...'

'Oi,' Frank yelled.

Claire and Gary jumped. The man finally stopped talking. He glanced back to his colleagues nervously.

'Listen, mate,' Frank said calmly, but with a hint of menace. 'I don't have time for this.'

'But, but...' the RCE man stammered, 'we're conducting important market research—'

'I said I'm not answering any of your questions, sunshine. You got a problem with that?'

Gary leaned across Claire to speak to the RCE man. 'I wouldn't get him angry. Not after what happened to the last bloke who did that.'

Claire frowned, but nodded in support.

Again, the man looked back and forth to his colleagues for guidance.

'Aw, bollocks to this.' With that, Frank pushed the man over.

'Frank,' exclaimed Claire.

'Bloody hell,' said Gary.

Frank watched the fallen man's colleagues flock to help him, then he rolled past the parked vans and sped off.

'And away we go,' Frank said. He was outwardly calm, but adrenalin was flowing through him.

Soon, he knew, it would curdle into regret.

'What the hell did you do that for?' Claire was asking.

'Aw, I barely touched him,' said Frank. 'And it worked, didn't it?'

'Blimey, Frank,' said Gary.

'Well, my back-up plan was to wallop him with your phone, Gaz, but I didn't want you passing out in shock.' He turned to the youngster and grinned. But Gary wasn't happy, offering only a brief, perfunctory smile in return.

Frank turned to Claire, but she was sitting with her arms crossed, staring out the window.

He sighed.

There's that regret, bang on time.

'I hit him,' Frank said quietly.

Claire turned slightly. 'Pardon me?'

'That's why I got fired from coaching Ian's team. The other manager laughed at Ian, so I put my fist in his face. And now I don't live with my wife and son anymore.'

Silence in the van as Frank drove on.

Then Claire started to make strange, muffled noises.

It took Frank a few seconds to realise that she was giggling.

Frank turned to her. 'You think that's funny?'

'No, of course not.' Claire tried to control herself. 'It's just... punching him in the face? Bit of an overreaction wasn't it? What was he saying, that his kid was better than yours?'

'Alright, alright, no need to take the piss.' But now Frank was smiling. 'He couldn't handle how... innovative my tactics were. You've heard of the Christmas tree formation?'

'Yes...'

'Well, mine's the cactus formation. Much spikier.'

Gary opened his mouth. Frank hoped that the lad was going to ask for more details about the cactus approach, but Gary seemed to change his mind.

'This other manager geezer thought it was hilarious,' Frank went on. 'Weren't him who was 3-0 down though, was it? And when he started laughing at my Ian doing a diagonal side-dribble – past four of his players, I might add – I just flipped. But like I said before, the sacking was mostly political.'

'I see,' said Claire.

They drove on in silence again.

It was Gary who finally spoke. 'So, with that guy just now, was *that* political as well?' he asked.

Frank and Claire looked at each other. Then Frank looked at Gary. The younger man's face remained impassive.

Then all three cracked up laughing.

'Good one, mate,' Frank told Gary when they'd all calmed down.

Could actually have a decent team here, he thought with a smile.

Presently, Claire said, 'Look.' She was pointing ahead. Frank and Gary saw it straight away.

A floodlight had appeared over the horizon.

8

IT WAS fair to say that young Ian Tuttle was impressed. Just as Susan
Clyne had known he would be.

Wembley's Games Room was a teenage boy's dream. A disused hanger
behind the stadium had been crammed wall-to-wall with arcade machines
and games consoles, both new and retro. The noise and array of flashing
lights was overwhelming, making Susan wince as she led a captivated Ian
through. Children were everywhere, as well as more than a few adults.

'So, what do you think?' Susan asked Ian, shouting above the noise.

The boy grinned. With ironic understatement, he replied, 'Yeah. It's
pretty cool.'

She led him to the main attraction. In front of a 70-inch 4K screen were two leather chairs, on which sat two young boys hammering away at control pads. A game of simulated football was unfolding at a blistering pace: the as-yet-unreleased latest version of *Ultimate Soccer Challenge* (*Ultima Soc* to its fans).

'Wow,' was all Ian could say.

'You'll have to join the back of the line, I'm afraid.'

'I'd queue overnight to play *this*. Look at those graphics... And they've got this season's kits.' Ian was physically shaking with excitement.

'I'll leave you to it, then,' Susan said, walking away. The screen so transfixed Ian that his usual good manners deserted him, and he forgot to say goodbye.

Susan didn't care. Indeed, she walked off with a big smile on her face.

The boy had forgotten all about charging his phone.

Despite the long queue it was Ian's turn soon enough. He was an expert on the previous *Ultima Soc* and, despite the excitement that a new edition induced, as usual the updates were minor – better graphics, revised kits and squads, smoother animation.

The gamers were playing winner-stays-on. Ian beat a 50-something man, who threw the Playstation 5 controller down in disgust as he left, and then the next player sat down.

Ian gave his new opponent a sideways glance and a polite nod. He was a tall and athletic man in his 30s, with designer stubble and long hair that was shaved on the sides and tied up in a knot. He had tattoo sleeves on both his forearms and was dressed in expensive nonchalance: ripped Dolce & Gabbana jeans, faded Fendi T-shirt, white leather Gucci hi-tops.

'Alright,' the man said in a thick Yorkshire accent. 'Kevin Maxwell. Nice to beat you.'

Ian's pulse raced. He had never been in the presence of someone so famous in his whole life.

Kevin Maxwell... Wow, if only Dad was here.

But he kept his cool.

'Ian Tuttle. And beat me? I wouldn't be so sure.'

'Ha, good lad,' Kevin replied. 'We'll see about that, won't we? And if you lose – *when* you lose – don't go giving me no "unfair advantage" twaddle just 'cause I'm an actual footballer.'

'Whatever,' said Ian as he selected his team.

'Hold on a tick,' said Kevin. 'Is this that new version?'

'Yeah. It hasn't even been in the shops—'

'Oh no, can't have that.'

Kevin went over to the Playstation 5 console and turned it off.

Cries of complaint rang out from the queue.

'Aw hush it, you lot,' said Kevin, now rooting around in a cupboard marked GAMES AND CONSOLES.

'What are you *doing?*' cried Ian. People were now turning on him as if *he* had any idea what this nutter was up to.

'Keep your keks on, just looking for... that's the badger.' Kevin retrieved a CD.

'What's that?' asked Ian.

'Couple of versions back. This one's much better.'

'Why do you wanna play that *old* one?'

Kevin ejected the current disc and replaced it with the one he'd found. 'This is the best version, trust me.'

'But... it won't even...' Ian stammered.

This was seriously embarrassing. And Kevin seemed completely immune to the torrent of abuse he was receiving.

What Ian had been trying to warn Kevin about now became apparent. The old version of the game wouldn't work on this newer console.

'Eh?' said Kevin, staring up at the blank screen.

71

'No backwards compatibility,' Ian informed him. 'That version's so old it's for the PS4, and not all of those games will work on the PS5.'

'Ah,' said Kevin with renewed hope. 'Think I saw one of them older machines and all.'

To Ian and the crowd's increasing disbelief, Kevin proceeded to unplug the Playstation 5, take out a Playstation 4 from the cupboard, plug *that* in, and turn the replacement machine on.

Kevin loaded the game then took his seat again, giving Ian the thumbs-up.

The boy just shook his head in disbelief.

It was when they went to select their teams that the penny dropped.

'There he is,' said Kevin as the screen changed to an animation of the two sides in the tunnel pre-match.

Standing with his fellow computer-generated players was a familiar figure.

'Look at *that* handsome fella,' marvelled Kevin. 'Obviously they couldn't go *quite* as good-looking as the real deal, would have distracted people from their game.'

The in-game camera dollied down the tunnel past the avatar Kevin Maxwell's blank, lifeless face. The real-life Kevin promptly stood up and turned around to face the crowd, his hands held aloft.

The onlookers forgot about being annoyed and erupted into applause.

Kevin milked the attention and didn't stop until Ian tugged at his T-shirt and said, 'We've started.'

The footballer span around and landed in his seat just in time to get a last-ditch tackle in on Ian's pixelated striker.

Kevin Diego Maxwell was brought up by working class parents in Driffield, East Yorkshire. As a child Kevin was interested in nothing but football. His dad got him into the game as soon as he could walk, standing side-by-side on the terraces of York City's Bootham Crescent cheering themselves hoarse, staying up together to watch *Match of the Day*. It was Max Maxwell who insisted on making his newborn son's middle name a tribute to his hero, Maradona, who had just demolished England using means both legal and illegal at the 1986 World Cup. Maxwell Senior idolised the mercurial Argentinean and refused to go along with the English public's consensus of hatred following the no. 10's infamous 'hand of God' goal.

But Max had inadvertently set his son up for a childhood of ridicule. Kevin's peers ganged up on him at playtime and administered humiliations involving his hand – forcing him to dip it in the toilet bowl, to put it up girls' skirts, to touch dog poo. And there was the name-calling – 'Argie-lover', 'hand-job', 'grease-ball.' Young Kevin was slight of build and pitch-marking thin so was no physical match for his tormentors. Whenever they got bored and let him be, Kevin practiced alone with a football in the corner of the playground. By the age of nine, he could replicate all of the tricks on his dad's *The Most Skilful Footballers... Ever* VHS; 73 minutes of opponents being left for dead by the likes of George Best, Johan Cruyff, Stanley Matthews – and, of course, a certain diminutive South American.

The schoolyard abuse toughened Kevin up. When he was ten, he decided to fight back, suffering a black eye and a bloody lip but nothing more. He was surprised at how inept the bullies actually were, despite heavily outnumbering him. It made young Kevin realise that a bit of front could go a long way and his tormentors soon moved onto easier targets. His fightback coincided with a growth spurt and by the time he started secondary school, Kevin had shot up half a foot. He joined the football team and was years ahead of all the other boys in technique, physicality and bravery. He would go for the headers others ducked from, take on every 50/50 tackle – and when he won the ball, which he invariably did, he had the skill and footballing brain to do something positive with it.

The bullying also influenced Kevin's personality. He learned how to answer the name-calling by entertaining people. Once he'd earned his first laughs he wanted more and more. He was the class clown, devoting more time to amusing his classmates than to his studies. His grades suffered, but it didn't matter – though his mum and dad went through the motions of chastising him, they knew that his heart was in his football. And Max Maxwell was thrilled.

Kevin was signed up by Aston Villa's academy at age 12 and he went pro upon breaking into the first team at 17. But his top-flight career turned out to be unsettled, comprising eight clubs to date and three more on loan. Managers rarely knew what to do with him – on the one hand, he was a tremendous box-to-box midfielder, the equal of Frank Lampard or Steven Gerrard, and was capped half a dozen times by the full England squad before he could drive. But just as prominent as his talent was his rebellious side – he was erratic, didn't follow instructions, and couldn't care less about formations or positional awareness. His discipline was poor too, always arguing with refs and getting carded for his reactions.

But he delivered the goods, winning the Premier League at three different clubs, the Champions League with two. The really serious problems came *off* the pitch.

'Kevin, would you mind if I asked you something?'

They were playing *Alien War*, shooting down screens of invaders with plastic assault rifles. Ian had won on *Ultima Soc*, prompting Kevin to challenge him to a rematch on a different game. Kevin beat him on a classic *Street Fighter 2* arcade (in straight rounds as Ryu vs Ian's Blanka) and they'd been touring the Games Room from machine to machine ever since.

'Yeah, ask away,' Kevin replied, hitting an alien queen with a well-timed grenade. 'I in't shy of a grilling.'

But Ian *was* shy. He knew that asking adults personal questions wasn't polite. But Kevin wasn't really an adult; it was like being with one of his schoolmates.

'Well, I was looking at the Premier League free transfers list the other day and—'

'And I'm on it.' Kevin started shooting down the aliens more aggressively.

'Well, yeah. I don't understand. How come you don't have a club?'

'Shit,' said Kevin. The alien queen killed both players with one swoop of her claw. 'Bitch. Thought we was gonna get away from her.' They holstered their guns.

Kevin immediately had his phone out.

'Better tweet about this,' he said.

'About *this*?' asked Ian. Between posing for countless selfies with fans, Kevin had already updated his social media accounts about 20 times since Ian had met him.

'Yeah, nearly got ten million.'

'Points?' Ian peered at the arcade's screen.

'No, you plum, Twitter followers.'

Kevin strode off, immersed in his phone. Ian trailed behind.

Now Kevin looked around the huge room. 'Owt else in here?' he said. 'Any driving games? Aw proper sound – *Urban Asphalt*.'

As they settled down into a double-car arcade machine, Ian ventured, 'So... why *don't* you have a club?'

Kevin's hand hovered mid-air, holding two pound coins to start up the game. He dropped his arm but kept looking at the coin slot as he spoke.

'You read the papers, mate? Online news and that?'

'Mostly I just check the football results.' Whatever Ian had picked up about Kevin Maxwell's troubles had come from his father. Frank Tuttle admired the player but only last week had slapped down his newspaper in frustration and declared, 'That idiot Maxwell should keep to expressing himself on the bloody pitch. He's just what this England team needs right now but he's doing himself no favours.'

Kevin put the pound coins down and turned to face Ian. 'You know about me history?'

'Yeah, two seasons at Villa, then—'

Kevin held up his hand. 'No, I mean when I *in't* on the pitch.'

Ian shook his head.

Kevin rubbed his temples with one hand and shifted his weight.

'Okay, lemme me give you a few choice headlines. "Embarrassment to the Max: Kev puts foot in mouth again." Let's see... "Gaffer docks Maxwell two weeks' pay over post-match comments." Then there was "Midfielder banned for five matches for Twitter outburst." Oh, can't forget "FA: Kevin has Maximus fine from us."'

Ian nodded along slowly. 'Sounds like the newspaper people find it quite funny.'

'Oh mate, don't get me started on them lot,' said Kevin, his fists clenching. 'When I were a kid just breaking through, they loved me. Built me right up. Then I realised – they only did it so they could knock me down.'

Kevin squirmed in his seat, pulling his T-shirt down where it had ridden up his back. 'Anyway, I say the wrong things, don't I? In interviews, on social media, to the magazines and papers. I'm always bleating summat daft. You know how when you see players asked questions after the match, they usually just say something dead boring?'

Ian nodded. He'd seen this on TV many times.

'I can't do it. I know that I'm supposed to tell the bloke with the mic, "Scoring's nice but the most important thing is three points for the team." But I always say summat like, "Yeah, I'm dead chuffed 'cause I'll get me goal bonus and if the team wins too then that's sound – reminds I gotta renegotiate me win bonus." I'm only being honest. They tried to give me this media training, but it did nowt. I still always... well, put me foot in me mouth.'

'They charge you for *that*?'

'No, the fines were for... speaking me mind. Saying what I really thought about other players, managers and, worst of all, the FA, slagging off how they run things. Now I'm known as a "PR nightmare," an expert at "bringing the game into disrepute." And I can't help reacting to them online clowns neither – some pillock says something to me on Twitter, I just have to fight back, breaking club policy. And then I find myself on the transfer list.' He stared into the middle distance. 'Only this time, looks like no one's interested in old Kev Maxwell.'

With that, Kevin rested his chin on his fist and just sat watching the screen. The game's demo mode showed a high-speed pursuit through a futuristic New York City.

Ian didn't know what to say. The boy was about to open his mouth to try something consolatory, when Kevin's demeanour changed completely. He spun around to face Ian with a huge smile on his face.

'Come on. I'm bored of all this. You wanna have a proper look round this gaff – take the Wembley tour what people don't normally get?'

'Awesome!'

9

A T THE same time that Ian Tuttle was getting acquainted with household name footballer Kevin Maxwell, his father Frank was driving his company van south parallel to the Thames River.

Frank glanced out his wound-down window, admiring the attractive residential area. He could see the sun glistening off the river's surface through the tree-lined side roads that branched off from Woodlawn Road. London's SW6 was as calm and tranquil as if it were out in the suburbs, rather than Tube Zone 2. Dog walkers greeted each other as they passed, and mothers parked their prams to exchange gossip.

As well as admiring the surroundings, Frank was hard at thought.

He was thinking about how they'd just solved the first clue, back at Emirates stadium. Was this proof that there *were* things hidden underneath the glossy surface world of football, secrets that they had never seen – because they hadn't ever gone looking for them?

Until now.

Frank took a right onto one of the side roads, Queensmill, and then an immediate left onto Stevenage Road. They were now within yards of Craven Cottage Stadium, the home of Fulham Football Club, situated on the north bank of the Thames.

'You have reached your destination,' Frank said, imitating a satnav. His companions Claire and Gary smiled, but their faces soon fell when they saw what was waiting for them.

A fleet of yellow RCE vans was parked outside the stadium.

Frank cruised past the vans and took the first left, coming to a stop on the curb of Finlay Street.

Claire was Googling 'Research Creating Excellence'.

'They seem like your average, run-of-the-mill PR agency,' she said, scrolling through the firm's website and holding her phone out to Frank and Gary. 'I mean, I've never heard of them, but there are loads of these kind of outfits.'

The trio got out. It was so hot that all three left their jackets in the van, although Gary held onto his rucksack. Frank led them back down the street that they had just driven up and they all peaked round the corner at the stadium.

'London's oldest football stadium,' commented Claire.

'One of many designed by Archibald Leitch,' Gary added.

'Such as Anfield, Celtic Park...'

'Mollineux, Villa Park...'

'Hillsborough—'

'Alright, alright,' Frank cut in, 'you're both football geeks, I get it.'

They ducked back around and stood at the end of the road.

'Here's something you two *won't* be so sure about,' Frank said. 'What the hell does one of these Halves even look like? And how are we gonna know when we find it?'

Claire and Gary thought about this.

'It'll be something old,' offered Gary.

'We'll know, Frank,' added Claire. 'I think when we find it, we'll just know.'

'I hope so,' said Frank.

He took out the tablet. 'So, let's see this next clue, then.'

Phase One

Clue Two (to find the first Half)

Within this location, a place for one person:
At peace ____
Next to nature ____
View of a king ____ ____

'Hmm,' said Claire, speaking for all of them.

Frank poked his head round the corner again. There were plenty of RCE vans but none of the actual employees were anywhere to be seen. Just a lone stadium steward – a portly grey-haired man in his 60s – who was manning the entrance to the Johnny Haynes Stand, which was next to a statue of the ex-player himself. Above the steward's head was a sign confirming that the next home game was this afternoon at 3pm.

Frank returned to the other two. 'What's that building inside that's got the "This is Fulham" sign on it?'

'That's Craven Cottage,' said Gary.

'For crying out loud, Gaz, I *know* this is Craven Cottage, but what's the bloody building with the sign on it?'

Gary looked to Claire for support. 'No, you don't understand...'

'I'm trying to get my lad back and you're playing silly buggers with me.' Frank wasn't in the mood to be patronised by some young wannabe football coach. This was the kind of character they had on staff now? And *Frank* had been fired?

'Frank, wait...' said Claire. 'Gary's right.'

'Eh?'

'The whole ground is called "Craven Cottage," yes, but there is also a pavilion building that is an *actual* cottage. It's where the players' friends and family watch the game, from the balcony.'

'Oh,' said Frank, embarrassed. He looked at Gary who, as usual, was taking refuge in his phone. 'Er, look, I'm sorry Gaz. Gary.'

Gary glanced up.

'I've been snapping at you all morning. I wanna, you know, apologise. I'm just tetchy 'cause I'm worried about Ian.'

Frank held out his hand.

Gary shook it and smiled thinly.

'Right, now that we're all friends again,' Claire said, 'let's figure this thing out. Frank, did you have an idea about the cottage?'

'Yeah, well, I dunno. If that's some special building inside the ground, then maybe what we're looking for is in there. And... isn't a king's home the cottage – like in the clue?'

'I think you mean palace, Frank,' Gary said gently.

'You mean, go all the way to South London?'

Gary and Claire shared a look, not sure whether or not he was serious.

Then Frank grinned. 'So, is the cottage worth a shot?'

Claire said, 'Well, the clue mentions a view and you'd think that the cottage's balcony would have a good one.'

Gary was nodding. 'And it would be peaceful, away from all the chanting fans.'

'"At peace,"' quoted Claire.

'So that just leaves the third part,' Frank said, looking at the tablet again. 'Nature.'

'Well, if it's made of wood, then that's from trees, right?' offered Gary.

'Good enough for me,' said Frank.

They crept together to the end of the road and peeked round the corner.

'So, are we going to... break in?' asked Claire.

'On a match day? Place will have security coming out of its ears, even this early,' said Frank.

Gary stared at Frank. 'You want to buy actual tickets?'

Frank rolled his head from side to side. 'Might have to.'

'No chance,' said Claire. 'My cousin is a Fulham fan. He rang me up last week to see if I had any FA comp tickets. I had to let him down – this match is sold out. It is the first home game of the season, after all.'

'Damn.' Frank rubbed his chin.

'There must be another way,' said Gary. Frank saw that he had his phone out again but resisted the urge to tell him to put it away and pay attention. The lad was probably searching for ideas online.

'If I still worked for the FA it would be easy to get in,' Claire lamented.

This gave Frank an idea. He saw that one of the RCE vans was parked further down the road than the others, outside of Bishop's Park. 'Follow me,' he said.

They crossed Stevenage Road and hid behind the isolated RCE van.

'The yellow shirt gang must all be round the other side of the ground,' said Claire.

'Or inside,' suggested Gary ominously.

Frank, meanwhile, was looking through the back window of the RCE van. He tried the door and found that it was unlocked. He pulled it quietly open, conscious of the steward not far away, and peered inside.

'I know how we can get into this ground,' he told the others.

Gary and Claire leaned in and saw what it was that had got Frank's attention.

'You can't be serious,' said Gary.

But Claire smiled. 'That might just work.'

It wasn't how Claire had imagined she would be spending the first Saturday of the new football season. But then today had been full of surprises, so why not roll with it?

'Small... that'll do for you Gary, right? Just slip it over your t-shirt. Frank, here's a large. I think I can get away with a small too, they're unisex.'

So here she was – in the back of a van with two men she had only just met, rooting through a cardboard box of yellow polo shirts and helping the men to find their sizes.

Well, she thought as she followed Frank and Gary back out into the sunshine, *makes a change from scanning Hootsuite feeds all day.*

'You okay?' Frank asked her.

'Yeah,' said Claire. 'I was just thinking... I just remembered that it's the Job Centre for me on Monday.' She smiled weakly.

Frank regarded her. Claire could see that he was trying to think of something consoling to say. It was sweet, really.

Finally, he ventured, 'Look, Claire. Nothing's gonna stop me getting my boy back, but if there's something dodgy going on in football as well then, I'm gonna to get to the bottom of that and all. We *all* are.' He looked to Gary, who had his nose in his phone again. Undeterred, Frank persevered. 'And I bet by the end of it all, whoever messed up and fired you is gonna come back tail between legs.'

The pep talk made Claire feel better. 'You think?'

Frank winked. 'Guarantee it.'

'Besides,' added Gary, 'you can't just turn up at the Job Centre. You have to fill in a form online and make an appointment first.'

'Thanks for that, Gary,' said Claire.

She and Gary hopped down onto the pavement. When Frank followed, his trailing foot caught something on the floor of the van.

They all looked down. Frank had knocked a box over and spilled its contents onto the road.

Franks reached down and picked up a sheet of paper, headed INTERNAL RCE MEMO: NOT FOR EXTERNAL DISTRIBUTION.

'Here,' said Frank, showing the paper to the other two, 'cop a load of this.'

The three of them read the brief memo.

Verbal data gathering questions for fans:

1. *Do you support a specific football team or just follow the game?*
2. *Are there any football rules you would like to change?*
3. *Is there too much advertising in football?*
4. *Do you watch most football games on TV or in a stadium?*
5. *Is winning the most important part of football?*

Report any controversial answers to your line manager so they can feed them into the long-term research project.

Note: See separate documentation for questions for those in the football profession.

'Sounds like the stuff that yellow-top bloke was asking me earlier,' said Frank.

'Hmm,' said Claire. 'Interesting that there's a question about how important winning is. Suggests that they're interested in fairness.'

'There's one about changing football's rules, too,' added Gary. 'Like all those Twitter rumours, saying the announcement will be about a rules change...'

'And what's "the long-term research project"?'

Frank pocketed the memo. 'This could come in useful,' he said.

The trio moved away from the van to stand in the shadow of Craven Cottage Stadium, all of them now wearing the familiar yellow polo shirts over their own tops.

'Alright,' said Frank, stealing a glance at the steward, who was reading the match day programme. 'What now?'

'What do you mean?' asked Gary. 'This is *your* cunning plan.'

'Yeah, um, but how exactly do you think we should...' Frank trailed off.

'Oh, for crying out loud,' said Claire. 'Just follow my lead you two.'

She pulled a compact mirror from her handbag. Glancing at her reflection, she muttered, 'That'll have to do.' Then she led Frank and Gary towards the steward.

The man looked up from his programme when he saw the pretty young woman approaching him with her two male colleagues in tow. She was smiling broadly, so instinctively he returned the gesture.

'Hi,' said Claire.

'Hello, miss,' the man replied.

'Just popping inside for a bit,' said Claire.

'All of you?'

'Uh, that's right.'

'We were told that you lot aren't allowed inside until later. When the fans start turning up. Bit early yet, isn't it?'

Claire thought on her feet. 'That's true. But... we also want to speak to the catering staff in the ground. Find out... which flavour pies are on sale today.'

'Which... pies?'

'Oh yeah. The half-time pie is crucial, surely you must know that.' She gave his large belly a prod in what was designed to be an affectionate, flirtatious gesture.

But the man frowned, not sure how to take the comment.

'Yeah, looks like you've eaten them all,' blurted Gary.

Frank shot daggers at him.

Claire tried to dig her way out. 'Ha-ha, no, it's quite serious actually, um, because we're researching fans' match day experience and the quality and variety of pies is the number one factor determining whether they have a good one. Match day experience, that is.'

The steward stared at her, then at Frank and Gary in turn, both of whom just grinned inanely, imitating the RCE employees that they had met earlier.

The steward turned back to Claire. 'Really? The number one?'

'Yes, completely,' she nodded. 'Voted for by 78% of half the key demographics.'

'I voted for it twice,' added Frank.

'More important to the match day experience than... than how good the game was?'

'Oh, how good the game was *is* especially important, of course, but the pies are *especially* important.'

'Sometimes I don't even stay to watch the game if the pie's been crap,' added Frank.

Claire kept smiling, but covertly squeezed Frank's arm to indicate that more interjections were not required.

The steward eyed the three of them up. The permanently smiling faces, creepy and forced. The reliance on statistics. The dogged persistence.

They were marketing people, alright.

'Go on then,' the steward said. 'And it's true – I do love a good pie. If the steak and ales are up to scratch, ask them to save me one, will you?'

The three imposters rushed through the open gate. 'Will do, bye,' Claire called back.

The steward returned to his programme.

Frank, Claire and Gary passed the cottage, eyeing it up as they went, and turned right, entering the Johnny Haynes Stand. They stood in the concourse among the not-yet-open concessions booths and next to the exit to Block KL. The stand was deserted and eerily quiet.

'"Checking the pies"?' Frank asked Claire.

Claire held her hands up. 'It was the best I could come up with at short notice.'

'No, it was great. Couldn't have done better myself.' Frank noticed a pie-selling kiosk and nudged the other two. They shared a quick laugh.

'Yeah, pretty sharp,' admitted Gary. 'But we've got a problem, haven't we?'

No one had to say it out loud. Instead, they crept back to where they had come in and peered out. There was no doubt about it: the Craven Cottage cottage was securely locked up. The word that came to Claire was *impenetrable.*

Another problem was that the steward they'd just duped was standing only feet away from it.

'I could distract him again,' suggested Claire.

Frank scratched his nose. 'Don't think so, we were pushing our luck the first time. And one of his mates will no doubt be along soon.'

The three of them returned to the stand. Now they could indeed see other stewards, milling about at the far end.

'So, what next?' asked Claire. The stewards were making her nervous.

'Let's look at that clue again,' said Gary.

Within this location, a place for one person:
At peace ____
Next to nature ____
View of a king ____ ____

'It wants *three* answers,' Gary said.

'That's true,' agreed Claire. 'And the third answer is two words.'

'*Three* places?' Frank was sceptical.

'Not necessarily,' said Claire, 'Let's be systematic. "Within this location," so that's got to be inside the stadium.'

'Right,' agreed Frank. 'So, we were right to pull that stunt and get ourselves inside.'

'Yeah. And "a place for one person."'

Gary frowned. 'Where can there only be one person? Is it... to do with the referee? There's only one of him. And Claire's blog was about refs...'

The other two pulled *maybe, maybe not* faces.

Then Frank got it. 'Of course,' he said.

'What?'

'I can't believe we didn't see it straight away. Come on.' With that he turned on his heel.

The other two chased after him.

Moments later, they were confronted with the pitch.

Frank had a huge smile on his face. He extended his arm in a sweeping gesture. 'All these seats. How many people sit on them?'

'Well that depends,' said Gary, tilting his head, 'on whether someone has a season ticket, or—'

'I mean at any one time.'

'Well... one.'

Frank raised his eyebrows.

'So, the answer is a specific seat,' said Claire.

'Reckon so.'

'And the three answers...' Claire started.

'Identify the seat.' Gary finished.

'Gotta be,' said Frank.

They made their way down the steps. Frank said, 'So you got four things that identify your seat: stand, block, row and seat number. Looks like that last part of the clue gives you both row and seat.'

Claire stopped. 'Wait, are we sure we're even in the right stand?' she asked.

'Nope,' said Frank. 'We're not.'

'How do you know?' asked Gary.

'Because I've already worked out part of the clue.'

This Ian kid was alright, Kevin had decided.

Sure, he asked a lot of questions, but that was normal when meeting a celebrity. And at least Kevin knew that his answers weren't going to get him in trouble – Ian hadn't once got his phone out to update his socials. It was nice to have a conversation where the other person focused on you exclusively, and this had even prompted Kevin to leave his own phone in his pocket for durations of longer than 60 seconds. The kid hadn't even asked for a selfie – which had upset Kevin at first, but he was coping.

The pair were circulating Wembley's inner administrative corridors, which Kevin had led them into through a door marked STAFF ONLY. The footballer was now looking for another door – and they had completed almost a full circuit of the ground already.

Meanwhile, Ian had been taking advantage of this opportunity to cross-examine a real-life player.

'Getting to the heart of the matter now, aren't you mate?' Kevin smiled in response to Ian's latest question. 'You're more probing than the BBC.'

Kevin was pleased to see Ian beam with pride.

'*This* is the reason I'm here today.' Kevin stopped walking and rubbed his thumb against his first two fingers.

'Money?'

'Bingo.'

'But I thought footballers were all rich. Why do you need more money?'

Kevin laughed, then realised that the boy was serious.

'I got a few quid, sure,' Kevin said. 'But what they don't tell you is that no matter how much you have coming in, you can always spend it. And all them fines for running me mouth off don't help much, neither.'

'So how does being here today earn you more money?'

Kevin started to walk again, and Ian duly followed.

'Well, mate,' the footballer explained, glancing at each door as they passed it, 'when you want a famous person, a celeb, to turn up to your event, you have to pay them. It's called an appearance fee. Usually you have to give your agent his cut, but luckily I currently represent myself.'

Kevin was glad that Ian didn't enquire as to what had happened to his last agent.

Instead the lad asked, 'So they've invited you to be part of the Family Fun Day?'

'Uh, not exactly. But they *will*, when they realise how I can help them.'

'How can you help them?' The boy maintained his polite tone, but even someone as self-absorbed as Kevin could appreciate that Ian was getting tired of walking past the same network of grey pipes and hazard notices, broken up by unpainted brickwork and the occasional closed door.

Yet rather than acknowledge that they'd been on the move for ages or admit that they were lost, Kevin took the opportunity to move onto his favourite topic.

'I've got plans, mate. Endorsement plans, using me name.'

'Your name?'

'Energy drinks: "Giving You Performance *to the Max*." Footie boots: "So You Can Kick It *to the Max*." Cars: "Driving You to the..." actually, that one could use me whole name, split up: "However *Well* You Drive, You Need Power. *To the Max*."'

'I... think I get it,' Ian said.

Kevin could tell that the kid was well impressed.

'So, whatever the FA want to plug, or whoever they're partnered with or whatever, I can raise their profile big time.'

'I've got an idea,' Ian said. 'You know what you *should* do.'

Since he'd warmed to the boy, Kevin gave him his best interested face.

'You should read out this big announcement thing. Everyone's going to be listening to that.'

Kevin stopped abruptly and turned to Ian. 'Mate, you should be an agent.'

The lad put his hands on his hips defiantly. 'No way, I'm gonna be a player.'

Kevin couldn't help but chuckle. 'Don't worry, I in't laughing at *you*,' he clarified. 'It's just that most agents start off saying exactly that.'

'Then what happens?'

'Then they figure out there are different meanings of the word "player" ... Anyway, reading this announcement thing – not a bad idea, that. Cheers, Ian.'

Then Kevin finally found what he'd been looking for. 'Ah, that's the badger,' he said, indicating a door that had TO MEDIA CENTRE printed on it.

Kevin opened the door and let Ian through into another bland corridor. This one was only short and led straight to another door, guarded by two burly security guards.

Kevin rocked up confidently. 'Alright, boys,' he said, flashing his most winning smile.

The guards were unmoved.

'You must be new. Professional footballers are allowed to come and go as they please in any FA building, including this here national stadium. So, if you don't mind...'

The guards still didn't budge. 'Are we supposed to let *any* player through?' one asked the other. 'Even *him?*' The man jerked a thumb at Kevin then made an open and closed *yak-yak-yak* gesture with his other hand.

His mate shrugged. 'What do we care? Great thing about this one is he don't humiliate no one but himself.'

The other guard laughed. Kevin joined in too, controlling his emotions.

The guards weren't finished. 'Oi Maxwell, remember when you said, "Security at football stadiums is run by morons and ex-prisoners"?'

Both guards laughed again, with a hint of menace this time, while again Kevin joined in through gritted teeth.

He said, 'I were dead young then, and had just got yanked to the floor by ten of your lot, all 'cause I were standing on the advertising hoardings celebrating a goal.'

'Yeah, that was at Newcastle,' the first guard remembered. 'I was at that game. You could have ended our kid's career with that tackle in the second half.'

'It was a 50/50 ball,' Kevin explained tersely.

'Yeah, 50/50 my arse,' the man said, glowering at him.

Kevin cleared his throat. 'Boys, I'm really enjoying this chat, but I've got a VIP here, the, er...'

'I'm the president of FIFA's son,' Ian cut in, 'and we're wanted upstairs *now*.'

Kevin's intense stare and Ian's brattish tone convinced the guards. 'Alright,' said the first, swiping his key card. 'Go on.'

The door swung open and the uninvited visitors marched through. 'Thanks a million,' Kevin murmured without looking up.

As the pair started up a metal staircase, the second guard regained his cockiness and piped up after them, 'Good luck finding a new club, Maxwell. Sure you'll be fine.'

'Yeah,' his mate joined in, '*Big* fine.'

Cackles of laughter rang out as Kevin and Ian climbed.

'Just ignore those guys,' Ian said softly.

Kevin brushed it off. 'Great save back there, mate. That were like Pete Harrington against Norway in the World Cup.'

Ian laughed. 'I'm a striker, not a goalie. Although I wouldn't mind being England captain.'

Kevin checked his phone. When he saw that his last tweet had been favourited 57 times already, he smiled. He switched to his home feed.

'Hey, the latest rumour about this announcement whatsit is that they're gonna increase the number of players in a team. That's perfect: "Need to *Max out* your team? *Well* You Better... er..."'

'Oh, so you don't know what the announcement is about either?'

'Hmm?' the footballer was now browsing his Instagram account. 'Nah. But when we tell this lot in here that Kev Maxwell is gonna read it out, they'll show us it straight away.'

Finally, they reached the top of the stairs. This set of guards took one look at Kevin and let him and Ian straight through the final door.

Kevin had been in Wembley's Media Centre a couple of times before, but Ian gasped audibly. The footballer patted him on the back and led him inside.

But right away they were stopped in their tracks.

'That's far enough, Mr Maxwell. Come with me, please.'

O VER at Craven Cottage, Frank was explaining to Claire and Gary which of Clue Two's three answers he had figured out. If correct, they would be closer to identifying a specific seat – and finding the first of the two Halves.

The three of them were standing halfway down Block KL, out in the sunshine. Sprinklers worked the pitch, creating rainbows and accentuating the freshly cut grass smell. Frank reflected on how pure and full of anticipation the pre-season pitch seemed, before a tackle had been made, before a refereeing decision had been disputed, before a goal had been scored. It was a newly poured pint or a bulging polystyrene takeaway box. It was joy still to come.

Presently Frank turned to the other two. He tapped something into the tablet and then showed them the screen.

Within this location, a place for one person:
At peace PUTNEY
Next to nature ____
View of a king ____ ____

The answer PUTNEY turned green.

'The Putney End,' Claire said while tying her hair up again, it having come loose with all the running around.

Frank grinned. 'I'm surprised you football nerds never got it straight away.'

'A stand... of *peace?*' Gary said, sipping water from a bottle he had taken from his rucksack.

'As in, no aggression or...' Claire was equally stumped.

Frank put them out of their misery. 'Fulham used to have a neutral stand. Not really home and not really away.'

'Of course,' Gary realised.

'Good work, Frank,' said Claire.

Frank looked across the pitch to the Riverside Stand. Two stewards in orange hi-vis vests were staring across at the three intruders.

Frank pursed his lips. 'Hey,' he whispered.

'What?' asked Gary.

'We better play it cool.' Frank was still looking at the stewards.

Claire and Gary followed his gaze.

Frank said, 'We just have to seem... legit.' Slowly, Frank raised a hand and waved at their observers.

One of the stewards waved back. The other raised his radio to his lips.

'Doesn't look good,' said Claire.

'Come on,' said Frank. 'Let's keep on the move. Make it look like we're busy working.'

As they made their way down the steps, Frank stole another glance at the stewards. They had now been joined by another colleague.

'Busy working on *what,*' said Gary, 'is the question.'

'Maybe we're doing a ground survey and recording the results in the tablet?' suggested Claire.

'Good enough for me,' Frank said.

The trio now pantomimed performing inspections as they descended the steps. Gary made sure that each seat went down and returned to its upright position. Claire was checking that the rows were all labelled properly. Both leaned into Frank to report their results and he duly pretended to tap on the tablet.

After a few minutes of this, Frank looked up again. The stewards had gone. He didn't know whether this was a good or a bad sign.

'Alright, enough of all this,' Frank said. They were now only a few rows from the pitch. 'Let's get in the right stand and start thinking about those other two clues.'

Currently, they were still in the Johnny Haynes Stand, one of the long sides that met the Putney End, which was behind a goal. The three of them were by now at the end seat of the bottom row, so they only had to cross diagonally onto the pitch then straight off again to enter their target stand.

'Where did you hear about the neutral stand stuff?' Gary asked Frank as they crossed.

'On this TV report a while ago. Remember they used to have that statue of Michael Jackson? He was pals with the chairman back then, the Egyptian bloke.'

'Mohammad Al Fayed,' Claire said, being careful not to catch the hem of her dress as she crossed over the advertising hoardings.

'That's him, the Harrods chap. He'd just sold the club and so they were showing the statue being torn down and then some Fulham fan was going on about the friendly atmosphere here, how they even had a neutral stand before the stadium was all-seater.'

As they started to climb the steps of the Putney End, Claire got an idea. 'Frank, that last part of the clue...'

'"View of a king"?'

'Yeah. What was Michael Jackson's nickname?'

Recognition spread across Frank and Gary's faces.

Gary said it. 'The King of Pop.'

Claire gave the thumbs-up.

'But wait,' said Gary. 'What are we gonna enter as the answer? "Michael Jackson" isn't a block or a row or a seat.'

This gave Frank and Claire pause for thought.

'So, we're looking for just one out of these thousands of seats,' said Gary as he looked up and across the stand.

Frank said, 'Come on, let's think it through. "View of a king..." Well, what would a king's view be like?'

'Good,' said Claire. 'Like we were saying earlier.'

'Right,' agreed Frank.

'Close to the pitch? So he can see all the action?' suggested Claire.

Gary wasn't so sure. 'You'd expect a king to be high up, wouldn't you?'

'Yeah, near the top – that's what I reckon,' said Frank. 'Come on.'

As they carried on up the steps, Gary got his phone out. 'I'll look into that other clue, "next to nature."'

'Good lad,' said Frank.

The three of them trotted up the steps and were soon at the top, row ZZ.

'Definitely a good view up here,' commented Claire.

'Good enough for a king?' asked Frank.

'Guys...' said Gary looking up from his phone. 'I think I've got this *nature* clue.'

As Gary led the way across the back row, Frank kept an eye on the Riverside Stand – not only were the three orange-vested stewards back, but two more had joined them. Again, one raised his radio. Frank looked down the rows of their own stand, expecting to see new stewards arriving there at any moment.

The three got to the end of the back row. They had now gone from the bottom right corner of the Putney End to the top left.

'Let's hear what you've got, Gaz, and sharpish,' Frank said, indicating across the pitch towards the stewards. 'I think we're gonna have company soon.'

Gary gulped. 'Okay.' He pointed out between their own Putney End and the adjacent Riverside Stand. 'Over there.'

Claire and Gary looked, but couldn't see anything.

Frank looked around again. Stewards *were* now spilling into their own stand.

'Gaz, time is of the bloody essence here. What's this nature clue?'

'It's right there.' Gary pointed again. 'We're "next to nature."'

Then Frank saw it. 'A *tree*? In a football ground?'

'The only tree within any English professional ground.'

Claire double-checked what block they were in. 'P7,' she said.

Frank tapped 'P7' into the tablet and the answer box turned green.

'Good work, Gary,' said Claire.

'Yeah, nice one Gaz,' said Frank shakily. He was more concerned about what he was seeing below them: five stewards were now climbing the steps of their stand with purpose.

'So that's two out of three, Claire was saying, 'but there's still one answer to get. We've got the block and think we're in the right row – but which seat in it?'

'I don't know,' Gary said. He and Claire had seen the approaching stewards now and were suitably panicked. 'Which has the best view – "fit for a king"?'

'I don't think we've got time to try them all out,' Frank said.

Then Claire had a thought. 'Frank, do you remember exactly where the Michael Jackson statue was?'

Frank shook his head. 'But it was on the outside and it weren't the same side as that Johnny Haynes statue we saw when we came in.'

Claire said, 'Gary, see if—'

'On it,' said Gary already tapping on his phone.

'Excuse me,' came a voice from below them. It was a steward, less than 20 rows away.

They all pretended not to have heard him. 'Come on, Gary,' implored Claire.

Gary's fingers were sweaty, slipping all over his phone's screen. 'Okay,' he gasped. 'I think I've found something.'

Excuse me,' The stewards were now 12 rows away. This time it was impossible to ignore them.

Frank turned and addressed the leader. 'Sorry mate, official RCB business.' He pulled on the logo on his stolen polo shirt.

'RCE,' corrected Claire.

'I'd like to see some IDs, please,' insisted the steward. He was six rows away now and Frank observed how his pals were moving to block off any escape routes.

Gaz, come on!

'Got it,' Gary said. He pointed directly ahead, between the Riverside Stand on their left and the Hammersmith End behind the opposite goal. 'It was out there, beside the Thames.'

'Right.' Claire crouched down at the end of the row and peered out towards where the statue would have been.

'Claire...' Frank warned her. The persistent steward was striding right toward them.

Claire, still crouching, blurted, 'End seat. Has to be.'

Frank immediately dropped to the floor and looked under the seat.

Gary took the tablet and entered the row and seat numbers. 'They're correct, they've turned green.'

'*Oi,*' yelled the steward. Frank could hear their pursuers stepping up the pace. He knew he had only a few seconds to find whatever was under the seat.

As it turned out, a few seconds was enough.

'You two,' Frank said from the floor, 'get down here, quick.'

Without hesitation, Claire and Gary joined him on the ground.

And by the time the five stewards had arrived at the end seat of row ZZ in Block P7 of Craven Cottage's Putney End, the three suspicious characters in ill-fitting yellow polo shirts had disappeared.

Frank heard a loud *click* from above him.

'No turning back now,' he said down to Claire and Gary.

There had been a trapdoor under the seat, not obvious unless you were looking for it. Frank had opened it outwards into the aisle, and after he had let the other two in, he followed and closed it. It had locked shut. Frank could now hear the stewards above trying to prise it open and cursing.

They were in a shaft in complete darkness, holding onto the rungs of a wooden ladder, with nowhere to go but further and further down.

'How did you know we needed the end seat?' Frank asked Claire.

'I just realised,' she said from below him, her voice hesitant while she concentrated on climbing, 'that "view of a king" might not mean a view *good enough* for a king, but a view where you could *see* a king. The end seat would have given you the best view of the Michael Jackson statue.'

They climbed on.

'Aw, it really stinks in here,' moaned Gary.

'Yeah yeah,' said Frank. 'You try having a kid – you get used to a bit of a pong.' Frank was more concerned about whether the old wooden rungs would hold – so far, so good, and no splinters either.

Claire shivered. 'Temperature's dropped, too,' she said. 'What do you think this was for – I mean, originally?'

'Gas works?' Frank suggested. 'Underground mineshaft? Old part of the tube network?'

In other words, I haven't the foggiest, love.

'Here we are.' Claire had reached the bottom, which was firm but wet, covered with half an inch of water. She took a step back and helped Gary down.

Frank joined them, then rummaged around in his jeans pocket and found a book of matches from last night in the bar. The memory of lighting flaming sambucas made him feel queasy, but he was too excited to let his hangover bother him.

Frank struck a match.

'Oh wow,' said Claire.

Frank extended his arm to reveal a grimy and narrow stone tunnel, about seven feet high but only a few feet wide. In the flame's limited light, it soon rescinded into darkness.

'Only one direction to go,' said Gary.

'Seems like it,' Frank said. He held the match up. 'Haven't got many of these, so let's get a move on.'

The tunnel was only wide enough for single file, so Frank led with Claire next and Gary bringing up the rear.

'Something I've been wondering,' said Frank.

'What?' said Gary.

'Why the hell do these Custodian people keep these two Half things hidden? If they're so important, like if they're safeguards or what have you, you'd think they'd put them front and centre.'

'I know,' said Claire. 'I've been thinking the same thing, it doesn't make any sense. I guess they must have their reasons.'

'Yeah, but what – shit.'

Frank had stumbled over something. Claire collided with him and Gary in turn bumped into her.

'What is it, Frank?' asked Claire.

'Something on the floor.'

Frank got down on his haunches and moved the match around his feet. He found it: an old football boot. He picked it up.

'Wow, it's ancient,' Claire said.

The wet boot was clumpy and heavy and had much larger studs than its modern equivalents.

Gary gave it a squeeze. 'Wouldn't fancy running around in a pair of those,' he said. Then he noticed something else on the floor. 'What's that?'

Frank lit a new match from his current one and gave it to Gary.

Gary side-stepped past Frank. He crouched down and illuminated a large round object. With an effort, he lifted it up with his other hand. It was an old laced-up football.

Gary passed the football to Frank, who felt its weight and said, 'Heading this beast must have cost you a couple hundred brain cells.' He dropped the ball and it landed with a splash.

'What *is* this place?' Claire wondered.

Frank lit another match and gave it to her. She held it low, revealing hundreds more objects scattered on the wet floor.

'Looks like some sort of graveyard for discontinued football gear,' Frank said.

'Under the oldest ground in London...' mused Gary.

They looked on, fascinated by the piles of physical history laid out before them. As well as boots and balls there were nets, shin pads, shirts and shorts... all discontinued and all worse for wear.

'Come on,' Frank said. 'These matches are running out and the clock's ticking. Let's keep going – and watch your step.'

Finally, they reached the end of the tunnel. Frank felt around the wall and found more wooden rungs.

'Another ladder,' he said over his shoulder. He held his match aloft, but it only illuminated a few feet above his head.

'So, if the exit's up there, then where's the first Half?' asked Claire.

'Did we miss it?' asked Gary.

'Start feeling the walls,' said Frank. 'And the floor too. There has to be *something* here beyond someone's old football boot collection.'

Frank lit matches for everyone, and they began to search.

'Wait a sec...' Gary said. 'I think I've found something. Look.'

He held his match to a wall and with his free hand began to trace a line in the wet clay. Something made from a harder stone had been embedded into it. Gary found a corner and then carried on tracing the edge.

'There's something there,' Claire said excitedly.

'Yeah,' agreed Frank. 'Here.' He gave her his match.

Soon Frank and Gary had traced all the way around a rectangle about the height and width of a magazine.

'It's some kind of... stone slab,' said Gary.

'A tablet,' said Claire. 'In the old-fashioned sense, like the Ten Commandments.'

'Gaz, see if you can get your fingers under it,' Frank said.

He and Gary managed to get purchase and slowly but surely worked the tablet free. It was thicker than a magazine – two inches of solid marble. Muddy water streamed down from the gap it left and Frank and Gary stepped aside to avoid getting their trainers wet.

The water did hit Frank's match. 'Shit,' he said. He let Gary take the stone, wiped his hand dry on his trousers, and took his matchbook out again. 'Last two. Better make them count.' He struck both and gave one to Claire, keeping the other for himself.

Gary held the stone tablet to the faint light.

'Oh my God,' whispered Claire.

They stood in stunned silence, the only sound the faint dripping of water.

'It's so *old*,' marvelled Frank at last, gently touching the surface. It was cold and delicate and left a thin layer of dirt on his fingers.

'More than 150 years,' said Claire, touching it tenderly.

Frank rubbed his dirty fingers together. 'How you know that?'

Claire and Gary shared a smile. Gary said, '1863. The year the football rules were recorded. Right here in London.'

'This is from *that*?' asked Frank.

'Without any doubt,' Claire replied firmly.

Frank held his match closer to the tablet's surface. 'It's got writing carved on it.'

'Yeah.' Claire was awestruck.

'What does it say? What does it say?' Gary could barely contain himself.

'Go on,' Frank said to Claire, his voice quivering.

Claire exhaled, trying to remain calm. 'Hold it still, guys.'

The writing was engraved deep into the stone. Tracing a finger over the letters, Claire slowly read out loud.

'"Sacred Half the First."' She stole a glance at the others. '"And ever shall it remain, that no prejudice must affect the arbitrator…"'

'"Arbitrator"?' said Frank.

'It must mean referee.'

'Oh yeah. Go on, there's more.'

'"This man of integrity must not be swayed by riches or the party's status and must always act according to his best judgement." That's it.'

'"Parties"?' said Frank. 'Something about end-of-season parties?'

'No, Frank,' Claire said patiently. 'I think that means *teams*. The two sides playing.'

'Oh,' said Frank.

Gary said, 'It's saying that referees must always make decisions that they believe to be correct, from their "best judgement."'

'Right,' said Claire. 'And the first part, about riches and status. I think it's saying that refs shouldn't be "swayed" by how big or wealthy the clubs are.'

'So, not give all the decisions to the big teams?' asked Frank.

'Right.'

'Claire... your blog...the stats about biased refs...' said Gary.

She just nodded gravely.

'So, if this is one of football's sacred, unbreakable safeguards, or Halves,' Frank said slowly, 'then that must mean that this announcement today is gonna go against it.'

'Ow.' Claire had neglected her match and let it burn down to her fingers. She shook it off and in doing so knocked Gary's side of the tablet, making him drop it.

'Bloody hell,' said Frank as he caught Gary's end, preventing the stone from hitting the floor.

'Sorry, guys,' said Claire.

'It's okay. Look, this is the last match, so we better scarper northwards. Let's put this thing in your bag, Gaz.'

Gary opened his rucksack. With Frank's weak flame guiding her, Claire carefully placed the stone tablet inside, making sure to not damage the electronic tablet that was already in there.

Then Frank's match went out.

'We'd better take off these tops as well,' said Claire.

In the darkness, they all removed their yellow RCE polo shirts. Gary held his rucksack open, but Frank took all three shirts and flung them back down the tunnel as far as he could.

'They can stay here, along with the rest of the rubbish.'

Frank grabbed the first rung of the new ladder. 'Onwards and upwards, eh?'

They ascended the shaft in silence, each digesting the discovery they had made deep beneath South West London.

This could actually be something big, Frank thought. *And what if only us three rats up this drainpipe can stop it?*

A bonk on the head told Frank that he had reached the top. He touched the ceiling. 'Metal,' he said down to the other two. He traced around the circular edge and added, 'Think it's a manhole cover.'

'So we're gonna come out *in the middle of a road?*' Gary gulped.

'Hopefully not,' Frank said. 'But we ain't got no choice, have we?' He pushed the manhole cover upwards.

It wouldn't budge.

'What now?' asked Claire. 'We go back?'

'No way,' said Gary. 'Those stewards looked nasty.'

'We're *not* going back,' Frank insisted. He pushed up with all his might. Nothing. Then he brushed his fingers all around the cover's edge, looking for a latch or an opening. He found none.

So he banged with his fist.

'It's not a door, Frank,' Gary said. 'No one's going to—'

The crack of light streaming in cut him off mid-sentence.

A hand reached down and touched Frank's shoulder. Frank grabbed it and was helped out into the August sunshine.

A squinting Frank was relieved to be in the open air again after his brief sojourn underground. As he adjusted to the light, he saw a pavement, then railings with grass behind them. He'd been right – the exit was a manhole. There was no traffic on the quiet side street, but Frank moved off onto the pavement anyway.

He then turned to see who had helped him. The man was in his late 50s, grey-haired and goateed, suit and tie. He was now pulling Claire up from the hole, with Gary already topside.

Bloke looks like police, Frank observed.

'My name's William Fullarton,' the man said, addressing them with a stern, bureaucratic bluntness. 'I'm the Football Association's chief fairness officer.'

'You're from the FA's Department of Fair Play?' said Claire, examining Fullarton.

'That's right,' Fullarton confirmed. 'Claire Butterfield?'

'Yes...'

'And Gareth Ward?'

Gary nodded, glancing at Frank and Claire.

Fullarton turned to Frank. 'So that makes you—'

'Yeah yeah, Francis Tuttle, pleased to meet you and all that.' Frank smirked. 'So, did we make it all the way to Australia or what?'

Fullarton didn't react.

'I see where we are,' Gary said. 'That,' (he pointed to the grass) 'is Bishops Park. Which means,' (he took a couple of steps back and looked to his right) 'the stadium is just over there.' Frank and Claire saw that they were indeed only down the road from Craven Cottage. All of the RCE vans had gone.

Fullarton spoke again. 'As my knowledge of your identities no doubt suggests, we've been watching your little gang all morning.' Only now did Frank, Claire and Gary notice that Fullarton wasn't alone. Two silver BMWs with blacked-out windows were parked up Ellerby Street. Next to each stood a man in a black suit and sunglasses.

Now Fullarton glared at Frank. 'You have an item that does not belong to you.'

Gary gripped his rucksack tightly.

'You what?' asked Frank mildly.

Fullarton's eyes narrowed into probing slits. 'You know what I'm referring to.'

'Don't have a clue, mate.'

'Frank...' said Claire.

'Are you gonna show some ID?' asked Frank. He thought of something else. 'Hey, is it you lot who are holding my boy?'

Claire laid a tentative hand on Frank's arm. 'Frank, please, it's okay. I know about the FA's fairness team. They're...'

'The good guys?' asked Gary, moving away from the brewing conflict to underneath a shade tree.

'Something like that,' said Claire.

Fullarton showed his open wallet to Frank.

Frank glanced at the ID and shrugged.

'You have, do you not,' Fullarton said, putting his wallet away, 'an item that is the property of the FA?'

Frank looked to Claire, who nodded. He then regarded the two other FA men – big blokes, standing only yards away, watching his every move.

Frank exhaled loudly.

'Fine,' he said. 'Gaz?'

Gary took out the electronic tablet and handed it to Fullarton.

'Thank you.' Fullarton pocketed it. 'Now,' he said, 'what did you find in that tunnel?'

'Nothing,' Frank said immediately.

Fullarton scowled. 'I don't have the power of the police, Mr Tuttle, but I can turn you over to them.'

Frank scoffed. 'For what?'

'Theft. Withholding stolen property.'

'I didn't steal anything – I found that bloody device and I was gonna return it today.'

Now it was Fullarton's turn to smirk. 'Of course. And you're telling me that you didn't pick up any souvenirs during your subterranean excursion?'

Frank didn't answer.

Fullarton changed tack. 'You and I want the same thing, Mr Tuttle.'

'What's that then?'

'To protect the game.'

'Maybe, but that's not all.'

'I know. And I can help with the other matter, too.' Fullarton made a gesture to one of his officers and the man opened a car door.

Two people got out. The first was a man who even someone with the most cursory knowledge of football would have recognised.

The second person made Frank's eyes light up.

'Ian!'

'Dad!'

Son ran up to father and they embraced.

'You had me worried, mate.'

Ian pulled away and let it all come out. 'I'm sorry Dad, I know I'm not supposed to go off with strangers, but they seemed okay and they had these uniforms on, and I *was* a little mad at you but not really, and then they took me to Wembley and that's where I met Kev and he's *so* brilliant and he paid for us to play loads of games and—'

'Alright, alright,' said Frank, patting his son on the arm. 'Tell me about it later.'

'Hi, Ian,' said Gary. Frank detected a note of guilt in the young man's voice.

'Hi, Gary.' Ian then remembered something. 'Hey Dad, Gary told me it was okay if I left training on my own because it looked like you weren't turning up.'

'Oi, no one likes a grass, mate,' Frank chastised. But he glared at Gary as well.

'I'm sorry, Frank,' Gary said. 'You *were* pretty late, and you know he's an independent lad.'

Cool it, Frank. Don't fly off the handle.

'Fair enough,' Frank said. 'Don't matter now.'

Meanwhile, Kevin had approached the group and was holding a hand out to Frank. 'Kev Maxwell. Great lad you've got there.'

Awed, Frank shook the footballer's hand. 'Thanks. He's alright when he does what he's told.' Frank squeezed his son's shoulder. Kevin shot the boy a wink, which Ian returned.

Kevin then gave Gary a brief 'alright, mate' and without waiting for a response turned straight to Claire.

'Hi,' the footballer said with his best lopsided grin. 'I'm Maxwell. Kevin Maxwell.'

'I know you are,' Claire said evenly, holding her hand out to be shaken.

'You'll've seen me on TV and at matches and all that.' Kevin held onto her hand with both of his and maintained eye contact.

Claire pulled away and coolly replied, 'The reason I know who you are is because you just introduced yourself to Frank and he's standing right next to me.'

Frank stifled a chuckle.

'Oh,' said Kevin. He was deterred for but a moment. 'Good one,' he said, smiling again.

And, despite herself, Claire smiled a little back.

'Well then,' said Fullarton, gesturing his two drivers to get into their cars, 'now that everyone's acquainted, why don't I buy us all some brunch?' He let his professional veneer slip for the first time. 'I'd love to hear what everyone's been up to this morning.'

Frank and Claire exchanged a look. 'Okay,' Frank told Fullarton. 'Sounds like a plan. Cheers.'

'Fabulous, and I know just the place. Mr Tuttle, you can follow my two cars in your van.'

'Come on, Dad,' said Ian. 'I'm famished.'

Frank put his arm around his son and they all left the scene.

'THAT certainly is an interesting theory, Mr Tuttle,' Fullarton said. He took a huge bite out of his bacon and jalapeño cheeseburger.

The group had secured a table in a pub on Long Acre, near Covent Garden, and they were tucking into their late breakfast/early lunch – all except the FA drivers, who waited outside beside their BMWs.

Frank still wasn't sure if Fullarton was on the level, but conceded that the geezer had at least been good enough to take them somewhere that did proper grub.

'Interesting – but you think it's total bollocks,' Frank said, taking a sip from his hair-of-the-dog pint of Stella; now that the pace of the day had slowed down, his hangover was making itself known again.

Fullarton wiped his fingers on a napkin and said, 'Mr Tuttle, do you know where we are right now?'

Frank looked around. It was the kind of unassuming place you could just wander into and catch a football match with a drink.

'A pub?'

'Yes. But not any old pub.'

Claire nearly dropped her chicken Caesar wrap. 'Wait, is this...?'

Gary put down his lemonade and looked around. 'It's not...?'

'It is,' confirmed Fullarton. 'The Freemasons Arms was formerly The Freemasons Tavern. Where an historic event took place.'

'What was that then?' asked Kevin. He was the only one who had ordered a healthy meal: green salad with no dressing.

'The recording of the official football rules,' Claire told Kevin. They were sitting next to each other – Kevin had made sure of it. 'The ceremony took place in the attic above our heads.'

'That wasn't even the last century, but the one before that – wasn't it?' asked Ian. His dad nicked a chip from his plate and then acted all innocent.

'That's right, in 1863,' Claire smiled at the boy.

But Kevin was unimpressed. 'That's all well and good,' he said, stabbing a pile of kale with his fork, 'but I know loads better places to eat round here that don't serve all them carbs and refined sugars you lot are shoving into your gobs.'

Patiently, Fullarton explained. 'We're here because I want you all to realise that I take the integrity of football very seriously. I have great respect for its traditions and the sincerity under which its rules were established.'

'So, is it true?' asked Gary. 'About The Custodians? A group formed by the men who wrote down the rules, which exists to this day and which has hidden two safeguards to be found if the game is ever threatened?'

'And that they created a quest called "The Campaign,"' picked up Claire, 'that must be followed to find the safeguards – the two Halves?'

'And that you can achieve true footballing enlightenment by completing The Campaign?' finished Gary.

Fullarton looked at the stone tablet that was sitting on the table. It was in front of Ian, who had declared himself its protector.

Now Frank helped his son to prop it up.

Fullarton examined the heavy stone. 'Hmm...' he said vaguely.

'What?' asked Ian.

Fullarton was gentle with the boy. 'I'm afraid I just can't be sure.' He turned to the adults. 'It will need to be sent away for authentication.'

'Okay,' said Claire. 'Authenticate it. But it *has* to be real.'

'Does it?' Fullarton stroked his beard, still peering at the tablet.

Claire was indignant. 'Of course it's real. It was right where The Campaign said it would be.'

'Or could it be an elaborate hoax?' Fullarton looked straight at her.

Claire didn't reply.

Clouds of doubt shifted over the table.

But Ian said, 'No, that's... that's ridiculous.'

'More ridiculous than it being true?' asked Fullarton. 'Master Tuttle, we live in an era of pranks and hoaxes – the internet has opened up thousands more routes for people to discuss their so-called evidence. Unsurprisingly, conspiracy claims have sky-rocketed as a consequence.'

Ian was getting upset. Frank gave Fullarton a black look.

'Look, I have to deal with facts,' said the FA man, holding his hands up. 'I've heard the legends too, same as anyone who works for the Football Association.' He looked at Claire.

'*Worked* for,' she corrected.

'My apologies. All I'm saying is if this is a genuine century-and-a-half-old artefact from a landmark event in history, maybe I can get on board with

115

your claims. But until I know that for sure, I have to take this at face value –
an oddity, a trinket, but not conclusive evidence.'

Silence from the table. A barman asked if anyone wanted anything else.
No one did.

Then Gary asked, 'So how long will this authentication take?'

Fullarton rolled his head from side to side. 'I'd say, based on the size and
weight... two to three weeks.'

'Two to three *weeks*?' Frank nearly choked on his hot dog.

'But the announcement is *this afternoon*,' cried Claire.

'Look, even if it *is* genuine,' said Fullarton, 'you can't just march into
Wembley, headquarters of the Football Association of England, brandishing
an old piece of rock and accuse them of corruption.'

'You're right,' said Frank, casually wiping his mouth and examining his
pint. Then he looked up and added, 'We need *more*.'

'The second Half...' Claire said quietly. Her eyes met Frank's across the
table.

'Yeah,' said Frank. 'Not forgetting this "true meaning of football" and
"enlightenment" stuff, too.'

Ian was fidgeting in his seat. 'Do *you* know what the announcement is
going to be about, Mr Fullarton?' he asked.

Fullarton shook his head. 'I'm as much in the dark as the rest of you.'

Frank gave Fullarton a sceptical look, which the fairness enforcer
ignored.

'And what about this PR agency, these Research Creating Excellence
people?' asked Gary.

'Never heard of them,' Fullarton said.

Again, Frank made it clear that he didn't believe the man.

'Excuse me,' Fullarton said. He took out his wallet and stood.

Kevin watched Fullarton head to the bar and then turned sharply to the
others. 'Listen you lot. Don't give up on this.'

'What's the point?' sighed Gary. 'Fullarton's right, we've got nothing.'

'Yeah, but, no, but... listen,' stammered Kevin. 'I found something out at Wembley.'

'*We* found something out,' corrected Ian.

'Sorry mate. Me and Ian, before your man grabbed us and escorted us from the flipping premises.'

'Yeah?' said Frank.

'Yeah,' said Kevin. 'But we need – oh, eh-oop.' Already Fullarton was on his way back from paying. Kevin hushed and quickened his tone. 'We need that tablet back. The computer one. We've got to carry on and get that other... whatsit.'

'Half,' said Claire.

'Yeah, that's the badger,' Kevin beamed at her.

'Are we sure we trust this guy?' Gary asked, indicating Kevin. 'He could be in on it.'

'You what?' Kevin said.

'And he is known for... how do I put it? Shooting his mouth off?'

Frank leapt to Kevin's defence. 'Now wait a sec, Gaz—'

'Everything okay here?' Fullarton was retaking his seat and putting his wallet away.

'Fine,' said Claire absently.

'Yeah,' said Frank. 'Just got a little heated arguing over who's gonna win the Premier League.'

Gary had retreated to the safety of his mobile while Kevin just shrugged and pulled out his own phone.

Fullarton smiled back at Frank. 'That's why I love working in the game. Nothing else stirs up so much passion.'

Kevin caught Claire's eye. Gave her a look that implored her to believe him.

Claire studied Kevin's face carefully.

Then she said, 'Excuse me,' to the table, stood up and turned towards the toilets. 'You gentlemen finish up. I'll meet you outside.'

They were assembled outside the Freemasons Arms: Frank, Ian, Gary, Kevin and Fullarton. The pub's Central London location on the corner of Acre Lane and Drury Lane meant that the group had to constantly shift to let the hordes of Saturday shoppers and tourists stream past them towards and away from the West End.

Claire still hadn't returned from the pub's ladies' room.

Fullarton addressed the group.

'I recommend you all go home,' he said. 'Forget about this business. Find a radio or a TV and tune in to the FA's announcement just before 3pm – I'm sure it will be nowhere near as Earth-shattering as you fear.'

'Oh yeah?' said Frank. He had started to respect Fullarton, but still didn't fully trust the man. 'You sure about that?'

And then Frank saw it: a moment's hesitation.

This bloke knows more than he's letting on.

But, cool as anything, Fullarton replied, 'Of course I'm sure.' Then he cleared his throat and glanced across the street to his two drivers, waiting obediently beside their BMWs. 'Well, it was nice to meet you all, please give my regards to Miss—'

Just then, Claire appeared.

'Oh, Miss Butterfield. I was just saying to your friends that—'

'That you're going to help us?' Claire's voice was quivering.

Fullarton was startled. 'Um, I'm afraid not. I was just explaining—'

Claire flung her arms around Fullarton and started crying. He turned beetroot red while the other four exchanged bemused looks. The FA drivers adjusted their sunglasses.

'Oh, I know you're just doing your job,' Claire sobbed. 'But it's just been such a rough day. *First* I get the sack, *then* we lose the tablet... I just don't know if I can cope.'

Fullarton, stiff as a goalpost, gave Claire a couple of perfunctory pats on the back. 'There there. It's okay. I know it's been hard.'

Claire withdrew and stared into Fullarton's eyes. Tears were running down her face. 'It has, it really has.'

Fullarton stepped back. 'Um, look, obviously I know senior people in the FA. I'll ask around, see if I can find out what happened with your job.'

'You'd do that for me?'

'Of course.' Now Fullarton was starting to enjoy being chivalrous. He patted his pockets looking for a tissue, but Claire was already dabbing her eyes with her own.

Meanwhile, Frank noticed that Kevin was watching this little scene closely.

Fullarton reached into his breast pocket. 'Please take my card,' he said, handing it to Claire. 'My work and mobile numbers are on it.' Fullarton gave a card to Frank while he was at it, who accepted with a curt nod. 'And here,' he turned to Claire again while taking out a notepad and pen, 'why don't you give me *your* number? So I can get in touch if I find anything out.'

Kevin started to scowl.

Claire finished wiping her eyes and put the tissues back in her bag. She then took Fullarton's pen and wrote her mobile number on his notepad. 'Thank you,' she said, touching Fullarton's chest tenderly. 'You're such a kind man.'

Frank saw that Kevin was about to say something and gave him a cautious look. Kevin hesitated, screwed his face up, pulled out his phone, and began checking his social media accounts.

Fullarton, meanwhile, was stammering. 'I'm... I'm just doing my job. If you've been fired with no explanation – well that's hardly *fair play*, is it?'

Claire laughed hugely.

Kevin could no longer hold back. He spoke without looking up from his phone. 'Right, so we'll be going now, eh?' He marched off without waiting for an answer.

Frank, Ian and Gary nodded their goodbyes to Fullarton and followed after Kevin.

Claire said, 'Yes, we should go.' She gave Fullarton one final smile and then caught up with the others.

Fullarton headed towards his BMWs, waving to Claire over his shoulder.

The group entered the underground car park in which Frank had left his van.

Kevin stopped and confronted Claire. 'What the hell was all that?' he demanded.

'What was all what?' Claire asked.

'All this being flirty with that bloke?'

'What's it got to do with you?' Claire had her compact out and was checking her reflection. 'Well hello, Miss Panda Eyes,' she muttered as she walked on.

The others followed her, an exasperated Kevin bringing up the rear. They soon reached the van.

The men (and boy) waited for Claire to finish fixing her appearance. She was struggling with the light and moved under the nearest halogen.

Frank coughed. 'Um, so Claire, what was the, uh...'

'Why the performance?'

'Yeah.'

Satisfied that she looked presentable again, Claire clapped her compact shut.

'Right, well, I thought that it might be useful to this quest we're all on if we still had this.' She produced the electronic tablet from inside her denim jacket.

The others gasped.

'You got it back,' exclaimed Ian, hopping from one foot to the other.

Frank was as excited as his son. 'Good stuff.'

'Oh no,' moaned Gary. 'We're in trouble now.'

The others ignored him.

Kevin was still pouting. 'So you weren't, like, *really*—'

'Upset? Come on, Kevin, you're a footballer. You should recognise pretending to be hurt when you see it.'

They all laughed, Kevin with a self-deprecating smile.

'But what happens when Fullarton notices that the tablet's gone?' asked Gary.

'Never mind that, Jerry,' said Kevin.

'Gary.'

'Whatever. How the bloody hell did you do it, Claire love?'

'Well, I knew that none of you boys would think anything of a woman taking a long time in the bathroom,' said Claire.

'That *were* dead long, even for a girl,' said Kevin.

'So, I knew I had time.'

The others were confused. 'Time for...' started Frank.

'While we were eating, I noticed through the window that there was a PC shop on Drury Lane. So, I got an idea. Instead of going to the loo, I snuck out the fire exit and...' She showed her palms in an *and-there-you-have-it* gesture.

Ian said, 'You bought another tablet and swapped it in Fullarton's pocket.'

'That is bloody brilliant,' said Kevin.

'Thank you, thank you,' Claire said as she gave them a little bow.

'You better keep the receipt,' said Gary, 'and hope that you get the other one back from Fullarton in a returnable state when this is all over.'

'Yes, thanks Gary.'

'Alright then,' said Frank, taking the tablet from Claire. 'Let's get onto the next clue. Three o' clock's getting closer.'

'Just a moment, Frank,' said Claire. 'I think we should let Kevin finish what he was saying earlier.' She turned to the footballer. 'Back in the pub. You were about to tell us what it was you and Ian saw in Wembley that convinced you that The Campaign is real.'

121

Everyone faced Kevin. He looked to Ian, who nodded to indicate that it should be Kevin who tells the story.

The footballer cleared his throat.

Claire was chuckling to herself. She was thinking about how England international Kevin Maxwell had reacted to her flirty performance with FA fairness enforcer Fullarton outside the pub.

He can't be that bright, she thought as she sized the footballer up in the artificial light of the underground car park. *And what's he playing at, coming over all possessive?*

But she put these thoughts to one side and listened to Kevin's story.

'Alright,' he was saying. 'So, me and Ian were walking into that Media Centre, this massive place full of computers and TV screens what overlooks the Wembley pitch.'

'It's like the NASA headquarters,' said Ian.

'Yeah. It were buzzing, full of people running around, typing on computers, all of that malarkey.'

Claire nodded. She, of course, could picture it exactly. She wondered if her desk was empty or if the FA had already got a temp in.

Kevin continued. 'Like I say, we were only there a couple of minutes before Billy Big Balls Fullarton got his hands on us, but we still saw two things. First, there were this woman, not bad-looking, dark hair and right tall, pacing about on her phone like she owned the place.'

'Susan Clyne,' Claire spat. 'My ex-boss.'

The bitch that fired me.

'I actually met her earlier,' Ian said. 'At the Fun Day. She was the one who showed me the Games Room, where I ran into Kevin.' Ian turned to Claire and sheepishly added, 'I thought she was really fake.'

Perceptive boy, Claire thought.

'Well, anyroad,' continued Kevin, 'this Susan seemed like she had her boss on the other end and he were having a right go at her. She were saying summat like, "I'm sorry, but we're getting it back and we're gonna wipe its hard drive pronto."'

The others digested this.

Then Frank asked, 'And what was the second thing you saw?'

'There were this huge room with a big table in the middle and one wall made out of glass.'

'Conference Room One,' said Claire.

'Yeah, it looked like a boardroom or summat. And all these important people were being shown inside by this mob wearing yellow polo shirts. Horrible bright things they were, wouldn't see me dead in one of them.'

Frank, Claire and Gary shared a quick glance.

Gary asked, 'How did you know that the people in the boardroom were important?'

It was Ian who answered. 'You could tell. They were being treated like VIPs, like royalty.'

'And the clobber,' said Kevin. "These weren't no off-the-rack suits, I can tell you. Top-end designer all the way. And they were right international-looking, talking all different languages and everything. So yeah, they was shown into this conference room and there were this huge screen, and you could see what were on it: one of them PowerPoint presentations.'

'What did it say?' asked Claire.

Kevin looked at Ian. 'It were summat like, "Rule changes... association football something..."'

Ian picked up the thread. 'I got a good look at it. It said: "Association football rule changes to enhance worldwide marketability."'

Kevin nodded in agreement.

The others stood open-mouthed.

'"Enhance worldwide marketability…"' It sounded to Claire like something the FA would come up with alright, but it didn't ring any bells with her.

'Right,' said Frank. 'We got no time to lose. Let's see what the next clue is and get moving sharpish.'

'But we can't all fit in the van,' Gary said while cleaning his glasses on his tracksuit top.

Frank thought for a moment. Then he addressed Kevin. 'Listen. Why don't us lot carry on with The Campaign and you use your connections in the game to see if you can find anything out behind the scenes.'

Frank rummaged around in his pocket and took out the memo that they found in the RCE van earlier. He unfolded it and pointed to the last line. '"See separate documentation for questions for those in the football profession,"' he read aloud. 'That mean anything to you?'

Kevin examined the memo but frowned and shook his head.

'That still leaves four of us but a van with three seats,' said Gary.

'Claire should come with me,' Kevin said quickly.

She gave him a pointed look.

'Well, can't be a good idea you running around all these stadiums, what with the FA being pissed off at you and that. You should stay out of the limelight.'

Claire smiled wryly at the footballer.

'Out of the limelight' – with a Premier League player? With Kevin 'headline-magnet' Maxwell, no less?

She took her time replying, making him wait.

What the hell, she decided. *Could be fun.*

'Alright. Two heads are better than one.'

'Sound. And I know just the man we need – for starters, I'm sure he'll have summat to say about this thing.' Kevin waved the RCE memo in the air.

'Good.' Claire turned to Frank. 'We better swap numbers.' Frank nodded.

'Yeah,' Kevin said, 'you, me and Frank should all swap numbers. You know, just in case.'

Claire rolled her eyes. 'Fine.' When they were done, she added, 'Now can we please get out of this car park before we all die of carbon monoxide poisoning?'

'Yep, let's get going,' said Frank. Ian and Gary jumped in the van.

Frank put his hand on the driver's door handle, then hesitated. He turned to Claire and Kevin. 'See you later, then.'

'Good luck, Frank,' said Claire.

'Same to you. And if it looks like everything's going tits up, we'll meet back in Pippa's Café.'

'Don't worry, Frank,' said Kevin, 'I'll look after Claire.'

Frank grinned at Kevin, clearly starstruck. Claire, meanwhile, just ignored the comment, safe in the knowledge that at least *she* was immune to a footballer's charms.

'Frank,' she said, as he went for the van's door again.

I don't want to be melodramatic...

But she decided to say it anyway.

'Be careful.'

Frank was a little taken aback.

'You too,' he replied with a firm nod.

SUSAN was nervous.

She was in her office signing off some expenses forms. But her mind was elsewhere.

Everything will go according to plan, she tried to reassure herself.

The punters down at the Family Fun Day were being stimulated into a frenzy by all the adrenalin, sugar, flashing lights, music and celebrities. RCE were doing what they were supposed to. And the tablet situation was in hand.

All seemed well.

But still she worried.

So much of this whole thing depended on predicting how people would behave. And despite market research, surveys and data crunching, algorithms and demographics, you could never *really* tell. What's more, Susan understood that 'the general public' was more than just many individuals collected together. It was its own beast. She often recalled a term coined by writer and philosopher Aldous Huxley: 'herd intoxication.' Where individuals cease to think for themselves and get caught up in the crowd, following its whims no matter how hysterical. It was a tactic used by extreme political movements to make otherwise sane people lose their rationality and be seduced into a feeling of strength, empowering them to shout and rant along with the larger group. It could be witnessed week in, week out at any football stadium: the security of being among thousands of others who followed the same cause.

But relying on people to follow the herd could still backfire. A collective was still made up of individuals. And individuals were much less predictable.

Susan watched the flock of happy faces running around below her on the pitch. And she wondered.

'Letting the tablet get out was foolish,' a voice from behind her said.

Susan shivered involuntarily. Didn't he ever knock?

'I know,' Susan replied tersely. Just as in the Media Centre last night, she couldn't bring herself to look at him. 'It seems it was left out in the open on its way to magnetic deletion. But, as I told you earlier, the situation is under control.'

She sensed him moving into the room, closer to her.

'It's back in our possession?'

'Yes. Fullarton is on his way here with it right now.'

'Will he... access it first?'

Her boss was only feet away now. She thought about his whisky breath and shuddered.

'No. Fullarton is very by-the-book.'

'So... no harm done?'

Susan forced herself to turn to him. As usual his face betrayed nothing, was set as rigid as wood – or a wall, to coin his old nickname. He was handsome – *too* handsome – and immaculately tailored, looking younger than his 50-odd years. Then of course there was the towering height that had served him so well in his former career, accentuated by his unfalteringly straight posture. But despite how presentable and camera-friendly he appeared to the rest of the world, to Susan he always gave off a creepy, otherworldly vibe, as if he were a giant who was only pretending to be human: Frankenstein's monster, or Lurch from *The Addams Family*.

And yet here we are, Susan thought bitterly.

She cleared her throat. 'No, no harm done at all. They've learned nothing, or at least nothing that won't sound like another crazy conspiracy theory.'

She watched his face briefly approximate satisfaction then revert to neutral. Then it twitched at a new thought.

'We *are* keeping an eye on matters, though?' he said.

'Don't worry,' said Susan. 'I'm taking care of it.'

He stared at her. Susan shivered again, dreading what his next change of expression might be.

But she only got that media-friendly grin. 'Good. Excellent. Right, if you'll excuse me, the dignitaries are waiting for the next part of their tour.'

He left.

Susan stared at her office door for a long time.

Frank would be the first to admit that he'd learned about most things in life through football. Like Kevin and Claire, he had a football-mad father, who would take him to games at Brisbane Road to cheer on their beloved Leyton Orient. Whenever he wasn't away with the army, the senior Tuttle would let young Frank accompany him to his local to watch televised games; the boy would join the men in the smoky pool room in front of the wall-mounted TV, fascinated by the banter and camaraderie of the adults, assimilating his way into adult culture watching match after match.

It was through football that Frank had his first kiss, which came at a school disco. It was the last song, and everyone was dancing in a circle to New Order's World Cup 1990 anthem 'World in Motion.' Frank found himself locking arms with Kelly Linighan; they were the only two who knew the whole John Barnes rap and started reciting it to each other. When the song changed, they locked lips. Kelly became Frank's first girlfriend.

Though not academically gifted, Frank did okay at Geography – he could name the European cities that had decent football teams. He wasn't bad at History, either – so long as the events coincided with key developments in the game.

So, it was true to say that football had taught Frank a lot.

But never anything about flowers.

'Flowers?' Gary Ward asked from the van's passenger seat.

'That's what it says,' confirmed Ian, who had the FA's tablet on his lap and was sitting between the two men.

The trio were travelling southwest down Piccadilly with Green Park on their left and central London's streets on their right.

Ian finished plugging his mobile into the cigarette lighter charger, then again read the tablet's latest clue – labelled 'Second Half, Clue One' – to his father and his football coach.

'"Go where the old flowers show."'

Far too easy, surely? thought Frank.

'Has to be Chelsea,' he said.

'"Flowers show,"' said Gary. 'Yeah, Chelsea Flower Show.'

Frank could see that Ian was disappointed, that the lad had hoped for more of a challenge.

'Well, it might not be,' Frank said. 'Is there somewhere else in London known for flowers?'

'Come on, Dad,' sighed Ian, picking at a loose thread on his football shirt. 'Where else can it be?'

Neither Frank nor Gary could think of anywhere.

So, Ian typed CHELSEA into the answer box and, to no one's surprise, it turned green.

The screen changed to the next clue.

Chelsea FC is a rival of the club Frank and Gary visited earlier, Fulham. In fact, Fulham were actually the first to be offered Chelsea's home, Stamford Bridge Stadium, back in 1905, but they declined, and Chelsea have been at 'the Bridge' ever since.

Frank, Ian and Gary walked through an outer gate and down a slope. Opposite the stadium itself was a long wall of memorials depicting the club's success, which groups of tourists were examining and taking photos of. One popular display was a team photo with a space missing for a fan, which today had a queue of schoolchildren eager to be photographed among the Chelsea first team. There was also a bright and striking mural of all of the club's kits since the turn of the century.

Gary and the Tuttles stopped on the forecourt and stood between the stadium on the right and the outdoor museum on the left.

Ian had the tablet. 'Alright,' he said swiping the device to life. He read the new clue out loud. '"When the old met the new." And there are six spaces to fill in, like a crossword clue.'

'"When the old met the new..."' repeated Gary.

'Six spaces, eh?' Frank rubbed his chin.

'A number,' suggested Gary. 'Or a six-letter word.'

'Must be,' agreed Frank. 'Well, there's a bunch of pictures and stats about the club over there,' he pointed at the wall. 'Could tell us something, maybe a word or a number that keeps coming up. You two check that out.'

'What about you, Dad?'

Frank turned to the right. 'I'll look at the actual stadium, starting with Peter Osgood.' He pointed to the statue of the ex-Chelsea legend. 'He's *definitely* old.'

They separated and got to it.

Osgood was holding a football against his hip. Frank looked all around the statue. He rubbed his hand on its warm surface and examined the podium. He inspected the striker's face and followed his eye-line. Nothing seemed significant; his surname was six letters, but that was it.

Frank then walked around the stadium's exterior, making a mental note of any six letter words or numbers – on the directions, on the signs, on the posters.

When Frank re-joined Gary and Ian, their slumped shoulders spoke volumes.

'Anything?' Frank asked.

'Not a badger,' answered Ian.

'The only six-digit figure we could find was the original seating capacity, 100,000,' said Gary. 'Didn't work. Then we put in a few six-letter words.'

Ian took over. 'Bridge, Drogba, Hazard, Essien...' He trailed off, implying a long list.

'But...?'

Ian and Gary shook their heads.

'What about you, Dad?'

Frank spoke with an optimism that he didn't feel. 'Well, I didn't get much in the way of numbers, but I've got some more six-letter ex-players. Osgood, of course, but also Vialli, Clarke, Harris...'

Ian tapped on the tablet as his father spoke, but none of the half dozen names Frank reeled off were correct.

Well, that's me all out of ideas, thought Frank.

'Do we need to go inside, Dad?' asked Ian. 'Like you did at Craven Cottage?'

Frank turned to the stadium. 'Are they...'

'No,' answered Gary immediately. 'Away to Everton. We'd have to break in.'

Frank exhaled. He scanned the outside of the stadium, trying to take it all in, trying to make a connection.

'I Googled anything "old" about the club,' Gary was saying, 'to see if any six-letter or -digit answers came back. Financial figures, record-holders, that sort of thing, but...' He trailed off.

The three of them stood there in the Stamford Bridge forecourt at a loss. Tourists swerved around them. The sun retreated behind a cloud.

'Wait,' said Ian. 'Dad, why don't we go visit Grandad? He's only down the road from here, isn't he?'

Frank raised his eyebrows. 'Your grandad?'

'Yeah, think about it.'

Frank looked back at the stadium, then at the memento wall. They were spent resources.

He went over the clue again in his head.

'When the old met the new.'

Maybe Ian was right.

But... could he really face going to see his old man?

Suck it up, Frank. It's all you've got to go on.

'Come on then,' Frank said, giving Ian a playful push. 'We can be there in five minutes.'

Father and son turned back towards the road.

'Um, so what's going on?' asked Gary as he caught up. 'Obviously I'm excited to meet a third generation of the Tuttle men, but... why?'

'I'll explain on the way,' said Frank over his shoulder.

Well, Dad, here I come.

13

ACROSS London, England midfielder Kevin Maxwell and ex-FA communications manager Claire Butterfield were speeding around a leafy Kensington suburb in Kevin's open-top bright green Ferrari 250 GTO.

Claire was trying to drink a Starbucks chai latte, but Kevin's driving was making this impossible. The footballer was the original boy racer, tearing down the quiet well-to-do streets, swerving around cyclists and cutting up other motorists.

'Hey,' Claire shouted, trying to be heard above the industrial hip-hop blazing from the stereo.

'This is a custom set-up,' Kevin yelled back. 'The car was a signing-on gift from the Sheikh a couple of seasons back. Pimped it out since: 55hz bass, full surround sound, reinforced suspension... the works.'

'It's very nice.'

'What?' Kevin was driving one-handed while trying to keep his hair in place.

Claire just glared at him. Eventually Kevin got the hint and turned the volume down.

'I said, "It's very nice."'

'*Nice?* Do you have any idea what one of these bad boys costs?'

'I don't care how much it costs, but I do care that there's no cup holder.'

'So?'

'So, where the hell am I supposed to put my coffee?'

Kevin shrugged.

'Is the idea that the car goes so fast that you don't have *time* for coffee?'

Kevin faced her. 'Look, when a car has—'

'Watch out!'

Kevin swerved to avoid a teenager who had run into the road to retrieve a Frisbee.

Claire's drink flew into her lap.

Kevin yelled back at the teenager. 'Why don't you play a proper sport, tosser?'

The youth gave Kevin the finger.

'Oh, great,' said Claire examining her dress.

Now Kevin saw the mess. 'Why'd you go and do that?'

Claire bit her lip. 'I don't suppose you have any tissues in this penis-on-wheels, do you?'

'Um...' said Kevin.

'It's fine, I've got some here.'

She got busy wiping her dress. Kevin slowed the car down and started paying attention to the road. 'Sorry about your outfit,' he said.

After she had cleaned herself up, Claire asked, 'So *who* are we going to see?'

'Me mate, Donno.'

'Stuart Donaldson?'

'Yeah, Stu Donno.' Kevin glanced sideways at her.

Claire was like a star-struck schoolgirl. 'Wow, I don't believe it.'

'What?' Kevin snapped.

'He's *only* the record holder for number of Premier League goals in a season. And number of hat-tricks in a season. And consecutive matches scored in.'

Kevin gripped the wheel hard. 'Yeah, he did have that one decent year.'

'More than just one. Wow, Stu Donaldson, *Donno*. I can't believe I'm going to meet him.' Claire reached into her handbag and took out her makeup kit.

Kevin pouted. 'He in't won two Champions Leagues though, has he? Or been on the front cover of *Footie* magazine a record eight times?'

Claire snorted as she applied her lipstick. Kevin went into a full-on sulk.

In the silence, Claire grinned to herself.

Presently, Kevin turned into a gravel drive.

'We're here,' he muttered.

They had arrived at the entrance to a gated community of mansions. The immaculate grounds, the marble fountains, the sports cars – everything screamed money.

'Wow,' said Claire.

'In't so great here,' said Kevin as he crawled the Ferrari up to the gate. 'Apparently the mobile reception's crap. And I heard the milkman's always messing up your order, bringing semi-skimmed when you asked for skimmed, running out of soya.'

Kevin leaned out and pressed a button on the intercom.

After a short wait, a screen came on to reveal a powerfully built black man in his 30s, wearing a gold silk dressing gown with 'S.D.' sewn into the breast.

The man peered at the screen. 'Yeah?'

Kevin pressed the button to speak. 'Donno, The Donninator. How you doing mate?'

A pause. 'Who is this?'

'It's me. It's Mini.'

Kevin turned back to Claire to explain. 'Nickname the boys gave me. "Mini" because of "Max"' because of me name? So it's... whatjacallit... ironic.'

Claire nodded patiently.

Donno was answering again. 'Who? Listen, if you're from the press, speak to my publicist. I'm sick of being asked about this bloody FA announcement.'

Kevin rolled his eyes at Claire and pushed the button once again. 'No, it's me, Kev Maxwell. Come on Donno, stop messing about.'

Donno squinted at the screen. 'Oh.'

Kevin smiled at Claire awkwardly. She raised her eyebrows.

Then Donno said, 'This is private property, please leave immediately.'

'Come on mate...'

'You hear this?' Over the intercom came the sound of two buttons being pressed on a cordless phone. 'That's the first two nines. Reverse that ugly car away in ten seconds or I'm gonna press nine again. Understand?'

'Oh, come on, Donno—'

'I've gotta stay away from you, Kev, for my career. I can't associate with a PR time bomb.'

Kevin was crestfallen. Claire went to say something, but then saw him regain his confidence in a flash.

'Are you *sure* that's the reason?' Kevin grinned.

'What you mean?' asked the other man.

'Well, you were always jealous of my dribbling skills. Yeah, you could thump a ball hard, but everyone knew that *I* was the star player.'

'Bullshit,' said Donno. 'The only dribbling you're good at is after three pints of shandy, you lightweight.'

'You wanna talk lightweight? Remember those two birds after Southampton away? Yours told me after that on the pitch was the *only* place Dangerous Donno could put in a performance.'

'At least I never had to pay any of my birds just so they'd stick around and listen to me yacking on.'

Kevin glanced back at Claire, yet still got his comeback in. 'At least with me, "Mini" don't *actually* mean nothing.' Kevin turned back to Claire and wiggled his little finger. She stifled a giggle.

No response from the intercom. The screen turned off.

Kevin and Claire waited.

The gate opened with a buzz.

Smirking, Kevin put the car into gear and rolled forward.

'What the hell was all that about?' asked Claire, watching the gate close behind them.

'Bants.'

'Bants?'

Kevin followed the road. 'Yeah. Bit of banter.'

Claire frowned. 'You were just slagging each other off.'

'It's the only way to get respect. You can have the cars and the bling and the clobber, but the only thing that really impresses the other lads is bringing the bants.'

As they rolled up to a parking space, Claire considered her surroundings. It kind of made sense – in a world where money was so abundant that it had lost all meaning, these super-rich man-boys had come up with their own currency.

'Right-oh,' Kevin said, leaping out and taking off across the courtyard. 'His gaff is number 11, his old squad number.'

As they approached the huge and garish house – around which circled topiary shaped like footballs, trophies and the numeral '11' – Kevin explained,

'Donno's been doing media work for years, even before he quit playing.' He held up the RCE memo. 'If anyone knows about this, it's him.'

Gary had never heard of the Royal Hospital Chelsea, but as Frank pulled the van into the impressive grounds and crawled past an endless lawn towards a stately home, it became clear to Gary that there was more to this place than the name suggested. All the old codgers milling around suggested something closer to a luxury retirement home.

Blimey, he thought. *Old Man Tuttle must have a few quid.*

'It's like *Downton Abbey*, isn't it?' Ian said to Gary, who smiled back at the lad.

Gary noticed that Frank was being unusually quiet, gripping the wheel tightly and keeping his eyes fixed on the road.

He thought better of commenting on this.

Frank parked in front of the mansion, next to a sign saying ENTRANCE TO MAIN QUARTERS.

As they got out, Gary could hold his tongue no longer. 'I still don't know why we're here.'

'You'll see,' said Frank. Gary saw Ian trying to catch his father's eye, but Frank remained distant, striding out in front ahead of the other two.

As they approached the entrance, Gary noticed a platoon of OAPs in bright red uniforms marching past in military formation.

The penny dropped.

'He's a Chelsea Pensioner,' Gary said as they entered the building.

Frank grunted in the affirmative.

'No one knows more about football than my grandad,' Ian said proudly.

Gary nodded to him, then consulted his phone. He knew he risked another chastising from Frank, but this time the Luddite ignored him.

Chelsea Pensioners are British army pensioners, Gary read to himself. It seemed that any connection to Chelsea Football Club was tenuous at best.

But since they'd come up short at Stamford Bridge, Gary could understand why they were now giving this a shot.

And he *was* intrigued to meet the man who had raised the great Frank Tuttle.

After speaking to reception, the trio came to the Nelson Suite. As they approached the door, Gary wondered what kind of impression they would make in such posh surroundings. A boy wearing a dirty football kit, a middle-aged man who looked like he had slept in his clothes and Gary himself in tracksuit and muddy trainers.

They entered a vast, expensively decorated social room, kitted out with priceless rugs, furniture and wall hangings. Men of pensionable age were sitting reading books, or playing billiards, or listening to music. Many smoked pipes. Huge widescreen TVs were showing black and white films and horse racing.

'Wow,' Gary said. 'This room is bigger than my whole flat. How much does it cost to retire into this place?'

'Bugger all,' answered Frank. 'Army perk.' He saw that Ian was looking around in wonder. 'Don't even think about it. If you want to travel the world, do it kicking a ball, not getting shot at.'

'How will we even find him in here?' Gary asked.

'It won't take long, trust me,' Frank said.

He was right. Moments after stepping into the room they heard a commotion.

'And I'm telling *you*, you are wrong wrong wrong!'

Albert Tuttle thrust his finger at the other man's face.

'Oh God,' murmured Frank as he, Gary and Ian watched from across the room.

White-haired and slight of build, the senior Mr Tuttle was not physically imposing, but his passionate anger more than compensated. The present target of his ire was a rotund man who was trying, and failing, to show no fear.

'Calm down, Bert,' the man was saying. 'I was only repeating what everybody else knows about the player.'

'*Everybody*? Please excuse me, I didn't realise that *every*body knew this to be a footballing fact.' Albert's sarcasm could cut through steel.

'Wow, Grandad's really angry,' commented Ian.

Frank turned to Gary, 'If you're thinking about making any comments along the lines of "I see where you get it from now, Frank" – don't.'

'The thought hadn't crossed my mind,' Gary replied with a smirk. The two of them shared a rare moment of camaraderie.

Ian carried on watching the scene unfurl, fascinated. He'd never seen his grandad at full throttle before. He knew he was passionate about football – but this was something else.

Frank, however, was apprehensive. He had barely spoken to his father since The Incident, beyond strained pleasantries to keep up appearances. Certainly, he hadn't visited his old man or picked up the phone. Frank had always felt like a failure to his dad, even before the recent unpleasantness, because he hadn't realised his ambition to coach football for a living.

But they were here now. Frank led Ian and Gary around the other OAPs and approached Albert.

The man he was arguing with had now regained some confidence. 'The fact remains,' he said, 'that Bobby Moore lifted the World Cup. That achievement can't be beaten. End of discussion.'

'There will *always* be a discussion,' declared Albert, 'as long as there are those with the courage and the wits to stimulate one.'

The other man was exasperated. 'That you can deny him being the best ever England captain is—'

'But I do deny it. Moore's contribution has been hugely overinflated due to the '66 tournament. On the other hand, another man in the modern era belied the misconception that a goalkeeper cannot be an effective captain and completely changed the fortunes of an underachieving—'

'Hi, Grandad.'

'Hi, Dad.'

Albert's manner changed completely. He forgot about his argument and approached his family, limping slightly from the hip that had taken loose shrapnel in Belfast in '70. The other man, meanwhile, rolled his eyes and returned to his game of checkers.

Albert gave Ian a hug then shook Frank's hand.

'So nice to see you both.'

'Thanks, Dad. Still tearing the place up, eh?'

'Oh that?' Albert grinned mischievously. 'Passes the time, doesn't it?'

'This is Gary,' said Ian. Gary shook Albert's hand respectfully.

'Nice to meet you, Mr Tuttle.'

'Gary's my football coach,' said Ian.

This interested Albert. 'Oh, I see, a quite noble profession. Well done.'

'Thanks very much.'

Frank felt bile rise in his stomach.

Here we go...

'My Francis always wanted to be a coach,' said Albert, right on cue. 'He used to spend hours on the living room rug with his Subbuteo men, lining them up and giving team talks. You remember that Francis?'

Frank screwed his face up in embarrassment.

'He used to *be* a coach until...' Albert trailed off, unable to hide his disappointment.

'Dad, please. We're not here to talk about that.'

'Francis Gordon Tuttle not wanting to talk about football.' Albert winked at Ian. 'This is a first.'

Frank was struggling to stay composed. 'No, listen, it *is* about football. But... is there somewhere we can go?'

'Of course. Follow me.'

143

Moments later the four of them were sitting on comfy sofas in Albert's spacious living quarters, drinking tea from a pot.

'Now then,' said their host, taking a sip. 'How can I help?'

Frank filled his father in on the events so far, from last night in *Bar Onze un Côté* (the abridged version) right up to needing a six-letter word or number related to Chelsea Football Club.

'I see,' Albert said.

Ian showed him the tablet. 'Grandad, do you think you can help us out with this latest clue?'

Albert put on his reading glasses and peered at the screen. '"When the old met the new."' He smiled. 'I can see why you came to a relic like me. What's all this about?'

'Have you heard about this three o' clock FA announcement, Mr Tuttle?' asked Gary.

Albert nodded.

'We think that it has something to do with a football rules change that will jeopardise the game.'

'Mmm,' said Albert leaning back and stroking his chin. 'Rule changes. Yes, there have been plenty of those over the years. I remember when substitutes were first permitted, in 1958. My father – your great-grandfather, Ian – he thought this meant the game had gone soft. "If they can't play on, just leave 'em for the worms" was how he saw it.' Albert chuckled to himself.

'Yes, rules evolve,' he continued. 'But things like substitutes, golden goals, video assistant refereeing... changes often come along – sometimes staying, sometimes not. But it's the core of the game, the fairness – *that's* what matters.'

'That's exactly what we're *talking* about, Dad,' Frank said. 'We think that the FA is going to change football so that it no longer *is* fair.'

Albert frowned. 'Well, that wouldn't do at all, would it?' He sipped his tea and stared out the window. 'Nowadays it's more about the money, the TV rights and everything else. The game's gone international and made some companies very rich. And good luck to them. But my father once told me something else: "Football must stay balanced between being a sport and a business." I wish more people would remember that.'

Frank leaned over and touched Albert's arm.

'Dad. We need to solve this six-letter or six-number Chelsea clue and find the second Half. Please, can you think of anything, anything at all?'

14

'AND THIS is the security system, connected directly to the old bill so I've got a plod here in five minutes flat... And this is my Persian rug, from pre-season in the Middle East. Nice geezers out there, don't touch a drink though... Oh, and *this* was a retirement gift from...'

Slumped on the white leather sofa on the other side of his former-teammate's living room, Kevin watched moodily as Stuart Donaldson gave Claire the grand tour.

As they left the room, Kevin called out, 'There were a rumour all them rugs was fake.'

'How would you know?' Donno called back without stopping. 'The gaffer left you at home after one of your Twitter tantrums.'

Kevin hesitated – and that was enough to miss his comeback window.

So, he went back to drinking his iced tea and staring moodily at a life-sized framed print of the homeowner receiving some award or other from David Beckham.

He couldn't deny it, Donno had pretty good bants.

Just home advantage, that's all.

Kevin scanned the colossal living room, which doubled as a shrine to Donno, and reflected on how things had changed. Back in the day, bants would stay away from the public and within the dressing room or on the training ground, where it belonged. Before social media exploded, things had been great for Kevin. He was known as a joker, a bit of a loose cannon, but more of a laugh because of it. The class clown, like back at school. Now, his loose tongue and fidgety thumb had made him *persona non grata*.

And now clubs were obsessed with this media training and making sure the players didn't say anything outside of the party line. Where was the fun in that? Kevin had taken the classes along with the rest of them, but he couldn't absorb all the monotonous drivel. 'Repeat after me,' the teacher the club had brought in would say. '*We're just taking it one game at a time. We're just taking it one game at a time…*'

What a load of cobblers. At these sessions, Kevin's mind would drift, usually to his self-promotion ideas. When a class was over and one of those media trainers or sports psychologists would ask him what he'd learned, he'd fake it and just tell them what they wanted to hear. That soon got rid of them.

Kevin swirled the ice around in his glass. Why was he so down? It had to be more than jealousy about Donno's Player of the Year trophies and the dozens of photos of him with celebrities. And sure, Kevin didn't currently have a club, but he'd been in this position before and something had always turned up.

Did how he was feeling have anything to do with this scavenger hunt he'd got himself mixed up in today? Unlikely. It was probably all twaddle anyway. People outside of the game looked for injustices everywhere and loved coming up with crackpot theories. The ones who played football for a living just got on with it.

A shrill voice from the other room snapped Kevin back to the present.

'No? *Really?*'

It was followed by high-pitched laughter.

Of course, Kevin realised. That was it.

Her.

For a footballer – young, famous, good-looking, rich, in peak physical condition – attention from the desired sex came easily. This was great when you first broke through as a player. But Kevin had started to find it all rather boring. The lithe bodies, the perfect skin, the pouting lips – it was still appealing, but he had found himself wanting more. He would never admit it to the other lads, but he wanted actual conversation, interaction on a non-physical level. The last one he picked up, a model-slash-actress named Siobhan, was great fun while downing cocktails at the Ivy, but the next morning round his penthouse flat when he'd asked her about her interests and ambitions, she'd looked at him like he was a serial killer and made a run for it while still half-undressed.

This Claire, though... now Donno was leading her back into the room, him still showing off, her still giggling away. Here was a girl – no, a *woman* – who was a real looker but who you could actually talk to as well. She didn't just sit there in awe of him and nod while he blathered on. She seemed to have, well, a good personality. Weird how that was usually the thing you said about the ugly ones, and yet Kevin had started to wonder whether it was the missing ingredient that made someone truly attractive.

'Wasn't it, Kev?' Donno was saying.

'Eh?' Kevin looked up to see Donno and Claire plonking themselves down on the other sofa.

'Blimey, away with the fairies this one. Explains why he's no good one-on-one with a defender.'

Kevin was back in the room. 'The only thing you're good one-on-one with, Donno, is... well, there's a lady present but...' He made the universal 'wanker' gesture.

'That's rich, coming from the geezer who once got caught—'

'Gentlemen, *please*,' said Claire, putting down her empty glass and straightening her dress. Both men's eyes flicked to her legs. 'I'd love to sit around all day listening to you guys "bant it up" or whatever you call it, but time is of the essence here and we really need some help.'

She smiled at Donno and handed him the RCE memo.

Donno examined the folded sheet of paper. 'Yeah, I've seen this logo before. These people were giving out some questionnaire things to players last season.'

'*I* never got one,' moped Kevin.

'You must have been on suspension, Min.'

'Oh. Yeah, probably.'

Claire implored Donno to carry on.

'Yeah, we came into training one day and had them under our pegs. Here, I think I've still got mine – I did my answers online.'

Donno jumped up, crossed the room and began rooting through a sideboard drawer.

While their host had his back turned, Kevin pouted at Claire.

'What?' she said.

Kevin responded by doing a silent imitation of her: listening to Donno, fawning over him, being impressed and giggly.

'Oh, grow up,' said Claire.

Kevin carried on with his impression and eventually Claire had to stifle a laugh. He stopped just in time to not get caught.

'There you go,' Donno said on his return, handing a crumpled piece of paper to Claire.

'Didn't know you could read, Donno,' Kevin commented.

'I can read a defensive line to stay onside, not like some—'

'Boys, please,' said Claire. 'Honestly, you're competing and bickering like a couple of kids. Who's the best? Who's won the most? Who cares! You do know that rather than trying to beat each other all the time, it would be much more impressive if you pooled your resources into something constructive, like charity work or something.'

Donno and Kevin thought about this.

Then Donno said, 'I donated 50 grand to Kiddies with Cancer last year.'

'Yeah?' retorted Kevin. 'Well, you didn't do three marathons in one season for three different—'

'Oh, I give up.'

Claire turned her attention to the questionnaire Donna had given them. 'Interesting,' she said. 'Very interesting.'

'Sorry to tell you this when you've come all this way, but I'm afraid I haven't got the foggiest idea how to answer your riddle.'

On hearing his father say this, Frank downed the rest of his tea and clattered the cup back onto its saucer. He was ready to leave Albert's posh apartment at the Royal Chelsea Hospital right there and then.

'That's alright, Grandad,' Ian said. 'We'll figure it out.'

But then Albert had an idea. 'Well, there is perhaps something...' He stood up, his knees cracking.

'Careful, Mr Tuttle,' said Gary, standing also.

'Do you want a hand?' asked Ian, rising too.

But Frank stayed put. He knew that his dad was too proud to accept help.

And indeed, Albert said, 'No, no, I'm quite alright.' He steadied himself on the arm of the sofa then moved off into his bedroom.

'Dad?' called Frank after him. 'What are you doing?'

'Keep your hair on, Francis,' replied Albert from the other room. 'I'm not having one of those "senior moments."'

Albert returned holding a blue item of clothing. He handed it to Ian, who unfurled it.

'It's a Chelsea shirt,' he said.

'That's right,' said Albert. 'Someone from the club came round once handing these out.'

'Why are you giving us this?' asked Frank.

'Have a look at the collar,' said Albert.

Frank did. 'It's red. So what?'

'Chelsea Pensioners...' said Gary.

Albert smiled.

Gary continued, 'This kit was to celebrate the Chelsea Pensioners. The red symbolises their uniforms.'

Albert nodded.

Frank took the shirt from Ian and examined it. He regarded his son, who tilted his head, then Gary, whose face was equally quizzical.

Then Frank stood up and said, 'Well, Dad, thanks very much for this. You've been a great help.'

'I'm sorry I couldn't be more—'

'No no, really, thanks a bundle. Come on you two, we're off.' Frank hurried them towards the front door.

'Bye Grandad,' said Ian, waving as he went. 'See you soon.'

'Drop by any time,' said Albert, sitting back down and causing his knees to crack again. 'Bethan as well. Such a lovely girl, Francis, I can't believe you two can't—'

Frank was already halfway out the door. 'Yeah yeah, no time to talk about that. See you later, Dad.'

Presently, they were outside in the open again. The sky had clouded over, making the day seem a lot later. The same red-jacketed parade from earlier now stood in a four-three-three formation on the lawn, practicing a rifle salute.

As they walked across the car park, Frank exhaled sharply. 'Well that was a waste of time. Grandad's obviously... not all there anymore.'

'Dad!' exclaimed Ian, nearly dropping the Chelsea replica shirt.

'It's part of life, Ian,' Frank said gently. 'People get old and their... faculties start to go. I'm just glad he's where he can be looked after.'

Frank led them to the van in silence. Ian was devastated; Gary gave him a sympathetic look.

Minutes later, they were turning out of the grounds onto Royal Hospital Road.

Frank drove with no particular destination in mind. The mood in the van was thick.

They didn't get very far before grinding to a halt at the side of the road.

'Eh?' said Frank. He checked the fuel gauge – empty. 'What? I filled her up yesterday.'

All three jumped out. Frank found the fuel cap open and traces of petrol under it.

Along with a single strand of yellow cotton.

'Siphoned,' Gary said. 'By those RCE bastards.'

'What we gonna do now, Dad?' Ian asked.

'Call the AA,' said Frank, replacing the fuel cap.

'I mean, about The Campaign.'

Frank leaned against the van and sighed. 'Maybe Fullarton was right. Maybe we should all just go home.'

Gary and Ian looked at each other. Neither knew what to say.

Frank took the Chelsea shirt from Ian and used it to wipe the petrol from his hands. 'Changing kits every season,' he muttered. 'Costs the fans a fortune.'

Then Frank stopped.

'Ian,' he said, staring at the shirt.

Ian looked up. 'Yeah, Dad?'

Frank turned to his son. 'How many boxes on that answer again?'

'Six...' Ian took the tablet out from his kit bag.

Frank dropped the Chelsea shirt and got out his phone.

Gary asked, 'Are you phoning the AA?'

'Nope,' Frank said, getting excited as he tapped away on the screen. 'You're not the only one who can Google.' Seconds later he said, 'Got it.'

Frank took the tablet from Ian and entered something into it.

His excitement spread to the other two. 'What is it, Frank?' asked Gary.

'Dad, come on,' cried Ian.

'Ha,' said Frank triumphantly. 'Looks like I was wrong about old Albert Tuttle.'

'What did you put in?' asked Gary.

'It was a number that it wanted, but not *one* number. It was a football season, the way you can write it as six digits.'

Gary and Ian thought about this.

'You mean,' said Gary slowly, 'the full year of the first one, then forward slash, then the last two digits of the second one?'

Frank nodded.

Like 1997/98, or 2000/01.

Frank held up the tablet. The answer box was now green.

'See – 2010 to 2011,' Frank said. 'Or 201011. The season that the Blues played with the Chelsea Pensioners shirt. When the old met the new.'

While working for the FA, Claire had encountered plenty of footballers. She knew what they were like on the whole: show-offs. The competitiveness, the materialism – it came with the territory and frankly she found it tiresome.

So she was disappointed that legendary ex-England striker Stuart 'Donno' Donaldson turned out to be much the same, and although she was curious to see his mansion and wanted to be polite, ultimately she couldn't care less about from where he got his Ming vase and what vintage were the wines in his cellar.

She wanted to get on with uncovering a football conspiracy – and now that Donno had produced another set of Research Creating Excellence questions, targeted at players instead of fans, she felt that they might finally be getting somewhere.

Claire was sitting on Donno's designer sofa poised to read out the contents of the questionnaire he had just given them. But before she spoke, she examined the man who was sitting opposite her.

Is Kevin Maxwell the same as every other footballer? she wondered.

He certainly seemed to be. Yet there was something about him, a sweetness. Yeah, he was good-looking, that was a given, but she suspected that there were more layers underneath that chiselled surface.

Or maybe she was just imagining things.

Claire cleared her throat and then read out the questions.

1.   *Is there anything you would change about football?*
2.   *Does how the fans feel matter to you?*
3.   *Would you be happy to start playing to new rules?*
4.   *Do you think the game's current rules are fair?*
5.   *Does the game being fair matter to you?*

When Claire had finished, she looked at Donno.

After deliberating a moment, the ex player said, 'I didn't really take it that serious, none of us did. I just banged out my answers while waiting in traffic because this mob kept coming round hassling us. They were always wearing these nasty tops...'

'Yellow ones?' asked Kevin.

'Yeah, yellow. Cheap looking. They said that by giving our answers someone would win a Lamborghini. The younger lads were excited by that but, well, I've already got a Lambo, and a Merc, and a Porsche, so...'

'They should have made the prize something actually useful to you lot, like *The Little Book of Playground Insults*,' mused Claire.

'Eh?' Donno and Kevin replied in unison.

'Never mind... Hmm, so here we have more questions about football being fair.'

Donno and Kevin stared blankly at her.

'Interesting,' Kevin said eventually.

Claire persevered. 'Did no one in the dressing room wonder why you were being asked about these things?'

'Well, no. I mean, it's not like it mentioned our wages getting cut or anything.'

'I see,' Claire said. 'So, what did you put?'

'For what?'

'How about the first question?'

Donno strained to remember. 'I think... for the first one... I put... "Don't know."'

'"Don't know,"' Claire repeated.

'Yeah.' Donno sank back into his sofa's luxurious leather.

'What about the second one?'

'I think... I put... yeah. The same thing.'

"And for... the rest of the questions? Same again?'

'Yeah.' Donno put his feet up on the round glass coffee table (which, of course, had the pattern of a football etched on its surface).

'And, let me guess, any of the other players who bothered to fill this in, they probably put...'

'"Don't know" as well – yeah, far as I know.' Donno shrugged. 'Look, last year was my final season, so what did I care anyway?' He began examining his fingernails to check if he needed a manicure.

'Right,' Claire said.

'I would have put the same thing, I reckon,' Kevin said.

Claire gave him a wan smile then sighed.

So, what now?

Kevin suddenly jumped out of his seat. 'Well, I guess we'll be off.'

'Yeah, I've got to finish getting ready anyway,' Donno said as he and Claire rose.

As Donno led his guests across his Tabriz carpet towards the front door, Kevin asked, 'So where you off to, then?'

With a casual wave of his hand, Donno said, 'You know this thing at Wembley today? The announcement? I'm reading it out.'

Kevin was aghast, stopping in his tracks as they reached the front door. '*You're* reading it out?'

'So you know what it's about?' Claire asked hopefully.

'Nope.' Donno had returned his attention to his nails. 'They wouldn't tell me, just that they'll have it ready for me on one of those autocues when I get there.'

'Well, can we come with you?' Claire asked, giving him her most winning smile.

But Donno was unmoved. 'Sorry, media work's my career now and I can't jeopardise it by bringing *civilians* to Wembley.' Donno directed this at Kevin – which Claire thought was a cheap shot.

Donno opened the front door and Kevin stepped through, only giving his host the slightest nod by way of goodbye.

Claire stopped in the doorway and watched Kevin shuffle towards his car. 'Donno, is there anything else you can think of about these questionnaires or the people that gave them to you?'

Donno pondered. 'Actually, there might be. I just remembered something.'

'Mm-hm?' Claire stepped over the threshold, giving Kevin another glance. He was leaning against his car, staring off into space.

Donno went on. 'I've seen another version of them questionnaires. Me and Mini's old gaffer got given one. I think it was especially for managers.'

15

THE NEXT clue was a really weird one.

Green square pranks (it's twisted).

Ian was mulling it over as he made his way with his dad and his new football coach to Sloane Square, the nearest tube station to his grandad's retirement home.

Ian didn't mind having to walk, but he wasn't happy that those yellow polo shirt-wearers had messed with their van.

I hope we run into those guys and Dad punches them in the face.

Still, they were on the move again and solving clues – and Ian was thrilled.

But this one had all three of them stumped.

'"Green square pranks"?' said Gary.

'That's what it says,' Ian confirmed.

'What does *that* mean?' asked Frank.

Ian saw the tube station up ahead. So long as they were still baffled by the clue, they wouldn't know where to actually go to when they reached it.

His dad was thinking hard. 'Footballers love pranks, banter and all that. Gaz, see if there are any really famous ones.'

Gary tapped away on his phone, looking left and right as the three of them crossed Holbein Place Road. 'Saving football is murder on a person's data,' he moaned.

'Well?' asked Frank presently.

'Lot of stuff about Wimbledon. The Crazy Gang.'

'Who were they?' asked Ian.

Frank answered, 'Well, you know that there used to be an actual Wimbledon Football Club in the Premier League? Back before they moved and became MK Dons?'

'Sort of...' said Ian. Being only 13, his knowledge of football's past was limited.

His dad explained. 'Back in the 1980s and '90s, the team's nickname was the Crazy Gang. They were the underdogs, beating Liverpool in the FA Cup Final in...'

'1988,' finished Gary.

'Right, '88. They had a load of characters in the dressing room, like John Fashanu, Dennis Wise, Vinnie Jones...'

'The guy who was in that X-Men film?'

'Probably.'

'Well, were any of their pranks... *twisted?*'

'They cut up each other's clothes,' said Gary. 'Set fire to their shoes, things like that.'

Ian frowned. 'I'd say that's definitely twisted.'

They had now reached the tube station. Sloane Square itself was across the street – actually more of a rectangle, tree-lined with benches and a fountain. The trio hung outside the station, pressed against the wall to avoid passers-by.

'So, what,' said Gary, 'you reckon we go to Wimbledon?'

Frank traced his finger along a tube map poster. 'It's down the District Line.'

Ian peered at the map. 'There's a Wimbledon Stadium down there?'

Frank sighed. 'We're looking at quite a few possibilities. Until recently AFC Wimbledon's ground was actually in Kingston. I don't know whether this quest is bang up to date enough to know that they've moved again.'

'But the *original* Wimbledon used to ground share with Crystal Palace,' said Gary. 'Maybe we're meant to go down to Selhurst Park.'

'Maybe,' considered Frank. 'Or maybe we need to go *up* to Milton Keynes.'

Milton Keynes?

Frank responded to Ian's confused face. 'That's where the current version of the original club now plays, as MK Dons.'

'And, of course, if the Campaign *is* up to date to the present moment,' said Gary, 'then we're going to need to go to Plough Lane.'

Frank nodded.

Now Ian was really lost.

'What's Plough Lane?'

'Where the old Wimbledon used to play,' Frank said, 'and it's been redeveloped and is now AFC Wimbledon's ground.'

They stood there a moment, weighing up their options.

'It can't be Milton Keynes,' said Ian. 'That's outside London, right?'

'Yeah, and the tablet said, "Capital instructions,"' Frank pointed out. '*Inside* the city.'

While Frank and Gary continued to debate where they should go, an advert inside the tube station caught Ian's eye.

He walked inside to get a closer look.

'"Green square pranks..."' he murmured.

And it was 'twisted'.

Are we missing something really obvious?

There was a woman in a Transport for London uniform by the ticket office.

'Excuse me?' Ian asked her.

'How can I help you, young man?' the woman replied. 'On your way to play football?'

Ian was thrown for a moment, then remembered he was wearing football gear and carrying a kit bag.

'That's right... um, do you have a pen I could borrow?'

'Of course,' she said unclipping a cheap black biro from her uniform. 'Keep it, we've got loads.'

'Thanks.' He took it and walked back outside.

'Ian,' said Frank, nearly bumping into his son. 'We thought you'd run off again.'

'I didn't run off in the first...' Blessed with a restraint that often eluded his father (not to mention his grandfather), Ian stopped himself from reacting. 'Dad, have you got a bit of paper?'

'Come on, we don't have time to mess around here any longer, mate.'

'Please, I just want to try something.'

Frank found an old receipt in his wallet and handed it over.

Ian turned the receipt onto its plain side, laid it down flat on a green electrical cabinet and began to write.

Frank and Gary exchanged a bemused look as Ian scribbled.

The boy held the receipt up.

He had written the words 'green square pranks' in a circle.

'Son,' Frank said gently, 'we know what the clue is. Now give me the tablet and we'll enter all the possible Wimbledon grounds one by one.'

'No, Dad,' Ian said, getting frustrated. 'Aren't you wondering why I've written the words out in a circle?'

'Um...'

'It's the best way to solve an anagram. Haven't you ever watched *Countdown*?'

'An anagram,' mused Gary. '"Twisted" ...'

'Watch,' Ian said.

He crossed the letters off from the three words one by one, each time rewriting the letter underneath.

The men's eyes widened.

'Oh my God,' said Gary.

Ian had made three new words, and when he entered them into the tablet, they turned green.

Ian span around and performed his usual goal celebration on the spot: clenched fist raised, mouth open in delight. He'd been doing it ever since he first watched his father's *Alan Shearer's Greatest Strikes* DVD.

Frank laughed at the weird looks they were getting from members of the public. He held Ian by the shoulders. 'Son, have I ever told you that I'm proud of you?'

'Not nearly often enough,' grinned Ian. 'Now come on, there's no time to lose.'

As the three of them moved through the barriers, they passed by the poster that had caught Ian's attention. It depicted the Tower of London and featured the slogan SEE KINGS AND QUEENS COME ALIVE.

The poster had made Ian think of Queens Park Rangers Football Club.

As usual, the London Underground was packed. Frank, Ian and Gary squeezed with the sweaty crowd onto a westbound Circle Line train. There were no free seats, so the men and the boy stood holding onto the yellow grab handles.

They had got as far as South Kensington station. Frank was examining a tube map as they pulled away.

'Three more stops 'til Notting Hill Gate,' he said, 'then we change onto the Central Line, get off at White City.'

'How long will it take, Dad?'

'Not long. And Loftus Road is only ten minutes' walk from the station.'

Ian was reading the tablet's next screen, tantalisingly labelled 'The Penultimate Clue (in two parts)'.

'What does "penultimate" mean, Dad?' he asked.

Frank frowned; he knew this one. 'Second to last,' he said.

'So, what do you think the *last* one will be about?'

'Dunno. But if it's the final stadium that it sends us to, then it *must* be Wembley.'

Gary agreed. 'Yeah, has to be.'

'But put that away for now, son.' Frank rubbed his temples, which had suddenly decided to remind him about his hangover. 'Let's just rest a minute. We can worry about the next clue when we get topside.' He glanced around at their fellow passengers. 'Besides, this is sensitive stuff, we better not talk about it in here.'

Ian nodded and put the tablet away again in his kit bag.

At Gloucester Road station more passengers got on. The extra bodies separated Frank and Ian from Gary.

Away from the other man, Frank took the opportunity to speak candidly to his son.

'Ian...' he started, ducking his head away from an obese man's armpit.

But Ian was also eager to talk. 'Dad, I just wanted to tell you...'

'What?'

'This has been the *best* day.'

Frank hesitated. 'Really?'

'I'm having so much fun.'

'You're not still... annoyed with me about this morning, or...'

The train stopped at High Street Kensington station. More passengers got off and on. Ian moved aside to give an elderly couple some space.

'Annoyed? Dad, come on, forget about it.'

'Really?'

'Yeah, 'course. But I have gotta say, you've been pretty weird since that stuff happened last season...'

Frank winced. 'I know, but I felt like... I dunno. I regretted it.'

'It *was* pretty funny,' Ian smirked. 'And that guy was a bellend.'

'Hey,' Frank said. 'He *may* have been a bellend, but I shouldn't have done what I did. Violence is never the answer.'

'Sorry, Dad. But you do know that all the lads on the team miss you?'

'They do?'

'Yeah, they've been asking about you, when are you coming back and everything. I mean, Gary's alright, but no one really listens to him. We all prefer you.'

Frank was thrilled.

'Dad?' It was Ian's turn to be coy.

'Yeah?'

'Are you and Mum... going to be alright?'

Frank thought carefully before answering. 'I hope so, son. I really do.'

'She still talks about you.'

'She does?' Frank was embarrassed. He evaded Ian's sincere face and glanced back up the train, searching for Gary. He found him and started to watch him; it was the first time Frank had seen Gary without his phone out.

'Mm-hmm,' Ian was saying. 'She talks about you a lot. And the other day, I heard her crying on the phone with—'

The train jolted to a stop, nearly knocking them over.

'Oh, you gotta be kidding me,' said Frank, holding onto a pole with one hand and Ian with the other. He couldn't believe what he was seeing.

Confusion and disorientation spread through the busy carriage. The stop was too sudden to be normal.

And then the lights went out.

'It's a terror attack,' someone yelled, ramping the panic up another notch.

'Hold onto me,' Frank told Ian calmly. Ian nodded in the darkness – illuminated by the blue glows of mobile phone screens – and gripped his dad's jacket.

'Dad, is it terrorists?' asked Ian.

'No, son, it's not terrorists.'

Frank was looking towards Gary again but now he couldn't see him.

What he did see were four figures barging through and heading this way.

Even in the dark, the bright yellow was unmistakable.

FA CHIEF fairness officer William Fullarton had not yet reached Wembley Stadium to return what he thought was the Association's missing tablet.

His encounter with Frank Tuttle and company this morning had been playing on his mind. He had been delaying his arrival at Wembley by taking care of some business that required him to stop off at certain sports centres – necessary work, but nothing that such a senior member of the Department of Fair Play need usually concern himself with.

And this one had to be his last stop. Club Des Sports, at David Lloyd Acton Park, was the only sports centre left on his list that he could conceivably tell himself was still on the way to Wembley.

Fullarton got out of his silver BMW. He left his driver behind in the car park and made his way to the reception of the centre's five-a-side football arena, passing the Astroturf mini-pitches in their cages as he went.

At the start of a new season, every sports centre in the country must hand in a report on its football facilities to the FA, confirming that standards of fair play are being met – lest they warrant an investigation. The deadline was weeks ago, but some establishments were tardy and needed to be chased with a personal visit.

The man on Club Des Sports' reception desk knew what Fullarton wanted as soon as he flashed his departmental ID. He had the report ready in a drawer and handled a bundle of loosely bound forms over. Fullarton received them without comment and turned to leave.

As he approached the door to the outside, the conversation of two five-a-side players at the vending machines made him pause.

'No, mate, I'm telling you,' said the one in the orange and turquoise striped football shirt, 'this announcement is gonna really bollocks football up. Haven't you been on Twitter?'

'Mate,' the other said, rolling up a sleeve of his black and grey shirt and reaching in to grab a Snickers bar, 'you're going on what Twitter says. That's like trusting Wikipedia. And who says it's gonna make the game worse? Maybe it's gonna make it *better*.'

'What, like VAR has?'

This had his friend stumped. 'Alright,' he said after a moment, 'so if it was that bad and everything, don't you think someone from the FA would stop it?'

His mate snorted. 'They don't care about the game. They're just a business, a profit-making business. Besides, big organisation like that, gonna be a ton of bureaucracy. No one's gonna have the balls to stand up against

168

that, they're all just getting on with their day jobs, following their procedures, keeping their noses clean. We all do it at work, don't we?'

'Excuse me, mate,' the other said. He was talking to Fullarton, who hadn't realised he was blocking the exit.

Fullarton mumbled an apology and let the two men out. He watched them head for their cars.

Travelling again now in the passenger seat of his FA BMW, the sports complex disappearing behind him, Fullarton took the tablet that had been causing so much trouble today out of the locked glove box.

When we're not leaving it lying around in bars, he thought as he examined the device, *we certainly take care of our equipment.*

The tablet looked like it had never even been used.

Fullarton knew that he was forbidden to view the tablet's content, that even a high-ranking member of the Department of Fair Play was not privy to the FA's most confidential information.

He glanced at his driver. Then he turned to the back seat where the other tablet, the stone one, was fastened securely with a seatbelt, like an infant.

Looking out through the windscreen again, Fullarton cleared his throat.

'Powell, I think I should check this device.'

The driver's eyes were unreadable behind his sunglasses. 'If you think that's best, sir.'

'It would be a shame to travel all the way to Wembley and find that it's faulty. That would make the Department of Fair Play look rather silly.'

'It could make many people look rather silly, sir.'

Fullarton opened his mouth but, not for the first time in his career, he resisted saying something that was best left unsaid.

He turned on the tablet.

And stared at a prompt to initiate first-usage set-up.

'Clever girl...' Fullarton murmured. He caught his reflection in the tablet's screen and saw that he was grinning from ear to ear.

'Powell.'

'Sir?'

'Change of plan. Take the next left.'

'So, not to Wembley, sir?'

'No,' said Fullarton.

'But it's only—'

'I know where the national stadium of English football is, Powell,' Fullarton snapped.

He sat there, staring out his window, brooding. 'No, not to Wembley,' he muttered to himself. 'Not yet.'

Despite his boss's mood, Fullarton's driver ventured one more question. 'Do you want me to lean on our sources to track down Tuttle and his friends again?'

Fullarton remained silent. He was deep in thought.

His driver waited.

Around the same time that Gary was suggesting that he, Frank and Ian might need to visit Selhurst Park Stadium for the 'pranks' clue, Kevin and Claire were actually entering its grounds in South Norwood.

They turned in off Holmesdale Road. The stewards assumed by his car that Kevin was a player and ushered him through. This pleased him no end, Claire observed.

Crystal Palace were at home, playing Kevin and Donno's old team, Wolverhampton Wanderers, and so the plan was to find the Wolves manager and see if he still had his edition of the RCE questionnaire – a second version that they hadn't yet seen.

The ground was overflowing with fans and Kevin and Claire joined the crowd of red and blue replica shirts. Kevin popped on a pair of gaudy designer sunglasses. 'So I don't get recognised,' he explained.

Claire was sceptical. 'Is that really going to make any difference?'

'Oh yeah. And we celebs proper value our privacy.'

As they made their way across the forecourt to the stadium, Claire observed Kevin peering over his sunglasses and making eye contact with several fans, who would then whisper excitedly to each other.

She gave him a wry look.

'What?' Kevin said, the picture of innocence.

When they reached the players' entrance, Kevin spied who they were looking for inside.

'Oi, Sid,' he yelled, taking off his sunglasses.

Sid McClane, a huge-bellied man in a club tracksuit, passed the door staff and approached Kevin and Claire.

'Mini Maxwell. What you doin' here, son?' asked Sid.

'Need a wee chat, gaffer,' Kevin replied.

'Come inside then, ya radge.'

They entered a reception area. Sid embraced Kevin and shook Claire's hand, then he led them off down a corridor.

'Look, Mini,' said Sid, 'Ah'm sorry aboot not renewing your contract, you know it wasnae my choice. That new chairman, he only wants youngsters, you didnae stand a chance.'

'It's alright Sid, some mug will come in for me. They always do.'

'Aye, that's the spirit. Just stay off them Tweetbooks and social networks.' To Claire he said, 'Always getting himself into trouble wi' his hands this one – and if it's no online then it's wi' the lassies.' Claire raised an eyebrow at that, and Kevin gave her another of his innocent looks.

The trio followed a sign towards AWAY CHANGING ROOMS. They were turning a corner when Sid's phone rang.

'Aye,' the big Scotsman said into it without breaking stride, 'you did read it right: 60 thou' a week, no a penny more. No, I didnae forget to put in an appearance bonus – the lad isnae *having* one. He gets well bloody paid to do his job, which is to play football matches. I'm no paying the lad *again* just for turning up.'

Realising that Claire and Kevin were within earshot, Sid continued with his voice lowered. 'Ah know you helped me oot wi' that other thing. Yeah, ah'm grateful, I know we'd both be up shit creek if they found out... But come on, your lad's hud two broken legs in five years. If he was a horse, he'd have been put doon by now... yeah... okay, that could work. Alright, call me back in ten.'

They now entered the away team's dressing room.

Footballers were in various states of undress. Banter filled the air as did items the men threw at each other, mostly shin pads and rolled-up socks. Dubstep music blared from a stereo.

Claire felt awkward in this testosterone-rich environment. There was a strong masculine aroma and many of the players were naked – and despite noticing her they remained unashamed.

They were more interested in Kevin.

'Mini Maxwell,' one heavily tattooed man said as he snapped a towel at Kevin – but missed and hit Sid.

'Eh,' yelled the manager.

'Oh no,' said the player in a thick Italian accent. 'Sorry my gaffer.'

His teammates (and Kevin) all cracked up.

Claire didn't know where to look and hoped they wouldn't be staying long in this sweat pit. To her relief, Sid moved them straight through towards a door at the far end. 'Bloody children,' he was muttering, rubbing his thigh. 'It's like working in a bloody zoo here.'

'Nice shot, Toni,' Kevin said as they passed the Italian.

The player laughed. 'Kevin, how come you no with us no more?'

'Yeah, Mini, ain't the same without you,' someone called from the showers.

'That's right,' came another voice, 'it's a lot bloody better.'

The whole room cracked up at this witticism and pelted Kevin with items of clothing. He threw back a pair of underpants which landed on the wrong person's face, to more hysterics.

'Come on through,' Sid told Kevin and Claire as he opened a door marked AWAY MANAGER'S OFFICE. 'Excuse these animals, miss,' he apologised to Claire as he hesitated at the door. 'If you let them oot onto the streets they'd soon be joining the foxes rummaging through bins.' Over his shoulder he added, 'Barely able to function in civilised society, this lot.'

'Didn't seem to bother your Sandra, gaffer,' called a voice.

'*What?*' cried Sid, spinning around on the spot. 'Who's talking aboot mah lassie?'

'Come on, Sid,' said Kevin, guiding his former boss into the office. It was tiny, windowless and bland, befitting its lot as a temporary home for managers just passing through.

Kevin gazed fondly back at the men with whom he used to share showers, pitches and team buses, and then closed the door.

Sid slumped down behind the desk and gestured for Kevin and Claire to sit across from him.

'Right, sorry again aboot all that, miss,' Sid said to Claire.

'Quite alright. I've seen it all before.'

'Hmm. Well anyway, how can ah help you Miss... eh, who did you say you were again, young lady?'

Kevin blurted out, 'Claire's from the FA.'

'Right,' barked Sid, now animated. 'Ah know why *you're* here. And let me tell you, missy, ah've got a bone to pick wi' you lot.''

Sitting opposite his ex-gaffer, Wolverhampton Wanders boss Sid McClane, in the away team manager's office at Selhurst Park Stadium, Kevin wished for the first time that he'd been paying a bit more attention to all this business he'd got caught up in today, otherwise he might not be at such a loss as how to blag his way out of his current situation.

But, as it turned out, Claire had them covered.

'Well, Mr McClane, I'm glad this doesn't come as a surprise,' she was saying.

'No, love, it don't,' Sid replied. 'Ah thought you lot would be turning up sooner, to be fair. Always checking up, aren't you?'

'Yes,' said Claire flatly. 'We are.'

'So, you must be here to take ya top-secret thingy back?'

'That's right.'

Kevin looked sideways at Claire. As Sid rummaged around inside a leather-bound club-branded organiser he had on his desk, she shot Kevin a wink.

'Here ya go.' Sid handed Claire a sheet of paper. Kevin leaned in and they both read it.

Donno had been right. It was on RCE headed paper and was directed at football managers.

But he had been wrong about one thing. This one wasn't a questionnaire.

'It's a list of instructions,' said Claire.

'Yeah,' agreed Sid, 'but a fat lot of good they did us.'

The instructions were headed PERFORMANCE-ENHANCING ROUTINES FOR FIRST-TEAM SQUAD.

'How come you look so surprised?' Sid asked Claire, the chair creaking as he leaned back. 'You lot at the FA endorsed it, don't tell me you havenae seen one before?'

'Oh, of course,' said Claire. 'Just that it went through a few redesigns. I would never have chosen *this* shade of purple.'

Kevin was really starting to admire Claire's blagging ability; it was a form of banter, and of course bants impressed Kevin more than anything.

'Yeah, well,' Sid was saying, 'like ah telt ye, it was a bloody waste of time.'

Kevin scanned the instructions. Long passages of text bored him, but he got the gist of it. It was a programme detailing how to 'psychologically prepare your squad to enhance its playing ability,' consisting of pre-match recordings and sessions with RCE representatives. It sounded to Kevin like the media training he was familiar with, although he'd never heard of 'mental conditioning,' 'suggestive meditation,' or something called 'intense focused repetition.'

'Hypnotism,' Claire whispered to Kevin when Sid was busy on his phone answering a text message.

Kevin frowned at her.

Claire folded the paper and put it in her handbag.

Sid got to his feet and started gesticulating wildly. '"Performance-enhancing" mah hole. We nearly got relegated – ah nearly lost mah job.' He turned to Claire. 'So, are you gonna explain yerselves then, or no?'

'Uh, yes,' Claire said. 'What I mean is, someone else will be along soon to formally receive your feedback.'

'Then why the bloody hell did you even come—' Sid's mobile started to ring. 'Excuse me.' He answered it. 'Mikey... What? Goal bonus? Bloody *goal bonus?* Am ah talking Hungarian here or what?'

Claire and Kevin took this opportunity to make a swift exit.

Back at Kevin's car, he was listening to Claire outline what she thought they'd uncovered.

'Brainwashing?' he said. 'You what?'

'It all makes sense,' Claire said, buckling her seat belt as Kevin started the engine. 'This Research Creating Excellence firm has been canvassing football fans and players to gauge their potential reactions to some upcoming rule changes. At the same time, they've been using hypnosis to condition players into being ready for the new rules, which will come into effect with today's announcement.'

'Okay... but brainwashing?' Kevin turned into traffic. 'That's a bit... science fiction, in't it?'

Claire shook her head. 'There's a whole industry dedicated to it. "Think Yourself Thin," "Become a More Positive Person." Companies make millions out of that stuff, there must be *something* in it.' Claire held up the three pieces of evidence that they had collected today. 'The FA really aren't taking any chances.'

Kevin thought it through. 'So, managers did all this stuff, the special music, the extra media training and all that, because they wanted their players not to argue about some new rules?'

'No, the managers were told that these were performance-enhancing measures – and when you have as little job security as they do, I imagine you snap up any possible advantage that comes along. But, like your old boss said, none of it really worked, it was all a smokescreen.' Claire went silent, tapping her fingers on the dashboard as Kevin watched her out of the corner of his eye.

'Hey,' he said eventually, 'there's summat else I don't get.'

'What?' asked Claire, still deep in thought.

'If they're going to all the hassle of doing this stuff with fans, players and managers, why in't they done it with refs? Them lot what actually carry out the rules.'

Claire frowned. 'That's a good question. Maybe they have. Maybe we'll find out.'

Kevin shrugged. 'Or maybe we won't, I dunno.'

Claire had her phone out.

'Who you calling?' asked Kevin.

'We need to learn more about hypnosis. I've got a friend who can help, in fact she works as a sports psychologist for...' She smiled and shook her head.

'For who?' asked Kevin.

'I was going to say, "for us." She works for the FA.'

17

THE PACKED London tube train was still stationary in the Circle Line tunnel with its nose just poking into Notting Hill Gate station, the only light from within it courtesy of the dozens of mobile phone displays that were dancing around like blue fireflies.

Frank was leading Ian by hand through the dark carriages. Confused and scared voices surrounded them as they forced their way through the crowd.

'Did someone pull the cord?'

'Are we under attack?'

'Shh, don't say that.'

But it was a different kind of threat that had got the Tuttles on the move.

The four pursuing RCE employees were shoving people aside to get to Frank and Ian. The leader was an intense young woman, whose yellow polo shirt was taut over her muscular shoulders. When Frank looked back her determined eyes locked with his.

'Dad, look,' cried Ian.

Frank faced ahead again. They had nearly reached the door right at the front of the train – it was still open, and it led out to the Notting Hill Gate platform.

Frank steadied his resolve and headed for the exit.

'Where's Gary?' Ian said, looking around frantically.

'I don't know, son,' Frank replied without slackening the pace.

'Do you think *they* took him?'

'He's an adult, he can take care of himself. We've gotta get out of here.'

Frank saw with horror that the door was starting to close.

'Excuse me.' Frank let go of Ian and barged his way past a group of men in West Ham United replica shirts. The door was only feet away, but it was nearly shut.

'Excuse me, pardon me.' Frank desperately scrambled around a pair of confused-looking women.

'Dad, you won't make it.'

'Yes I...' – Frank put a foot down – '*will!*' The door hit his trainer and stopped.

'Slip through, son,' Frank said when Ian caught up. The boy turned sideways and squeezed through the gap. He landed on the platform. People waiting for the train just stood watching him – no one wanted to get involved.

Ian got straight up and turned back to his father.

The door was pushing in on Frank's trainer, testing the soft shoe's resistance.

As Frank looked down at his foot, a memory flooded back: Bethan, one Sunday afternoon in Brent Cross Shopping Centre, telling him that a man in his forties shouldn't be wearing trainers all the time. 'Maybe a nice pair of loafers,' she had suggested, examining one.

Frank smiled through the pain in his foot. If he'd have followed his wife's footwear suggestion, the firmer shoe would have been a big help right now.

I promise, I'll make it up to you, sweetheart, Frank thought. *All of it. And I'll buy a pair of bloody loafers.*

A flash of yellow in the corner of his eye brought him back. The muscular RCE woman was nearly upon him and her three colleagues were close behind.

'Dad,' called Ian from the platform.

'I see them...' Frank said.

It was now or never. Summoning all his strength, Frank grasped the door. He needed to have a firm hold on it so that when he slipped his foot out the door wouldn't immediately ping shut. But the motor was too strong – the door was going to snap closed as soon as he pulled away. And Frank's sweaty grip was loosening.

'Here you are, mate,' someone said.

It was one of the guys in the claret and blue West Ham shirts, offering to help.

A woman wearing a blue Millwall shirt joined him.

'Cheers... thanks mate... ta...' said Frank, as more and more football fans in various teams' strips came forward and helped to hold the door open.

Frank yanked his foot out and squeezed through the gap onto the platform next to Ian.

The door snapped shut just as the RCE woman got there. She banged on the glass in rage.

Frank and Ian gave her the finger and then made a dash for the station's exit.

Claire looked around Pippa's Café.

Back here again, she thought.

She was sitting at a table with Kevin and Laura, her FA sports psychologist friend who had slipped out of Wembley to meet them.

All three nursed cups of tea while Laura talked about hypnotism.

'Do you know who are the most susceptible to being hypnotised?' she asked.

Kevin tilted his head. 'Morons?'

'No, although... well, no, it's nothing to do with intelligence. It's people who act without thinking.'

'Who lack empathy?' asked Claire.

Laura shook her head. 'Those who don't do much stopping and considering. Who just get on with things.'

'So, in other words, people who behave instinctively.'

Laura nodded.

Claire could tell that Kevin wasn't getting it.

She leaned over to Laura. 'Can you put it in footballing terms?'

'Okay.' Laura smiled. 'Kevin, it's the middle of a match. You're—'

'Hold up. Are we playing home or away?'

'Uh...'

'And are we talking a league game or cup?'

'At home in the league,' Claire said quickly.

'Okay,' said Kevin.

Laura continued. 'You're playing number ten and you run ahead of the striker, who then slides a through ball across the ground for you to run onto.'

Kevin grinned. 'Sound.'

'So, you're racing into the box to meet the ball's path – but the keeper's sprinting out.'

'The bastard.'

180

'What do you do?'

Kevin considered. 'Depends. How close I were, how close *he* were, the angle, whether there was any defenders...'

'Right, right. But are you actually *thinking* these things?'

'Nah, course not. I just run onto the pass and do whatever: smash it first time, take a touch and slot it near post, take it round the keeper, do a cheeky lob.'

Laura nodded. 'Right. You would act *without* thinking.'

'Yeah, I guess so.'

'Because thinking—'

'Means bottling it.'

'Exactly.' Laura addressed them both. 'Athletes condition their minds and train their bodies so they can perform without having to think. They go through hours of repetitive drills and exercises, creating muscle memory and making technique a reflex. Hence, they're especially hypnotisable – it's just a mental extension of what they're already doing physically.'

So that must mean...

'My God,' Claire said, 'it's always been hypnosis, hasn't it?'

'What are you saying?' asked Laura.

'The media training, making sure the players say the right things. That's why these Research Creating Excellence people thought that their scheme could work: it *has* been working for years.'

Laura reflected. 'You're right. The repetitive conditioning inherent in media training is a mild form of hypnosis.'

Something dawned on Kevin. 'Exccpt, you du get some footballers who it don't work on.'

'Of course,' said Laura.

Kevin raised his eyebrows and let the silence hang.

Claire and Laura stared at him.

'You're immune?' asked Claire.

Kevin shrugged sheepishly. 'Looks like it.'

Claire thought about this. 'So with you,' she said, 'not being able to robotically repeat the phrases they drum into you, about the team being the most important thing, take every game as it comes, all those clichés. Instead always saying what you feel, no matter what the consequences. It's not just that you like to clown about, *they genuinely can't condition your behaviour.*'

Kevin shrugged again. 'I just found that stuff really boring. Went in one ear and out t' other.'

'So, you do know what this means,' said Claire.

'What does it mean?' asked Laura.

'The FA has brainwashed this country's professional footballers into being unable to think for themselves. They're conditioned to adapt swiftly and without consideration or complaint to whatever instructions they're given, no matter how nefarious.'

Laura exhaled. 'Wow,' she said. 'The FA? Are you sure?'

'This RCE firm are working for them, Sid McClane confirmed as much. And today everything they've been plotting is going to pay off.' Then Claire realised something else. 'Kev, this means you're extremely valuable.'

'Try telling that to managers and chairmen of professional football clubs,' he grumbled.

'Not only do you have the status to get us into Wembley, but you're one of the only ones – maybe *the* only one – who can speak out against the rule changes on behalf of footballers. When Frank finds the second Half, and with you on our side, I'm sure we'll be able to stop the announcement.'

'I'm sure as well,' Laura said, 'that the hypnosis would have included a failsafe to stop the subject from taking any steps that could harm the FA's interests. So, yes, a footballer on whom it had worked wouldn't be able to help you like Kevin is today.'

Kevin nodded his agreement – but it was at Claire that he was looking, with intensity.

Claire blushed and turned away. She knew that she didn't look great: she was flustered; her hair was dishevelled after travelling in Kevin's Ferrari with the top down; she hadn't touched up her makeup for ages. Yet she was conscious that Kevin had been checking her out all day.

'We better get our arses over to Wembley then,' the footballer said finally.

Claire took his hand and gave it a squeeze.

'Right. But first, we need Frank.'

18

FRANK and Ian looked up at the home of Queens Park Rangers Football Club – officially now called the Kiyan Prince Foundation Stadium, but still widely known as Loftus Road.

It was the smallest stadium that Frank had been to today and the one whose club had the most nomadic history – this was QPR's thirteenth different address. Plans to move the club to a fourteenth and larger ground had often been mooted, but had yet to come to fruition.

The stadium was situated right next to a housing estate. A dog barked and a few cars passed by, but otherwise the scene was quiet. No one was in or around the ground since the team were obviously away today – to whom Frank didn't know and he was too tired to care.

Arsenal and Chelsea's grounds had immediately presented Frank with histories of their past glories. Fulham's had been full of quirks. But standing there before Loftus Road's South Africa Road Stand, there wasn't very much to help them with the latest clue.

'Gary might have had an idea,' said Ian. 'I wish I had his mobile number.'

'Never mind Gary,' Frank snapped.

'Why are you being so hard on him?' Ian asked moodily.

'Look, he's not here and we are, so we have to just get on with it. And don't take that tone with me, young man.'

Ian pouted.

Frank changed tack. 'Anyway, haven't teams come back to win after having a man sent off?'

'Yeah...'

'Well then. We just lost him in all that tube kerfuffle. I'm sure he'll turn up later – if he's got any sense, he's gone to meet up with Claire and Maxwell at the café.'

'But... what if *they've* got him?'

Frank looked right at his son. 'Come on, Ian. What will *they* do to him? What did *they* do to you?'

Frank watched as Ian considered this. He knew he was a smart lad and grasped the concept of regrouping and just getting on with it. Frank also knew from his own managerial experience that being down to ten men (or in this case, two) often helped refocus a team.

He said, 'Let's go over this new clue, then.'

Ian read it aloud from the tablet. '"The Penultimate Clue (in two parts). Part one: The journey you took shows where you must look. Make a number out of what you've done and join it to a letter from where you are to make a symbol."'

Frank frowned. 'Okay. So "journey" – it must be talking about all the running around that we've been doing today.'

'Yeah, I reckon so,' said Ian. 'And we want one number and one letter that when joined together make... something. So, what has our journey "shown" us?'

'It's shown *me* how to give myself blisters,' Frank moaned.

'Come on Dad, we need to think.'

So Frank thought. His head started to droop and he found himself looking down at his scuffed trainer, blackened on both sides from holding the tube train's door open. He suddenly felt exhausted, the hangover that he'd been managing to suppress threatening to re-emerge. He leaned against the stadium's wall and felt his eyelids get heavy as he stared across the road at Champlain House Estate. All he wanted to do was slide down onto his arse and have a good kip.

Is this all really worth it?

'Dad, don't fall asleep.'

Frank snapped his eyes open and looked at Ian. He was struck abruptly by how much he loved the boy, more than anything in the world.

More than the game?

Definitely. But as he stared at his son, with his oversized football shirt and socks that wouldn't stay up, Frank realised that the emotion he felt for the game and the emotion he felt for Ian weren't so distinct; they inhabited the same space, overlapped with each other. Football was family and family was football; separate, and yet the same. It also dawned on Frank that today was about more than being the hero who saves the game. It wasn't about the glory – it was about the youngsters, the next generation of fans. Whatever ugliness the FA had planned today would hit them the hardest and might very well take the joy out of football for good.

Not on my bloody watch.

Frank got a hold of himself. 'Okay,' he said standing up straight. 'Okay. Our journey today. Well, all day we've been running around football stadiums.'

'Right.'

'Stadiums and your grandad's place, but that was only because we couldn't figure out the Chelsea clue *at* Chelsea...'

'But how does where we've been make a number?'

Frank pondered this. Then he had a thought.

'Ian, can you Google a map of London that shows all the football grounds?'

Ian took out his phone and within seconds did just that. He found a simple map of the Capital that had each football team's stadium marked with the club's initials.

'Okay, so now what?'

'Can you make it so I can draw over it?'

'Sure, I've got an app for that.'

Ian took a screengrab of the map and then opened the app. He gave the phone to his dad.

Frank drew a freehand line over London with his finger, beginning where 'AFC' was marked and heading southwest to 'FFC'. From there, he made a short anti-clockwise curve to connect the line to the dot marked 'CFC.' Then it was a final short flick northwest to 'QPRFC.'

Frank took his finger off the screen. Ian examined his dad's handiwork:

'Um...' said the boy.

'Doesn't look like much, does it?' Frank admitted.

'It kind of looks like...' Ian squinted, 'a 1 on its side?'

'I suppose,' said Frank. 'It's a bit wonky, but I'm not the best at drawing. And maybe the map isn't to scale or something.'

'Well, it isn't close to any *other* numbers...'

They turned to look at a nearby map of Loftus Road Stadium's layout.

'Not seeing any 1s...' said Frank.

They both leaned in to study the stadium map closer.

Then Ian found it: the only mention of the number 1 on the whole map. 'There. On the Ellerslie Road Stand. Turnstile Block 1.'

Frank and Ian took a left onto Bloemfontein Road then another immediate left onto Ellerslie Road.

They were still in a residential area but had moved several rungs up the property ladder. This was a wide suburban street, full of old Victorian houses and well-tended trees. A couple with a baby loaded up a car and laughing kids on bikes rode past.

Turnstile Block 1 was at the end of the road. Ian and Frank walked briskly along the pavement, which was parallel to the stadium.

'You know,' Frank mused, 'I like an old ground that's right among the houses.'

'Why's that?'

'It's slap bang in the middle of the community. You can walk it from train stations, there are pubs all around... that's the way it should be. Not like the newer grounds.'

'What's wrong with them?'

'They're usually plonked out on some industrial park. And once you're there you're stuck there. No pubs nearby, nowhere to drink before the match.'

Ian looked at his father. 'So, you're saying that they're making it harder for fans to get drunk and rowdy.'

'No, just... you'll understand when you're older. It's all part of the match day experience. Instead we got bloody half-and-half scarves and so-called supporters who need the words to the chants up on the screen.'

Presently they reached a gate with a sign: TURNSTILE BLOCK 1. ELLERSLIE ROAD STAND BLOCKS R TO X. HOME SUPPORTERS ONLY.

The pair walked right up to the gate and looked left and right. The gaps between the bars afforded only a narrow glimpse into the stadium, where they could see the pitch and a few seats. The wall approaching the gate was just plain bricks.

They fell back again.

'Locked up proper tight,' said Frank. 'We're not getting in, that's for sure.'

'No,' agreed Ian. He read the sign again. '"Blocks R to X..." We need a letter for the clue and there are seven in this stand. How do we know which is the right one?'

Frank consulted the clue again. '"Make a number out of what you've done and join it to a letter from where you are to make a symbol,"' he read. 'Maybe... maybe it wants us to put them together... like, *draw* them together, like we drew over the map.'

'Okay,' said Ian. 'Trial and error then. Let's see if any of the letters R to X look like something when put with this 1 we've got.'

Ian took out his phone again and started to draw and erase, draw and erase.

Out of the letters on offer, only *S* made a recognisable symbol when combined with what they had already drawn:

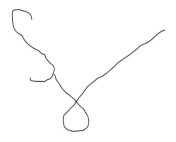

'That looks like... a pound sign,' Frank said.

'Yeah,' agreed Ian. 'The symbol for a pound.'

Ian entered '£' into the tablet.

And the answer turned green.

Father and son gripped each other and huddled round the screen as it changed.

The Penultimate Clue (in two parts)

Part two

You will find the second Half balanced exactly
between the two major forces that drive football.

'"Two major forces..."' Frank quoted. 'What does that mean?'

'And balanced... balanced *on* something?'

They were at a loss.

Frank glanced at his watch and cursed under his breath.

Then Ian snapped his fingers.

'What?' said Frank.

'Remember what Grandad said?'

'What did he say?' Frank still felt a pang of guilt over how he had misjudged his father's mental faculties.

'Something about... about how...' Ian strained to remember it word for word. '"Football must stay balanced between being a sport and a business."'

Frank didn't get it. 'So?'

'So, those are the two major forces, aren't they? The game itself and the business part for it all? And you need to have them balanced.'

Frank nodded slowly.

'Maybe Grandad was actually telling us something – maybe that wasn't just something his own dad said one time, *maybe it was an instruction*. Like him giving us the Chelsea shirt was.'

Frank didn't want to believe it. 'It's probably a coincidence, son.'

Ian frowned at him. 'Do you *really* think so, Dad? Does all the stuff that's happened today seem like a coincidence?'

Frank remembered how he'd felt in his van on the drive away from the Emirates, after they'd solved the first clue. It was the same way he'd felt when he was climbing up a creaking wooden ladder from a godforsaken tunnel underneath Craven Cottage, having just prised an ancient stone tablet from a wall.

And he knew in his heart that he felt it now, too.

Frank pursed his lips. 'Okay. You're right. So then, balanced between a sport and a business. If we're talking about finding something, then it has to be between two places.'

'Right.'

'And we've got the football bit covered here,' Frank gestured to the stadium beside them, 'so we've got to find the place between here and a business that's balanced.'

'Which must mean exactly the halfway point.'

'Right. So, let's try going from this stadium to a business and check halfway along the journey whether we can find this Half.'

Ian nodded excitedly.

'But what business...' Frank pondered. 'Well, your grandad was talking about money coming into the game...'

'And we've just made the pound symbol...'

'Then it has to be a bank.'

'Right.'

The two Tuttles regarded one another. 'Okay,' said Frank firmly. 'Let's give it a shot.'

'So, where's the nearest bank? It's just houses around here.'

Frank walked a few yards to the end of the road and looked right, down Loftus Road (the road) to where it met Uxbridge Road. 'That looks like a high street down there.'

'Come on then, let's go.' Ian was already off.

'Hold on,' his father called after him. 'You haven't spent the last 30 years in pubs, son of mine. You go, find the nearest bank and retrace your steps. I'll meet you halfway.'

'Got it.'

Frank watched his boy hurtle off.

Ian ran.

He ran because there was no time to lose. He ran because he was eager to find out if there really was a second Half, perhaps buried under the very ground his feet were now pounding.

But mostly, he was running because it felt awesome.

He skidded to a stop at the end of Loftus Road, where the quiet side-road met busy Uxbridge Road high street. He panted and looked around him at the bustling people, walking up and down, coming in and out of shops, talking on mobile phones, shouting across the street.

Where's the nearest bank?

Ian turned left and ran, swerving between people, looking both ahead of him and across the street. Eventually the shops ran out and became houses.

No banks.

Ian span around and sprinted back the way he came, passing the turning back up Loftus Road and keeping on until the shops ran out again.

No banks this way either.

How could there be no banks?

Ian was still full of adrenalin, but now something else was raising his heart rate: panic.

He turned around again and headed back up the high street. The panic subsided and a duller feeling replaced it: disappointment. He felt like he'd let his dad down. He knew that it wasn't *really* his fault, that he'd only been trying to help with this stupid Campaign quest thing. But the fact was, *he* had made the connection between what Grandad said and the clue at QPR's stadium and it had turned out to be completely wrong. His grandad hadn't been giving them a clue when he mentioned football's balance of sport and business, after all.

Ian was almost back at Loftus Road (the road), dreading the slow walk back up it to Loftus Road (the stadium) to report back to his dad. He could have phoned him, but he wasn't in a hurry to break the bad news. He could have run again, but he didn't feel like it anymore.

Ian stopped at the curb of Arminger Road to look left and right. He was about to cross, but before he did, he glanced to his right again. Something had caught his eye.

Across the street was a shop that he hadn't noticed before because he'd only been looking for banks.

The shop was called SHARIF POUND PLUS STORE.

And it was directly opposite Arminger Road.

Slowly, Ian turned to look up Arminger. Then he pulled out his phone and looked up his location on Google Maps.

Arminger Road was parallel to Loftus Road. But instead of carrying on and hitting Ellerslie Road as Loftus does, Arminger stopped before it got there, turned left and became Ethelden Road. That road lasted only about 50 yards before it took another left to become Ingersoll Road, which headed straight back down to re-join Uxbridge Road to complete the loop.

Ian nearly dropped his phone when he realised that the point at which Arminger turned left to become Ethelden was halfway between Sharif Pound Plus Store and Loftus Road Stadium.

Exactly between the two locations. You could even call it balanced.

His swirling emotions fusing into excitement once more, Ian scrambled to dial his father.

'Dad,' he gasped. 'I know where the Half is. Meet me there, I'll give you directions.'

19

BACK in Pippa's Café, FA sports psychologist Laura Granville was getting ready to leave.

'Claire,' she said awkwardly to her friend, 'you know I had nothing to do with this stuff, it's all news to me. Well, I mean, I knew about the techniques, obviously, but I had no idea the extent of—'

'Don't worry, I believe you,' Claire assured her. 'This goes a lot higher up than the likes of me and you – but we're going to get to the bottom of it.'

Kevin gave a supportive thumbs-up.

'Well, I'd better get back,' said Laura. She grinned wryly. 'I'll be lynched if I'm seen with you.'

'Yeah fugitive from justice, that's me,' Claire deadpanned. Then, more seriously, 'But thank you so much.'

They hugged.

'I'll let you know if I hear anything else.'

Kevin came round the table to shake Laura's hand. 'Thanks for everything, love.'

Then Kevin had a thought. 'Eh, wait a sec, Laura.'

She turned around.

'Am I the only one what ignores their media training?'

'You're the only one I know about.'

'So how come this hypnotism din't work on me?'

Laura shrugged. 'Hard to say. Athletes are prone because, like I say, the nature of their work means that they're more attuned to their instincts. But they also rely on ego strength, that core sense of their self – who they are, what they can do.'

'I think Kevin is well acquainted with the concept of an ego,' Claire said drolly.

Kevin raised an eyebrow. He beckoned Laura to continue.

'Well, you need a strong ego to perform on the pitch, to go through with your job.'

'You're talking about confidence,' said Claire.

'Yes, that can be affected by the ego. Now, hypnotherapy is often used to strengthen a weak or damaged ego, to help restore that sense of self in the patient. But in some cases, the reverse is true – the ego is *over*developed, and any attempts to access the subconscious using hypnotism prove to be futile.'

Kevin mulled on this. Claire tried to suppress a smile.

Eventually, the footballer said, 'So you're saying that I have so much of the ego and confidence and all that stuff that makes you a brilliant player, these brain experts couldn't get into my noggin no matter what they tried?'

Laura hesitated. 'That's... one way of putting it.'

Kevin snapped his fingers. '*That's* why no club's signed me yet. Bastards are worried they can't control me. I knew it had to be summat like that.'

Laura raised her eyebrows at Claire, who just smiled and shrugged.

When Laura was gone, Claire turned to Kevin. He was deep in thought, mumbling to himself.

'All I gotta do is show 'em,' he was saying. 'Show 'em I've still got it and they'll snap me right up...'

'You seem to have got your mojo back,' Claire observed.

Kevin brazenly put an arm around her. 'You know, Claire love, I reckon today is gonna turn out pretty alright for all of us.'

Letting herself get swept up in the moment, Claire put an arm around Kevin in return. 'I hope so,' she said with a smile. Their eyes met.

The door banged open. Kevin and Claire broke apart and turned.

It was Gary.

'Harry,' said Kevin. 'Alright, mate?'

'Yeah, good, fine,' said Gary distractedly as he arrived at their table.

Claire looked beyond him. 'Where's Frank? And Ian?'

Gary exhaled sharply. 'Can I get a coffee here?' he barked at the staff. 'Soya milk.'

A teenaged waitress approached chewing her pen. 'Don't got soya. Full or semi-skimmed.'

'Christ,' snapped Gary, slumping down onto an empty seat. 'Just black then.'

The girl returned to the kitchen nonplussed.

Claire and Kevin gave each other a look and then sat back down, facing Gary across the table.

'So, what happened?' asked Claire.

Gary busied himself playing with a ketchup bottle. 'We got separated.'

'How's that then?' asked Kevin.

'Some of those yellow nutters turned up on the tube and I lost Frank and Ian while trying to shake them.'

'Why were you getting the tube?' asked Claire. 'What happened to Frank's van?'

'It doesn't matter,' snapped Gary.

'Take it easy, mate,' said Kevin.

Gary exhaled again, rubbed his eyes. 'Sorry. It's just been a long day; I've been up since... God knows and all this running around and...' He sighed. 'I feel guilty about getting split up from the others. I never got their phone numbers, and I didn't know what to do, so I came here. I'm sorry.'

'It's alright,' said Claire. 'This is where we planned to meet, you did the right thing. I'm sure Frank doesn't blame you.'

Gary's coffee arrived. He sipped it too fast and recoiled at the heat.

'So, the other two haven't got here yet?'

'Nope,' said Kevin, now busy checking his mobile.

'But we found something out,' Claire said excitedly. 'Footballers have been hypnotised to go along with these new rules so they will adapt to them quickly and not question them. These RCE people were worried about how the players would react and so took no chances. They surveyed footballers and the public with FA-funded market research and have been manipulating the players' media training and giving managers pre-match instructions, all to condition everybody's behaviour.'

'Wow,' said Gary.

'Bastards,' said Kevin. Claire and Gary looked at him, but he was talking at his phone. He looked up. 'I've lost seven followers,' he said. 'Knew I'd gone too long without posting.'

Claire rolled her eyes and continued. 'But it turns out that Captain Tweet here is immune to the hypnotism. So, when Frank arrives, we need to get him and Kevin into Wembley to complete The Campaign and stop the announcement.'

Gary sipped his coffee and glanced at the wall clock. 'Well, we haven't got very long to do that.'

Claire drummed her fingers impatiently. 'I know, I know...' She got out her phone.

Gary snapped, 'Wait.'

Claire stopped. Kevin looked up.

'I've just remembered. It was the last thing Frank said to me. I don't know if he knew this stuff about him,' – he indicated Kevin – 'or not, but Frank told me that as soon as I got to the café, I should grab Kevin and meet him – Frank – inside Wembley.'

Kevin, bored now, put his phone away. 'Fine. Let's get on with it then.'

Claire was confused. 'But how is Frank going to get inside Wembley to meet up with you and Kev?'

'I don't know, we got split up before he could explain. But he seemed like he had a plan.'

Kevin was already on his feet. Claire stood as well. 'Alright then,' she said. 'We *all* go.'

'Ah, no,' said Gary. 'Frank said you should wait here, because Kevin was right earlier – it's too dangerous for you to be out in the limelight, what with the FA firing you.'

Claire reflected on this.

'I just want to call Frank, to... see if he's okay,' she said as she found his contact on her phone.

'Right, good idea,' Gary said.

Claire called the number and listened.

'Straight to voicemail,' she reported. She left a brief 'call me back' message then hung up. 'They must be on the tube again.'

Gary nodded.

Kevin said to Claire, 'We better get over to Wembley sharpish. I'll call you when I'm with Frank.'

Claire wasn't happy but she didn't see any alternative.

She stepped forward and gave Kevin a kiss on the lips. It was brief but sincere. 'Be careful.'

Kevin looked at her wide-eyed. 'Don't worry, I got this.' He winked. 'See you soon.'

Gary was already halfway across the café. Kevin turned to give Claire one last look, before following Gary out onto the street.

Claire waved after Kevin through the window.

Alone now, Claire sat back down. Her tea was cold, but she sipped it to give herself something to do.

Now what?

Minutes later, the door swung open again.

'Frank,' said Claire.

'Claire,' he replied. He and Ian made a beeline for her. She stood up and gave Frank a brief hug and squeezed Ian's shoulder.

'I just missed your call,' said Frank. Then he looked around. 'Where's Kevin?'

'Well he's with... he's with Gary, they already went over to...' Claire trailed off as she witnessed Frank's reaction.

He had gone as white as a Tottenham Hotspur home shirt.

Claire felt sick. Gary had been right here in this café not five minutes ago and she had swallowed all of his lies. Then not only had she let him go, but she'd let him take Kevin, their only hope of getting back into Wembley and stopping this whole debacle.

'I'm sorry,' she told the Tuttles.

'It's okay,' Frank said gently. 'You didn't know.'

Young Ian was having a hard time accepting the truth about Gary.

'I thought he was my friend,' he said with a cracking voice.

Frank put an arm around his son. 'Don't take it personally,' he said. 'I'm sure he didn't want to hurt you.'

The waitress poured them all teas, which they ignored.

'When did you realise he was working for the FA?' Claire asked Frank.

'I had a funny feeling about the bloke all day. But I didn't know for sure until I saw him pull the emergency cord on the tube.'

The other two gasped.

'And straight away,' Frank continued, 'the yellow mob was on us. And they didn't pay no attention to Gaz – they brushed straight past him and headed straight for me and Ian.'

Ian turned to his dad. 'You didn't tell me about all that.'

'There was no time, son. We had to get to Loftus Road and find the second Half. And besides, I needed you focused on your game – not distracted by off-field problems.'

'I'm calling Kevin,' said Claire with her phone already to her ear. 'It's ringing.'

But it went to voicemail. Claire left a message.

'I'll keep trying him.'

Frank nodded.

Claire composed herself. 'So, you think Gary's been working for them from the very start?'

'Must have been,' said Frank.

'But he was *helping* us,' said Ian. 'It doesn't make any sense.'

'He was negative most of the time,' Frank pointed out. 'Calling the whole thing hopeless.'

'Maybe he was told to make it look like he was helping us but to ultimately stop us,' Claire suggested. 'Or his orders could have changed as the day went on.'

'That would mean he was getting updates...' Frank snapped his fingers. 'He was always on his phone. I thought he was just Facebooking. The sneaky little... he must have been texting back and forth with *them*. *That's* how those yellow tossers were always right on top of us.'

Claire said, 'Look, there's something you two need to understand about Kevin.' She explained about his resistance to hypnotism and what they had learned about Research Creating Excellence's mind-control programme.

Frank absorbed it all without comment. Claire knew that he had been through enough craziness today to not doubt her.

'But as soon as Gary found out about Kevin's importance,' Claire continued, 'he snatched him away.'

The trio sat thoughtfully for a moment.

Then Claire asked, 'So, *did* you find the second Half?'

Frank gestured to Ian, who put his kit bag on the table and unzipped it.

Ian reached inside and carefully removed a solid glass object. He held it up for Claire to see.

It was identical in dimensions to the stone tablet they had found earlier – comparable to A4 paper in length and width, but much thicker. Inside was a sheet of parchment, preserved inside its transparent tomb.

'My God,' said Claire.

'Can you believe this was in a normal street, buried under a tree?' marvelled Ian.

Frank held up his hands to show dirty fingernails. 'Had to keep a good look out for the neighbours. I was sure they were gonna call the old bill.'

Claire had to laugh.

Ian handed her the glass case.

'Wow,' she said, impressed. Her enthusiasm was infectious and made Frank and Ian smile again too. 'Heavy.'

Claire turned the glass over, confirmed that the back of the parchment was blank, and then read from the front side.

'"Sacred Half the Second."' She paused and cleared her throat.

'"Whomever has been trusted with the power to change football's rules shall not be hindered from doing so. And once it has been passed, symbolised by the next official kick of a ball, then no legal recourse can be taken to reverse it."'

Claire looked up. 'That's not good. It sounds like the FA and these RCE people have *carte blanche* to change the rules – even if their reasons are disreputable. And then, when today's matches kick off, the rules are legally sealed. This is terrible.'

Frank nodded patiently. 'Keep reading,' he urged.

'"However,"' Claire glanced up, '"from the party who is proposing this change, all members must be in agreement. If any of the party reverses his opinion before a ball is kicked, the change cannot go ahead and cannot be proposed again." So, this means—'

'All Dad has to do is persuade *one* of these rule-changing people before kick-off and the whole thing goes away.' Ian was bouncing in his seat.

Claire smiled at Ian. 'And you know what? I reckon he can do it as well.'

Frank waved his hand dismissively.

'So, was that the last clue?' Claire asked.

'No, the *penultimate*,' said Ian markedly.

'We typed in the name of the road where we dug this up,' said Frank. 'Then the screen changed again.'

Ian showed the tablet to Claire for her to read aloud.

'"So you may understand the true meaning of football – found in its sacred home." And underneath it says, "The Final Clue."'

Claire frowned when she read the clue. 'It looks like directions on a compass.'

Frank rolled his head from side to side, unsure.

'Or something buried again?'

Frank shook his head. 'Don't think so. We haven't figured it out yet, but I reckon it only becomes clear when you're actually inside Wembley.'

Claire nodded; that made sense. 'So the only thing is, how do we *get* inside Wembley and back together with Kev?'

The sound of the café' door opening stopped Frank before he could answer.

For the third time that afternoon, Claire watched someone she had met only hours before entering the café.

It was Fullarton.

205

'I called him on the walk down from the tube,' Frank explained as all three stood to meet the FA's chief fairness officer.

Before Fullarton could even open his mouth, Claire let rip.

'Fullarton, you have to see this. The Campaign is real, you've got to help us get into Wembley, we're running out of—'

She stopped dead when she saw what he was holding up.

It was the dummy tablet she had switched with him earlier.

'Look familiar?' Fullarton asked.

Claire's heart sank.

Fullarton scanned the café, then turned back to Claire and the Tuttles. 'Come with me.'

Fullarton had escorted Frank, Claire and Ian away from Pippa's Café and the foursome were now sitting on a picnic table out the front of The Torch pub on Bridge Road. From their side of the table Frank and Ian could see Wembley Stadium, less than half a mile away.

They hadn't bought drinks; this wasn't a social visit.

Fullarton was waiting for the others to speak first. He was holding the tablet he'd been duped by away from his face with his thumb and forefinger, like a football sock after a sweaty training session.

'I can explain—' Claire started.

'No need,' Fullarton said. 'I'm bound by the FA to retrieve our property and to administer the appropriate punishment upon those who commit crimes against us. Stealing from the Association invokes a three-year ban from all English football stadiums.'

They stared at him, jaws dropped. 'Even my lad?' asked Frank.

'*All* of you. And I *will* enforce it if you don't leave the Wembley vicinity immediately.'

Ian was on the verge of tears. Frank held his hand under the table.

Fullarton gave the tablet to Claire. 'I hope you kept the receipt, Miss Butterfield. Now, the real one?'

Frank rummaged through Ian's kit bag and handed it over.

'Thank you.' Fullarton checked it then pocketed it. 'So where are your other friends? Mr Ward and Mr Maxwell?'

'Gary's run off to Wembley, taking Kevin with him,' blurted Ian. 'He's working for *them*.'

Fullarton's eyes narrowed. 'Young man, please don't start talking to me about "them". You're beginning to sound like a football conspiracy nut and believe me, there are enough out there already.'

Frank was unhappy with the Department of Fair Play man's tone, but he managed to keep his voice even. 'Fullarton, you need to see something.'

Frank took the glass-encased parchment out from Ian's kit bag.

While Frank handed it over, Claire said, 'The second Half.'

Fullarton examined it passively.

'I've seen better fakes,' he said at last, 'and I've seen real artefacts that look less genuine. Without proper authentication, I still can't take any of this seriously. Now I must repeat my advice: *go home*. Because if you're seen within 500 yards of Wembley Stadium, the police will be on you in seconds. They've been given your photographs.'

With that Fullarton stood up, taking the glass-encased parchment with him.

'Wait,' Claire implored. 'Please, just listen for two minutes.'

Fullarton hesitated. 'You have *one* minute,' he said, sitting back down.

Claire and Frank (with the odd insert from Ian) quickly filled Fullarton in. The drinkers and staff paid the four of them no attention, but they kept their voices low, nonetheless.

'That's some story,' Fullarton said when they were done. 'Brainwashing through hypnosis?'

'Yeah, I know it sounds barking,' Frank admitted.

'On the contrary,' Fullarton said, 'I used to be in the armed forces, and they employed similar tactics on new recruits. To install aggression but with control. To numb pain and help us block out the horrors.'

'Young men heading into battle...' mused Claire.

'Indeed – except shooting with SA80 rifles instead of personalised football boots. Look, please understand, I'm not dismissing you outright. But as I alluded to Master Tuttle, when you deal with the delusional and the paranoid on a daily basis, you build up a wall of cynicism. People see hidden forces, agendas. No one wants to accept the things they don't like, so they search for someone to blame. The public are bad enough, but it's not as if football managers provide good role models. "The refs are against us; the fixture list is against us..."'

Fullarton sighed. 'When I realised that I had the wrong tablet, I obviously couldn't take it to Wembley anymore. But I also didn't try to track you down to reclaim the genuine article. Something made me hold back.'

The three looked at him hopefully.

'But as compelling as your story is, you still lack the one piece of evidence that would give me cause to act.'

'Which is?' demanded Claire.

'The announcement,' Ian answered.

Fullarton smiled. 'Clever boy you have here, Mr Tuttle. Yes. Your whole quest has been about preventing the FA's announcement from coming to pass, yet you still don't actually know what it is. So, all I see are two disgruntled ex-FA employees and one young man who's come along for the ride.'

The other three stayed quiet. All the fight had gone out of them.

Again, Fullarton stood to leave. 'I'm sure the announcement will be nothing like what you fear. Trust the game – it's strong, it will survive. It always does.'

With that, Fullarton turned and walked away towards Wembley.

Frank, Claire and Ian watched him go in silence.

It was Ian who broke it. 'Do you think he's right? That the announcement might *not* harm the game?'

Frank stared ahead and didn't reply.

Claire asked, '*Has* revenge been my motivation?' She turned to Frank. '*Is* this just about getting our own back on the FA?'

But Frank still just stared in silence.

At Wembley.

Claire and Ian looked at each other. Frank was so focused that neither his only son nor his new friend dared interrupt him.

Finally, Frank said, 'No.'

Claire and Ian waited.

'No, that's not it. This isn't just our paranoid, bloody... payback mission. Something bad is going down today and it's been coming for a long, long time. I finally understood everything at Loftus Road. It all boils down to one thing.'

'What?'

'Money. That pound sign clue was a warning: don't let money corrupt the game. If it becomes about nothing more than profits and international TV rights and sponsorships, then the handful of mega-rich clubs just get richer, increasing the gap, stopping anyone else having glory. Oh sure, a less fashionable club like Blackburn or Leicester can win the Premier League every 20 years or so as a freak occurrence, or clinch the FA Cup now and again, when the "big" clubs ain't prioritising it. But no way is it a level playing field, there's no actual fair play. If big clubs break the rules, they just buy their way out – pay a fine that's nothing, a slap on the wrist for them. All this cash has shifted the priorities of the people what run the game. "Football must stay balanced between being a sport and a business."'

Claire looked confused.

'Ian's grandad told us that,' Frank explained. 'Claire, son... today I reckon we're gonna find out what happens when the sport part disappears over the horizon and football becomes nothing but a business. And we'll always know that we could have done something – but we bottled it.'

20

KEVIN and Gary were trawling the same Wembley corridors that Kevin had dragged Ian around this morning, only this time the footballer was the one doing the following.

'Are you done borrowing my mobile yet, mate?' Kevin asked again.

'Nearly finished,' Gary replied as jovially as he could manage, while still pretending to tap away on the other man's smartphone.

'How about now?'

Gary winced.

Christ he's irritating – even by a footballer's standards.

Gary had no intention of returning the phone. And he wasn't sure how much more stress he could take today.

Being with Kevin had meant that getting into the stadium was no problem. And once inside, the footballer's status had granted them access to the labyrinth passageways that connected its back offices.

Gary had told Kevin that they were heading to meet Frank and the moronic player was gormlessly trailing along. But all the while Gary had to keep him distracted enough so that he would stop asking for his phone back. That stuck-up cow Claire had rung several times already, but luckily the first thing Gary had done was turn the device on silent mode.

'I thought you only needed to check your email,' moaned Kevin as they rounded yet another corridor. 'And where are we meeting Frank, anyway?'

Gary cursed inwardly.

Where is this room? Why is this stupid stadium so bloody huge?

'Sorry mate, I'll be done with your phone in a minute, thanks again for letting me borrow it. Most people wouldn't lend out their mobile, so I really appreciate it.'

Kevin puffed out his chest. 'Well, I've always been described as a man of the people. But, about meeting Frank—'

Gary looked right at Kevin. 'Hey, mate, didn't you mention earlier that you're interested in endorsing products? That sounds fascinating, why don't you tell me all about it?'

'Oh,' said Kevin. 'Yeah, I've got loads of ideas about that. Having "max" in me name could work with all kinds of stuff. Like, you know those extreme sports holidays...'

Gary tuned out. He focused on finding the right door while still pretending to be busy on Kevin's phone. Yet again Claire was ringing, so again Gary hid the screen from its owner and let it go to voicemail.

That bloody Claire. She was just like all the others: condescending a regular chap like Gary and worshipping arrogant pricks like Maxwell. The last thing Gary wanted was for the meddling bitch to get in touch with her new boyfriend and mess up Gary's plans.

Annoyingly, this meant that Gary couldn't now check his *own* phone to reread the directions to the rendezvous – Maxwell had to believe Gary's claim that his own battery had died.

Gary just hoped he would actually recognise the door when he finally saw it.

'Then there's the ads that could use me old training ground nickname, "Mini." So, the travel agents could sell "Mini breaks" ...'

It pained Gary to listen to this idiot's gibberish. In actual fact, complaining about players with other fans on football forums was one of Gary's favourite pastimes. He loved to highlight their vanity and perceived lack of intelligence to likeminded keyboard warriors, and the foot-in-mouth prone Maxwell happened to be one of his prime targets. Of course, when Gary had first met Kevin this morning he had been thrilled, but then quickly pushed his admiration down and reminded himself what he *should* feel.

Gary had one life principle: he hated anyone who played or coached football for a living.

At school, Gary had been a promising full back. He was good on the ball, had great positional awareness, won everything in the air. He was unstoppable.

That was until his vision deteriorated to the point that he was virtually blind without his thick heavy glasses, which were impractical for playing and made him hesitant to go up for headers or in for tackles. He tried every type of contact lens, but his eyes rejected them all. He even gave prescription swimming goggles a try, but they robbed him of his peripheral vision and made him feel self-conscious. Before he hit his teens, Gary knew that he would never be a professional footballer.

Eventually he managed to console himself by focusing on coaching. You didn't need an illustrious playing career to become a top coach, just look at Arsène Wenger or Jose Mourinho. And on the touchline, you could wear glasses. That was his path, he decided – *that* was how he would make the game his life. He earned a First-Class BSc in Sports Science and following university immediately applied to the FA's Young Coaches scheme. In the meantime, he looked to increase his experience – most recently in the role with Ian Tuttle's team.

But he'd graduated three years ago now and the FA had rejected every one of Gary's applications to the coaching scheme.

He had nearly given up hope. And then he received a phone call last night when he was sleeping in his tiny studio flat, with its view of Robert Pires.

'Hello?' Gary said into his phone, bleary from being awakened.

'*Gareth Ward?*' the caller said. It was the same muffled, disguised voice that Gary would hear with Frank and Claire in Frank's van less than 12 hours later.

'Um, yeah? Yes?'

'*This is the FA.*'

Gary sat up in bed and put on his glasses. Thoughts raced around his head. Did someone drop out of the coaching programme? Had they reconsidered his application?

'Hello,' he managed.

'*Listen carefully. I have all of your applications for our Young Coaches scheme in front of me.*'

'Right...'

'*Frankly, I think it's a disgrace that you've never been accepted.*'

Gary gulped. 'Okay...'

'*I assure you, Mr Ward, that the reasons have been entirely political. Your ability is without question.*'

'Yes... um, I see.'

'*But that isn't important right now. What is important is that you* can *get on that scheme.*'

214

Gary jumped out of bed and started to pace the room. 'Really? How?'

'*A situation has emerged where we need a contact, someone to take instructions, handle a fast-changing situation and report back live.*'

Gary rubbed his temples. This had to be a dream. 'Me?'

'*According to our records, you're a trainee coach with the Brent Bruisers boys' football team, correct?*'

'Yes, that's correct, I just took the role.'

'*Well then. You're our man. Help us out tomorrow and you will find yourself on that scheme on Monday.*'

Gary listened carefully as the caller outlined the plan and the part he was going to play in it.

'*Any questions?*' the caller asked finally.

Gary thought about it. And found that, yes, he did have a question.

Now, Gary was so close. It was fast approaching 3pm and he had done all that was asked of him. Yes, he had panicked on the tube, acted independently when the strain got too much, and he just had to get out of there. Hopefully he wouldn't be found out. But he had stayed in touch with his contact all day – following every contradictory instruction and resisting reaching out on social media. And now he was about to complete his day's work by delivering this rambling cretin, who was apparently important to the FA for reasons Gary couldn't care less about.

If only he could find the right bloody door.

Maxwell, meanwhile, had now moved onto recounting one of his Champions League Final triumphs in painstaking detail.

'There were nowt else for it. I dug in me right boot and did a cheeky chip from 30 yards. I knew it were bang on from the second—'

'God, don't you ever *shut up?*'

This did shut Kevin up, momentarily. He regarded Gary curiously. 'What's that, mate?'

Gary stopped walking and, in an uncharacteristic show of boldness, let all of his frustration out on the footballer.

'Because of factors outside of my control, I couldn't make it as a player. Meanwhile you coast from club to club, running your mouth off, ending up a millionaire. And having God knows how many girls in the process. It's just not fair.'

Gary's rant left Kevin nonplussed. 'Well mate, life's not—'

'No, but I'll tell you something else: whatever's going on today is gonna change the game forever and I'm gonna to be one of the first coaches to take advantage of it. I'm going to be part of the brand-new order of football – and you, *Diego,* are just a loud-mouthed has-been.'

Kevin frowned.

Then something seemed to click inside him.

Gary recalled hearing an interview with Kevin on *Sport Chatter* in which he revealed that while yes, he sometimes reacted to online abuse, years of terrace chants had left him immune to taking verbal insults personally. There was only actually one thing could really push his buttons – but he swore he would never reveal what it was.

Gary realised with dismay that he'd just stumbled upon it: Kevin's middle name, the focus of his childhood bullying.

Gary tried to backtrack, holding his palms out and retreating. 'Hold on, wait, I didn't mean...'

Kevin balled his fists.

Then the door that Gary was cowering next to burst open and Susan Clyne sprang out.

'I *thought* that was you,' she said to Gary. 'Why are you shouting? Do you *want* to alert security?'

'Thank God,' breathed Gary, hiding behind Susan.

'Oh,' said Kevin, recognising Susan from his brief visit to the Media Centre this morning. 'It's *you.* So, where's Frank?'

Susan ignored him.

'So, you managed to bring the footballer,' she said to Gary.

'Yes, I've brought him, I've done everything you said,' Gary whined. 'Am I done now?'

'Soon enough.' Now Susan turned to Kevin and switched seamlessly into PR mode. 'Hi, Kevin Maxwell? Wow, I'm a really huge fan.'

The flattery restored Kevin's dignity. 'Well, at least someone in this place has some taste.'

'Susan Clyne.' She shook Kevin's hand. 'FA director of communications and partnerships.'

'Communications?' Now Kevin was on full alert.

'That's right. Let's head to the Media Centre, where we can talk about using you as part of our public-facing team.'

With this she had Kevin rapt. She led him and Gary through the open door.

So close and yet so far, thought Frank as they crossed over the road from the pub to the bus stop.

It was over.

'You better get home to your mother's,' Frank told Ian with a glance at the bus stop's digital display: 223 DUE 2 MINS.

'It's not *my mother's*,' snapped the boy. 'It's *our* home. Why don't you come back too?'

Claire stood aside to give the father and his son some space.

'Your mum and I still have things to sort out,' Frank said softly.

'What things?'

'Grown-up, boring things.'

'Do you still love each other?'

Frank sighed. 'Yes, son, we do. It's just... complicated. Look, tell you what I'll do. I'll give her a ring later on, once all this fuss has died down, and I'll see if I can come over and we'll watch *Match of the Day* together. Sound good?'

Ian perked up. 'Yeah. Sounds good.'

'Alright then. Come here.'

They hugged.

'And Ian?'

'Yeah, Dad?'

'I never should have left you alone at Wembley.'

'No, Dad, I was okay, I wasn't—'

'But I didn't *know* you were okay. It was my fault that you ended up there in the first place, and after that I should have been focussed on nothing but getting you back. I'm sorry mate.'

Ian didn't say anything. He just hugged his dad again – and when they broke apart, he suddenly shot him a wink, making Frank laugh.

The number 223 was approaching.

'Dad, don't you understand?' Ian said as he got out his Oyster card. 'By taking The Campaign instead of running straight to Wembley, you *were* helping me. If you'd put me above saving the whole of football, *then* you'd have something to apologise for.'

The bus pulled up as Frank digested this statement.

'Go on,' he said. 'Get yourself home Ian Tuttle, before your mother has a heart attack.'

Ian smiled at last. 'Bye Claire,' he said while hopping on board.

'Bye Ian,' she said. 'Nice to meet you.'

The bus's door shut, and it pulled away.

Only when Frank had seen it disappear around the corner did he turn back to Claire.

'So then,' she said.

'So.'

'We gave it a bloody good go, didn't we?'

'Yeah, we bloody well did.'

'Maybe Fullarton is right, maybe the announcement really won't be anything bad.'

'Yeah, maybe.'

But Frank didn't believe it and he knew Claire didn't either.

'Um, you know Claire, I'm sure Maxwell will be fine. He, uh, he's quite a character.'

Claire surprised Frank by hurling her arms around him and squeezing him tightly. 'You're a good man, Frank Tuttle,' she said, her voice cracking.

Frank hugged back. And he was surprised to find that when he blinked, his eyes were wet.

OVER at Wembley, Susan was busy exploiting Kevin's eagerness to speak to someone who might be able to realise his self-promotion aspirations.

Her combination of interested facial expression and positive noises was working wonders: Kevin hadn't noticed that she was leading him down Wembley's never-ending corridors in the exact opposite direction of the Media Centre.

'So yeah, I'm happy to do whatever for the FA, and right now I'm totally available. Although if I *do* get signed by a club this season, which I'm sure I *will,* you can use me on a haddock basis.'

'An *ad hoc* basis,' muttered Gary. He was trailing behind the other two, struggling to hold his patience with how Susan was indulging Maxwell.

Susan shot Gary a hard look.

'That sounds perfect, Kevin,' she smiled back at the footballer.

Gary, meanwhile, also wanted her attention. 'So, listen, Susan, have you got my acceptance letter printed already, or—'

'Not right now, Gareth,' Susan said tersely.

'No, sure, of course... but we must need to get something down on paper? The coaching scheme starts on Monday....'

'Hey,' said Kevin, 'how come you two know each other?'

Susan didn't miss a beat. 'Gosh, Kevin, I've just had a thought. A name like "Maxwell" can surely be tied to advertising too. There must be a whole host of suitable products.'

'Well, funny you should mention that actually...'

Susan was relieved to have steered him back onto autopilot. Not just to stop Kevin asking more questions about Gary, but to shut up Gary himself.

It was only through sheer force of will that Susan was managing to hide the extent of her exasperation with young Mr Ward. Because secretly she was cursing herself for the unexpected consequences of her phone call with him late last night.

'There is something I was wondering about,' came the voice on the other end of the line.

Susan pinched the bridge of her nose. She watched an aeroplane pass across the dark sky over the Wembley pitch outside, taking people far away from here.

'Yes, Mr Ward?'

'Well, it's not that I'm not pleased, and it's not that I'm not grateful, or that I don't believe you – unlikely as it might be that the FA would call me up at midnight to talk about my place on a coaching scheme...'

'Please can you get to the point.' Susan checked her coffee mug. Empty.

'Well, how do I know that you are who you say you are? How do I know that if I do what you tell me tomorrow, when I turn up at St George's Park on Monday, they won't just tell me to get lost?'

Susan cursed inwardly. She hadn't counted on there being any resistance, that Gary Ward would be this insecure and distrusting. She was unprepared, and that wasn't like her at all.

You're losing him, Susan. And he could be your only chance.

'What if I were to tell you,' she stammered, feeling that with each second of silence he was slipping further from her grasp, 'what if I were to tell you that through me you would be working directly for a former England captain?'

There was a literal gasp down the line.

She still had him.

But at what cost?

Gareth Craig Ward had only emerged by chance from Susan's late-night trawl through the FA's files, her painstaking attempt to find anyone whose life overlapped with Frank Tuttle's. When she came across an application to the scheme that identified him as a trainee coach at Brent Bruisers, which she knew to be Tuttle's son's team, she dialled his number right away.

And so when during their conversation Gary seemed to be slipping away, when it became clear that his life of disappointment and regret had conditioned him to meet any positive development with disbelief, Susan had dropped the ball and resorted to a rookie marketing tactic. She'd name-dropped.

It had worked, of course. If she, with her level head and business acumen, had been so thoroughly taken in by the man who was really pulling the strings, then how could a worm like Gary Ward fail to be impressed? But not long after putting down the phone, Susan realised with a cold chill the extent of the risk she had taken by using classified information as bait.

Because Gary was, Susan found out to her horror when she began researching him online, a social media addict, a user of all the major platforms and with a history of messaging celebrities. She was worried that he would contact her boss, who was active online himself, so as well as texting instructions to him all day, she'd also been reminding Gary about confidentiality and how breaking it would put his place on the coaching course in jeopardy. And so far, it had worked: Gary hadn't posted online once or tried to contact *him*.

All in all, it had made for an extremely taxing Saturday.

But now, thank God, it was nearly over. And now she had Kevin Maxwell, she was one step closer.

Susan stopped the two men in front of an unmarked door.

'Huh,' said Kevin, confused. 'Is this a back entrance to the Media Centre?'

'Sort of,' said Susan. 'This is a... waiting room. We're just going to leave you here until we need you.'

'What... for *today?*' asked Kevin.

'Why, yes. I thought you might want to read the announcement out live on TV.'

Kevin's eyes were now the size of dinner plates. 'Bloody right I would.' Then he seemed conflicted. 'But... I'm supposed to be...'

'Supposed to be what, Kevin?'

'Oh – um, no, I mean, of course I'd love to. But I thought that Donno were doing that?'

'Stuart Donaldson?' Susan smiled mischievously. 'Well, I don't see him around here, do you?'

Kevin smiled back.

Footballers. So predictable.

Susan opened the door and let Kevin into a small furnished room. As he passed ahead of her through the threshold, she snatched the footballer's phone from Gary's hand.

'Oh yeah, this'll do nicely,' Kevin was saying. He had made a beeline for the complimentary drinks bucket.

'So just chill out here, watch some TV, make yourself a drink,' Susan said from the doorway. 'Someone will be down for you in no time.'

'OK, nice one,' Kevin said, plunging a scoop into the ice bucket. 'Sound voddy, love, Grey Goose.'

'Great,' said Susan. 'And you *have* read an autocue before, haven't you?'

Kevin looked up. 'Er, well, not really.'

'Oh,' said Susan. 'Well, the words move quite fast, so just be prepared for that.'

Kevin was replacing the cap on the bottle of vodka. 'Oh yeah?' He tried to seem casual. 'How fast?'

Susan handed a folded sheet of paper to Kevin. She put her other arm around him, leaned in close and whispered, 'No one's supposed to see this before 3pm... but it's nearly time now, so I think it will be fine.'

'What's this?' asked Kevin, a little uncomfortable with Susan's sudden closeness.

She pulled back. 'It's the announcement. Just go over it before you're called upstairs.'

'Cheers,' said Kevin, taking the paper.

'Okay-good-luck,' Susan reeled off quickly while shutting the door on him.

Outside in the corridor she strode away purposefully.

'Did you lock it?' Gary asked, catching up.

'Yes, I locked it,' Susan snapped.

If there's one person who could never *inspire a group of football players, Gareth, it's you.*

'I don't know what you're up to with Maxwell – that's your business,' he was saying now. 'I'm just glad that the moron's out the way, aren't you? Wasn't he getting on your nerves? So whiny and self-involved.'

'Takes one to know one,' Susan muttered as she sped on ahead.

In the little waiting room, Kevin had Susan's sheet of paper in one hand and his glass of vodka in the other. It was the announcement alright – and finally seeing it after all this build-up, he wondered what all the fuss had been about.

Kevin took another sip and frowned. There were more sheets of paper stapled underneath – and these other pages were *much* more interesting.

Kevin read through them all with his eyebrows raised.

He put his glass down and dropped onto the sofa.

And sat on something.

Kevin stood up and reached into the back pocket of his jeans. He brought out his smartphone.

Hello, mate. Can't believe I forgot about you.

Wait... so how did it get back into his pocket?

Kevin looked at his phone. He smiled when he saw all of Claire's attempts to reach him: missed calls, texts saying 'Get back to me asap.'

Then he looked again the sheets of paper.

I've defo got something to get back to you about, Claire love.

He quickly downed the rest of his vodka.

Claire trailed behind Frank as they entered Wembley Park tube station. Frank was keen to leave and she was too, but something was holding her back.

'Well, I need the Jubilee Line,' Frank said at the barrier. 'Gonna meet the AA at my van.'

'Metropolitan for me,' Claire said. But still she hesitated. 'I'm gonna hang around here a sec. Got something I need to do.'

Frank frowned but nodded. He held out his hand and Claire shook it.

They smiled wanly at one another.

Then Frank was gone.

Claire turned left, crossed the concourse and stopped at the familiar exit at the top of the steps.

The view of the stadium had changed somewhat from this morning.

The crowd had swelled to fill the whole of Olympic Way, a thick river of people that flowed from the station past her then down the steps. Hundreds of police, on foot or horses, bobbed around the edges, along with plenty of those scumbags in yellow polo shirts.

It was a struggle, but Claire managed to lift her head to look at the crowd's destination.

'What *happened* to you?' she whispered to her beloved Wembley.

She couldn't bear it. She turned away and ran towards the barriers.

As she passed through them into the station, Claire's thoughts turned to Kevin. She'd rung him at least six times and texted like mad – why wasn't he getting back to her? She was surprised at how hurt she felt – and how concerned.

She took out her phone for another check as she stepped onto the escalator.

No missed calls. No texts.

But as she held the phone, she received a picture message.

On opening it, Claire immediately span around and sped straight back up the escalator the wrong way.

She sprinted towards the Jubilee Line. When she reached its escalator, she took it down three steps at a time, calling out 'Excuse me' and 'Can you move, please.'

At the bottom, a train stood with its doors still open.

'Frank!' Claire shouted as she raced along the platform.

Just as the doors started to close, she heard, 'Claire?'

'Get off the train.'

'What? Claire?' She could see him now, moving from the centre of a carriage to its door.

'Get off the train.'

Frank pushed past a couple of men in rugby shirts and squeezed off as the door shut behind him.

Claire and Frank approached each other on the platform.

'What's going on?' asked Frank.

Claire gave him her phone while she got her breath back.

'Kevin... he sent me... this.'

Frank's jaw dropped.

The format of the FA document that Kevin had photographed and sent to her phone was immediately familiar to Claire. She was certain that what she was reading was genuine.

Announcement for first day of new football season
(to be read aloud before kick-off by a current or ex-footballer)

Good afternoon, ladies and gentlemen.

The governing body of association football in England, the FA, announce that they have entered into a binding agreement with the firm RCE, Research Creating Excellence. This is a deal designed to ensure the continued integrity and fairness of the game for years to come and to benefit you, football's millions of devoted fans.

From kick-off in a matter of minutes, commencing the first round of games of this new football season, RCE will assume power over the rules and regulations of professional football across England, comprising the Premier League and the three tiers of the Football League.

As a result of this exciting new partnership, the FA are thrilled to announce that they are offering a full refund of the cost of every already purchased football ticket for this weekend's games. Season ticket holders can claim the equivalent of one full-priced ticket for their club.

RCE employees are stationed at grounds across the country to answer any questions about this fantastic development and RCE can also be contacted via the FA's by way of the Association's contact details on their website.

Thanks for your time and good luck to your team today!

Claire looked at Frank, whose brow was furrowed. They were still on the busy Jubilee line platform, huddled in a corner.

'Well,' Frank said, 'they've made it *sound* good, but it doesn't really tell us anything.'

'It's ridiculous – farcical,' said Claire. 'How can the FA afford to pay back every single ticket-buyer? That's thousands, maybe *millions* of pounds – and I can tell you for a fact that the Association is still skint from the Wembley rebuild.'

'Hmm,' said Frank. 'So, they could only be that generous if they were getting even more money from somewhere else...'

'And if they *really* needed to sugar the pill. Which must mean that what's actually going on must be *so* bad that—'

She was interrupted by another beep from her phone. She opened up more photos from Kevin.

'Here we go,' she said.

The photos were of printed slides from a PowerPoint presentation, all of which were watermarked with the word CLASSIFIED.

<u>Confirmation of the FA/RCE deal</u>
<u>and</u>
<u>Five Year Plan of implementation</u>

Association football rule changes to enhance worldwide marketability

The 3pm kick-off today will trigger the implementation of the Football Association's ground-breaking partnership with RCE, an international conglomerate comprising sponsors of the English game.

The funds that the FA is receiving from RCE will enable us to not only pay back all debts related to the rebuild of Wembley Stadium, but will leave a substantial surplus. A minority of this surplus will be used to fund the Association's nationwide ticket refund initiative, the subject of today's announcement; the rest will be distributed internally.

Today's announcement will serve a dual purpose:

- satisfy the inconvenient necessity for transparency about RCE's legislative powers, in particular concerning refereeing, and

- boost the public's morale through monetary gain.

Paying out these ticket refunds will ensure a feeling of goodwill among supporters, as will the Family Fun Day PR event. Replenishing this feeling of goodwill shall become increasingly necessary when we begin to roll out RCE's planned rule changes, as detailed in the slides that follow.

Ten new rules will come into force at a rate of two per year at the start of each football season for the following five seasons. Each will be enacted with no prior notice to the public, and will come immediately following further positive announcements to the public that provide a monetary compensation – the exact details of the four future instances of compensation are still to be decided.

The ten new rules are as follows:

Year One

1. The FA has internally allocated the 20 Premier League sides a letter from A to T, ranging from the club with the highest global fan base to the club with the lowest. Referees no longer make judgement calls during matches. Instead the officials always rule in favour of team A over all others, team B over all except A, team C over all except A and B, and so on.

2. Every time there is a break in play (for a foul, throw-in, goal kick and so on), there is an additional three-minute pause to allow advertisers to broadcast commercials (with sound) on pitch side hoardings and on stadium screens, and on television (when a game is televised).

Year Two

3. Commercials (with sound) run constantly throughout matches at stadiums and across the bottom of TV screens, when a game is televised. All singing and chanting in stadiums is banned.

4. The six most globally supported clubs are exempt from relegation and guaranteed European football every season. Other teams can avoid relegation with a voluntary contribution to the FA/RCE.

    From this season onwards, 75% of games are televised and fixtures can be rearranged for TV with only 24 hours' prior notice.

Year Three

5. Building on the success of 'half-and-half' scarves, any game involving one or more of the Premier League's six most globally supported clubs is split up. One half is played at 12.45pm GMT and the second half later that same day at 5.30pm GMT.

6. Saturday 3pm kick-offs are outlawed.

    From this season onwards, 100% of games are televised.

Year Four

7. There are no more draws. Penalty shoot-outs will commence if a game is deadlocked after 90 minutes.

8. Teams must change both their home and away kits three times per season, with new designs every August, November and February.

    From this season, ticket prices nationwide are raised by 100%.

9. Premier League stadiums are required to have 90% corporate seating.

10. All football stadiums are alcohol-free and no business selling alcohol can operate within a three-mile radius of a stadium.

From this season, ticket prices are raised by 200%.

The actual changes to the rules will never be announced formally – only that season's monetary compensation to the fans will be declared. The changes will simply become apparent as the new season progresses. It is hoped that many fans will not even notice the new rules, or that they will be too happy about their compensation to care.

Any fans who are *not* happy with taking their compensation and accepting the changes will soon diminish in number as the rules are rolled out. The new rules are designed to gradually transform the profile of football supporters, with the goal of making it impossible for a certain type of fan to even exist by Year Five.

The Referees' Association and the Professional Game Match Officials Board (PGMOL) have received separate instructions on how to lengthen the VAR checking process, with the twin purposes of allowing extra commercials to air and to give the centralised VAR team the time to re-edit footage to 'correct' it. The two aforementioned bodies are assimilated into RCE with immediate effect, and in the long term the referee as a physical presence on the pitch will be eradicated and replaced with VAR on its own.

Negotiations are ongoing with world footballing bodies with regards to the international implementation of these rules, with both FIFA and the International Football Association Board (IFAB) expressing their enthusiasm. In England, the changes shall, of course, consequently affect the Women's Super League and both sexes' England national teams, about which details will follow in future correspondence.

Thank you for your time and congratulations on being part of football's new order.

Claire and Frank staggered back through the tube station in a daze, both reeling as if they'd been punched in the gut.

'They finally did it,' Frank said at last. 'They sold the game out.'

'So, Research Creating Excellence isn't really a marketing firm, it's a front,' said Claire.

'A front for what?'

'For whoever is really behind all this – these "international sponsors of the English game."'

As they turned a corner, Claire scoffed. '"The rest of the surplus will be distributed internally,"' she quoted. 'Ha, somehow I don't think they'll be putting it into the grass roots game.'

'It'll go back to the sponsors?'

Claire nodded. 'And to the FA's top brass. And if there's anything left, then no doubt it will find its way to those "six most supported clubs."'

'And what's all this about splitting up the big draw matches? And cutting three o' clock kick-offs?'

'Globalisation,' said Claire. 'It's because of the time difference. They want to maximise viewing figures for the teams that are most popular in the markets either side of the world – America and Asia – even if it makes a mockery of a football match as a sporting event. And as for three o'clock on a

Saturday... well, it doesn't equate to a good kick-off time anywhere in the world.'

'Except for here, where the game's actually being played, where it's been a tradition for decades.'

Claire nodded sadly.

'But how can they think that giving people a few quid back will distract them from having the game ripped apart?'

'It might. Ever noticed how politicians will reveal that tax is going up or benefits are going down at the same time that the news is already preoccupied with some other big story?'

'No...'

'Exactly.'

'But all these changes,' blurted Frank, 'they'll... they'll destroy the game. They go completely against its traditions and integrity and are gonna price out the average fan and...' Frank wore himself out just as the ticket barriers came within sight.

'Kevin and I were wondering earlier about whether referees have been targeted by RCE,' Claire mused. 'Now we know: human refereeing is being fazed out altogether. Too risky – you don't have to worry about whether you can persuade a computer to be corrupt, you just program it that way. God, I mean... there have been match-fixing scandals before, but if this goes ahead, *every* football match will be fixed.'

'Yeah,' added Frank, 'and not only that, it'll be *completely legal.*'

'Come on,' said Claire as they passed through the barriers and out of the station, 'you know where we need to go now.'

'Right,' said Frank firmly.

They hurtled down the steps but were stopped in their tracks as soon as their feet touched Olympic Way.

'Excuse me, miss,' a riot gear-clad policeman shouted above the crowd. 'We're under strict instructions that you two mustn't be allowed any closer to Wembley.'

Claire looked past him. Within the throng she saw a familiar grey-haired man in a suit, only yards away.

'Fullarton,' Claire called out.

'Miss, I'm afraid you and the gentleman will have to—'

'Leave it out, you jobsworth plod,' barked Frank. This made the officers turn on him – freeing up Claire to rush over to Fullarton.

'Oi,' the police yelled after her.

'Trust me, you lot,' Frank said, 'if you care anything about this game you're paid to protect, we're doing you a favour.'

Meanwhile, Claire had succeeded in luring Fullarton over to them and was showing him her photos of the presentation.

'No... it can't be...' Fullarton said. 'And these came from inside Wembley?'

'Yes, Kevin's there right now. Please, Fullarton, you have to get us into the stadium, we're running out of time.'

'But, but...' Fullarton stammered, 'can't be sure... must authenticate...'

'For God's sake,' snapped Frank. 'Fullarton, this is your chance to score a winning penalty. You can't over-think it, you have to go with your gut.'

Fullarton absorbed this.

'Officer Hill,' he said to one of the policemen. 'These two are to be taken past the crowds and straight into Wembley Stadium without delay.'

'Yes sir,' said the officer.

'Thank you, Fullarton,' said Claire. 'You made the right choice, you'll see.'

They turned to go with Officer Hill.

'Claire? Frank?' Fullarton said. They stopped. 'Just make sure you get to that Media Centre in time. And don't forget this.'

He brandished the FA tablet like a sword.

Frank took it. 'Right. We still have one last part of The Campaign left – "The True Meaning of Football." Cheers, Fullarton – William.'

They were off.

Fullarton watched as Frank and Claire followed Officer Hill and his colleagues through the mob and out of sight.

Then he headed off in the same direction. There was someone he needed to see.

22

WEMBLEY.

Although today they weren't, for once, here for a football match, Frank and Claire were still part of a huge crowd. They left Officer Hill and waded through all the people to the concourse inside, finding a space next to a betting kiosk.

Claire was talking to Kevin on her phone. 'Yeah, we're just inside the Bobby Moore entrance.' She frowned and looked at Frank. 'What do you mean you're locked in a room?'

Frank gave her a perplexed look.

'Well, have you actually tried it?' Claire rolled her eyes. 'Yes, put down your drink and check the bloody door.' She waited. 'It's *not*? Then get your skinny arse out of there and run like you're chasing a loose goal kick... What? Yes, "skinny arse" was a compliment. Now *move it.*'

Claire hung up and glanced at the clock on her phone.

'This is gonna be tight,' Frank said. But they were both excited, the adrenalin was flowing again.

Frank unfroze the tablet's screen and read aloud.

The Final Clue

To find the truth at football's core, take the pitch markings and add more.
Three lines intersect across the home of the game:

1. Royal Route straight through the
centre to First Way.
2. From the top centre south-southeast.
3. From the top centre south-southwest.

'Something about Wembley itself?' Frank wondered.

'Yeah, and the pitch markings...' said Claire.

'Royal Route is that road that goes around the stadium...'

Frank spied a discarded ticket for the Fun Day on the floor and picked it up. Then he grabbed a pen from the betting kiosk.

The ticket had on its back a Wembley map, showing the layout inside the stadium the roads that surrounded it.

'Right, here's Royal Route, on the west side,' Frank said. 'And First Way is here on the other side. "Straight through the centre" – that's gotta mean through the centre circle, right?'

Claire shrugged and nodded at the same time. Frank drew a straight horizontal line that cut the pitch exactly in half.

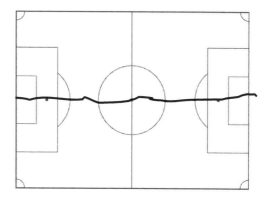

'Now,' Frank said. 'The other two have got to, what's it... overlap.'

'Intersect.'

'Yeah. One going diagonally from the top of the centre circle down and to the left, another down and to the right.'

Frank drew two diagonal lines all the way down to the edge of the pitch. They formed a triangle in the middle of the centre circle, which cut through the first line.

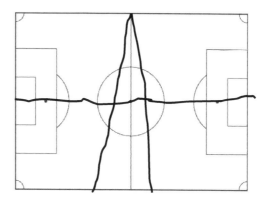

Frank and Claire stared at it. 'So, what does that tell us?' asked Claire.

Frank squinted.

And then he got it.

'I know what this means.'

'What? What is it?'

Frank scribbled three letters over the pitch.

Claire looked at his handiwork and smiled.

'Of course,' she said. 'That's what The Campaign has *really* been about all along.'

'Let's get to that Media Centre,' said Frank. 'I know exactly what I have to say to stop all this.'

Frank explained his plan to Claire.

'Okay, sounds good,' she said, 'but we still have to wait for—'

'Now then,' a voice startled them from behind. 'Did I miss owt?'

Claire was thrilled that The Campaign was back on and seeing Kevin again made her happier still. She threw her arms around the footballer.

'Eh up, what did I do?' he laughed, returning the embrace.

'You're here,' she whispered in his ear.

They broke apart, embarrassed in front of Frank.

'Plenty of time for hugs later, you two,' he told them with a grin.

'Right,' said Claire, clearing her throat.

She led the other two through the packed concourse, while Frank filled Kevin in on the last clue and the plan it had inspired him to come up with to stop the announcement.

'You think that'll work?' Kevin asked him.

'You don't?'

'I dunno, I mean this lot seem right determined. Your man, whatsisname...'

'Where is that traitor Gary?' snapped Frank, clenching his fists.

'Gone,' Kevin said. 'Off with this woman – that Susan, Claire's ex-gaffer.'

'Wait,' said Claire. 'Did Susan give you the PowerPoint slides?'

'Yeah, by accident, I think.'

'And she left you alone with them and your phone?'

'Er, I guess.'

'Why would she do that?' Frank wondered.

This does not add up, thought Claire.

'And why,' Frank continued, 'did she let you see the announcement early?'

'Oh, *well.*' Kevin was bursting with pride. 'Your woman said she wanted me to *read* the announcement.'

'Susan said *you* could read it?' asked Claire.

'In your face Stu Donaldson, eh?'

Frank and Claire regarded each other dubiously.

Claire said, 'Well, we need to get to the Media Centre regardless, so come on.'

'Hold up,' said Kevin stopping them. 'I've been walking around tunnels in this flipping stadium all day and I've finally figured out that that in't the quickest way to the Media Centre.'

'Of course it is,' said Claire. 'I've worked at Wembley for years.'

'Then you should know that we can just cut through there.'

Kevin pointed. They had come to a stop at one of the many entrances to the Wembley pitch.

Claire looked.

'Alright,' she said to Kevin with a wry smile. 'We'll give your way a try. Just don't go getting too cocky.' She ran past him down the tunnel towards the sunshine.

'As if I would,' Kevin called to Claire as he followed her. As he passed Frank, he shot him a wink.

Frank shook his head with a smile and ran after them.

The knocking on her office door jolted Susan. The combination of barely any sleep, too much caffeine and all-day tension had made her jittery. She reached for her ever-present mug of coffee; it was cold.

'Hi, Susan.'

Oh God, please not this again.

'I'm a little busy right now, Gary.' She didn't turn around. 'It may have escaped your attention but the FA is preparing to give an announcement that's going to change football forever.'

Gary moved inside. 'Exciting stuff. But what I wanted to talk about—'

'I have your acceptance letter on my laptop.' Now Susan swivelled in her chair to face him. 'All I have to do is print it and sign it and you're on the course.'

'So maybe, you could... do that now?'

Susan narrowed her eyes.

Gary soldiered on. 'I mean I did everything you wanted me to do, I followed your every instruction, whether it was helping them or trying to dissuade them, never once questioning you when you flip-flopped between the two, and I didn't post *anything* on social media...'

'And what about pulling the cord on the Underground? Was *that* something I wanted you to do?'

Gary hesitated. 'But... there weren't any consequences, were there? It was just getting a bit too much for me and I panicked, okay?'

'And ran.'

'And I ran, yes.'

'The RCE representatives are trained marketing professionals, Gareth. They could have handled the situation.'

Gary pouted.

Susan sighed. 'Just wait for the announcement to be over, Gary. Then we'll rubber-stamp this.'

'Okay. Thank you, Susan.'

'Until then, just stay out of the way. Do you think you can do that?'

'No problem.' Gary backed out of the room.

Susan thought of something else. 'Gary, actually... wait.'

He stopped, one foot out the door. 'Mm-hmm?'

'Tell me something.'

'Sure.'

'Who do you support? Which football team do you follow?'

'Oh. Well, that depends.'

'It... *depends?*'

'Well, the earliest I can remember is Man United dominating everything, so naturally I liked them. But then Arsenal had their 'Invincibles' side, so I switched to them. But I got sick of waiting for them to win the league again, so I moved on to Chelsea. But then Man City came onto the scene in a big way, and of course you've got Liverpool now, so—'

'Okay, that's enough.'

'Oh, and I forgot to mention—'

'Please Gary, stop.'

He shrugged and turned to leave again.

'Actually, just one more thing.'

Gary waited with his hand on the door handle.

Susan couldn't help herself. She had to ask.

'Do you think the game would be better if... if only the big clubs could win?'

Gary stared at her. 'Well, *yeah.*'

'Doesn't fairness matter?'

Gary regarded her as if she had suggested that football be played with a square ball.

'Fairness? Is *life* fair? No, it's survival of the fittest, Darwinism. Bigger clubs get more worldwide support: more merchandise sales, more TV money. It's inevitable that they will get richer and richer and eventually suck in all the idiots who support the crap teams. Then all the loser clubs will go bankrupt and finally it'll be only the big boys left. That's what *I'm* looking forward to, and I can't wait.'

Susan stared at Gary open-mouthed.

She turned away from him. 'Please leave,' she managed.

Gary left.

Susan got up and approached the vast window overlooking the pitch. She pressed her hands against it and stared down at all the families below her. She observed the myriad of replica shirts, some of which she didn't even recognise.

Then Susan turned to look through her office's glass wall into Conference Room One. The dignitaries her boss had been entertaining all day were in there again, enjoying exotic fruits and freshly ground coffee. She wondered how many years the people out there kicking balls through holes and munching on candy floss would have to work to earn what the men and women who funded RCE made in a week.

She was drawn back to her desk, to a framed photo. Susan with her husband and their two children, all wearing the shirts of non-league Bromley Football Club. The kids were so young – was that really the last time they had been to the football as a family? Yes. She had spent every Saturday since working, trying to make the game better. She hadn't just enjoyed it together with the ones she loved for years.

There was another knock at her door.

'Gary, for crying out loud—'

'Excuse me, Susan.' The voice was old, deep, full of gravitas.

William Fullarton was standing in her doorway.

'I'm sorry to barge in here like this,' he said. 'But I think you owe me an explanation.'

THE FAMILY Fun Day was still in full swing. Kevin, Frank and Claire were having to slalom their way around people and nearly got split up more than once.

'Look – that's the exit nearest your Media Centre.' Kevin was pointing across a patch of grass that was somehow empty.

'Let's do it,' said Claire.

They darted straight for the open expanse of pitch.

Frank glanced at his watch. 'Good idea this, Kev. We're gonna get there with time to spare.'

'Yeah,' agreed Claire, 'but that doesn't mean we can afford to—'

But before she could go on, they were stopped by a bald man in a tracksuit.

'Eh, you can't go across there, like,' he said in a thick Scouse accent.

Any irritation they felt quickly turned to awe when they realised who the tracksuit-wearing man was: ex-England manager Roddy Burnside.

'Gaffer,' said Kevin shaking the big man's hand. 'How's tricks?'

Burnside squinted in the sunshine. 'Eh, Mini Maxwell. How ya doin'?'

'Sound, sound. Just cutting through here on our way to—'

'Didn't realise you were turning out for me today, like.'

'Well, I...' Kevin observed their surroundings. They had ended up on the touchline of a mini football pitch, set up for a celebrity tournament. Both teams – an assortment of ex-players, pop stars, soap actors, journalists and reality TV personalities – were currently down the other end for a corner kick.

'Come on, Mini,' Burnside was saying. 'Don't worry about kitting up, just pop this spare shirt over your togs. And you don't need boots, it's just a kickabout.' The manager had a dark brown strip over Kevin's head before he could protest. The opposition were wearing green.

Frank and Claire grasped what was happening.

'Mr Burnside,' Frank said. 'It's an honour to meet you. But we need Kevin—'

'Course, I *say* it's just a kickabout,' Burnside was carrying on, 'but we're two-one down in the 80th and I want to flaming well win this thing, otherwise I'll be the laughing stock of the after-dinner circuit. Come on, I'll take off Smudger. *Eh, Smudger, get your arse over here.*'

Kevin gazed out onto the pitch. Saw the other players, his fellow celebrities. Saw the goals, the makeshift pitch markings. Beyond that, the adoring fans, clamouring to watch the spectacle. And a rolling TV camera.

Kevin turned to Frank and Claire, his eyes pleading.

'Kev, no,' said Claire. 'We don't have time.'

'Just five minutes,' he begged. 'Come on – if it gets too tight, I'll just catch you up. Job's a good 'un.'

'Kevin, please,' Claire implored. 'We've come this far; we can't take the risk.'

But Frank was patting Kevin on the back. 'Go on son,' he said, 'show us what you can do.' He looked at Claire. 'Just a five-minute cameo, on and off again.'

Kevin consulted Claire again. She shook her head in resignation.

Kevin ran onto the pitch, high-tenning the rock star who he replaced.

The England midfielder was pure magic. As soon as he received the ball he was on the move, feinting one way then the other, showboating for the crowd, before laying off a diagonal pass to the winger. He zig-zagged his run in order to take two Green defenders out of the game, then controlled a return pass on his chest and flicked it over the last defender. Then he shaped himself and connected with the falling ball sweetly on the volley, sending a rocket straight past the goalkeeper's outstretched hand and into the back of the net.

Kevin raised his hands in celebration and was mobbed by his teammates. The crowd went hysterical, chanting '*Maxwell, Maxwell, Maxwell!*'

But as soon as the opposition kicked off, Kevin's side were on the back foot, nearly conceding again.

Growing frustrated, Frank started to yell things from pitch side. 'Go tighter. One of you. Just play the simple ball.'

Throughout all this, Claire had been watching the clock on her phone more than the game, although Kevin's bravura performance had made her look up more than once. Now she was studying Burnside, who in turn was watching Frank as he barked instructions and gesticulated. When the manager tapped Frank on the shoulder, Claire assumed he was going to tell him to keep his trap shut.

Instead Burnside said, 'Hey mate, you seem to know what you're talking about. Why don't you take over? I'm knackered, fancy grabbing meself a nice pint of bitter.'

Frank's jaw dropped. 'Really? You want me to... coach the team?'

'Yeah, why not. Will be good for cameras, good for charity, like. And this way, if we lose, it's all your fault. But if we win, mind, I'm taking all the credit.'

'Right, of course.' Frank's head was spinning.

'Go for it, son,' said Burnside, moving swiftly away.

Frank looked at Claire for permission, just as Kevin had done. She sighed and made an exasperated gesture. 'If we've got time for Kevin to be Roy of the Rovers, I guess we've got time for you to be Mike Bassett.'

Frank grinned.

Then he cleared his throat.

This is it. Cool, calm, composed.

After all, Frank Tuttle was an experienced coach.

But never of B-list celebrities in front of a national TV audience.

Despite that, and the added pressure of filling in for an ex-England manager, Frank didn't panic.

He took a deep breath.

'Number three, what you *doing?* Track back on their seven. Stay tight, that's it. Two, *two.* Watch your man. Kev, *Kev* – run into the channel. Their right-back can't get near you, keep him occupied.'

The celebrity players glanced at this stranger bellowing orders at them and immediately responded to his authority. And it worked – the disorganised shambles quickly became a solid unit.

From his territory in central midfield, Kevin turned and gave Frank the thumbs-up.

Claire, meanwhile, stood with her hands folded across her chest – still tense about the ticking clock, but at the same time marvelling at the change in her two new friends. Each was in his element.

'Kev, come here,' Frank called out during a break in play.

Kevin trotted over and Frank handed him a sports drink.

'Gaffer?'

'Two minutes left. This lot are crap, we can do them.'

His player nodded, sucking on the bottle.

'We need to do a "fake playground."'

Kevin swallowed the sugary liquid. 'A what?'

'Here's how it goes.'

Seconds later, Kevin was trotting back over to his teammates. He got them into a huddle and passed on Frank's instructions.

Claire, who had overheard what Frank told Kevin, said to him, 'You have *got* to be kidding.'

Focused, his eyes never leaving the pitch, Frank replied, 'Just watch.'

And watch Claire did. As the Green side took their goal kick, Kevin and his Brown teammates broke formation and all chased after the ball, like a group of kids at playtime.

The Greens panicked. Every one of their outfield players copied their opponents and chased after the ball, which got lost somewhere in the mix of bodies.

Then a TV weathergirl from the Brown team hoofed the ball goalwards, towards space Kevin was already running into.

The Greens had all been pulled out of position, creating a huge gap in their defensive third. Kevin ran onto the pass, controlled it deftly with his left boot and then knocked it ahead to chase onto.

Only the keeper was left to beat. It was a race for who would get to the ball first.

Kevin was cool: back straight, legs moving in tandem. Judging by the onrushing keeper's speed, a regular shot would get smothered. The angle of the pass made a lob doable, but there was a better – and far more audacious – alternative.

All this went through Kevin's mind in less than half a second. The crowd merely saw Kevin 'Mini' Maxwell reach the ball a microsecond before the goalie and control it while spinning around 360 degrees, stealing the ball from the outstretched gloves and releasing it goalwards in one swift movement.

Kevin didn't watch the ball go in. While it rolled along the turf towards an empty net, he stopped still, faced the crowd and cupped one hand to his ear. And when the fans erupted, he simply tilted his head in their direction. Seconds later he was celebrating with his teammates.

The ref blew for full-time. The Browns had come from behind to win 3-2.

As the victorious team headed towards the technical area, teeth-whitened, fake-tanned, dyed-blonde TV reporter Tommy Edworthy shoved a microphone in Kevin's face.

'Blimey, proper quality cameo, Kev,' Tommy told him with his trademark Essex cadence. 'We all thought you were on the scrap heap, bruv.'

Still walking, Kevin opened his mouth to reply. But then he saw Frank on the touchline – his head shaking, his eyes imploring.

Tommy persevered. 'I better be careful asking you questions, Mini, know what I mean? Don't wanna lump you with another fine, eh geezer?' Again, he beckoned Kevin to speak into the microphone. 'Come on bruv, ain't like you to be short a word or ten.'

Kevin considered his interviewer. 'Tommy, I'm saying nowt. Go speak to the coach what won us the game.' They had reached the touchline and Kevin put his arm around his friend. 'Meet Frank Tuttle – tactical genius.'

Tommy, sensing a story, turned his microphone and cameraman towards Frank. 'Well then – Frank, innit?'

'Um, yeah, Frank Tuttle.'

Frank noticed with dismay that his interview was being shown on the huge Wembley screens.

'That was an... interesting approach, Frank,' Tommy was saying. 'It certainly confused the other team. Are you Roddy's assistant?'

'Er, no, I'm just a bloke.'

'"Just a bloke"? Like, from the crowd?'

'Yeah, Roddy popped off for a... for a break and I stepped in. I do have experience, coaching non-league, kids and that.'

'Well, Frank,' said Tommy with a glance to the camera, 'with tactics like that in your locker, I bet some Premier League managers wouldn't mind picking your brain. What you call that approach?'

'Er, well, that was the "fake playground."'

'Quality. And how exactly—'

'Eh, what's all this then?' Roddy Burnside was barging his way back into the limelight, wiping foam from his mouth. 'What about the manager for the *other* 80 minutes?'

Tommy turned the mic to him. 'Roddy, just the fella. Can you explain how this amateur league coach has just come in and...'

Frank and Kevin were thoroughly enjoying all this. But when Frank saw Claire's imploring expression, he came back to his senses.

'Come on,' he told Kevin. 'We've got a bigger job to do.'

'Right,' said Kevin. 'Just a sec.' He took off his brown shirt and made a show of throwing it into the crowd. This got the biggest cheer of the afternoon, which rang out behind Kevin, Frank and Claire as they ran towards the exit that led to the Media Centre.

24

SUSAN CLYNE knew that FA chief fairness officer William Fullarton wouldn't be as easy to fob off as the last visitor to her office, Gary Ward, had been.

'So then,' Fullarton was saying as he advanced inside, 'what have you got to say for yourself?'

'I don't have time for this. The dignitaries are waiting—'

'Then let them wait. I want answers.'

Susan glanced at her wall clock. 'About?'

'About a certain PowerPoint presentation.'

Susan cursed under her breath. She had been counting on Maxwell sending the PowerPoint slides to Claire and Frank; she hadn't reckoned with them reaching Brother Will.

Keeping her cool, she simply said, 'Oh?'

'Yes, "oh." You lied to me, Sister Susan.'

'Excuse me?'

'You told me that this announcement was a minor thing, a bone to throw to the public who were becoming disillusioned with the game. Now I discover that it's actually part of a plan to tear out football's heart – exactly what you and I have sworn on our lives to protect.'

'Shh.' Susan jumped up and closed her office door. 'Are you mad? You know that rumours already circulate this place.'

Fullarton didn't care. 'I have my day job and you have yours. But we're more than just employees collecting paycheques. We're supposed to be preserving the sanctity of the game against all threats. *And now you dare to betray us?*'

Despite the thick glass and closed door, Fullarton's outburst was heard in the open-plan office of the Media Centre. FA employees were now looking at them through the office's glass wall.

Susan pulled Fullarton into the corner away from prying eyes.

'Will, you have to trust me. I have this situation under control.'

'Do you?' spat Fullarton in an angry whisper. 'All day, *I* have been trying to control this situation, trying to protect FA property and to keep a lid on potential scandal. Not just in my role for the Department of Fair Play, not even because of my allegiance to The Custodians, but simply as someone who cares about the game. And all the while you've been using me to make sure that this... this *abomination* goes ahead?'

'Oh, so am I to understand that you've been breaking protocol today, Brother?' Susan mocked. 'Taking your time returning FA property, interfering with affairs with which you aren't supposed to be interfering? Not *you*, Mr By-the-Book?'

'When faced with an unprecedented threat,' Fullarton replied through gritted teeth, 'protocol no longer seems quite so salient.'

Susan gave Fullarton a sardonic *I'm-impressed* look.

'It's all over for you, Sister Susan. The Captain is already on his way and I would not be surprised if he has you excommunicated.'

'*The Captain is coming?*' Susan shook away her shock. 'Brother Will, please listen to me. I've been under a lot of pressure today, trying to keep many balls in the air. Tell me, Tuttle and Claire are in the stadium, right?'

'Yes,' said Fullarton slowly, eyeing Susan up. 'And I've been informed that they're now heading up here, to the Media Centre.'

Susan turned away from Fullarton. 'So, they will make it on time. The Captain was right about him.'

Fullarton was confused. 'But you've been... are you saying you actually want them to come here? What do you mean, "right about him"? Tuttle?'

Susan faced Fullarton again and fixed him with a mocking grin. 'Surely with all your experience and knowledge, you know to what I'm referring?'

Fullarton's eyes widened. 'You don't mean that The Prophecy has—'

The office phone cut him off. Susan read the caller ID: CONFERENCE ROOM ONE.

It was time.

At Wembley's Bobby Moore entrance, an elderly man dressed in impressive regalia was being escorted inside by three stewards. The stewards' manner indicated that the guest was held in the absolute highest regard.

'Where did you want to visit first, sir?' asked the youngest steward. 'I'm afraid the stadium is very busy right now, what with the Family Fun Day...'

'Quite alright,' the elderly man said. 'What good is an empty football stadium? Creepy places. Full of the ghosts of fans now absent, eerie with expectation of the next game. No, give me a full-to-capacity arena every time – this is quite wonderful.'

'Yes sir,' said the young steward. 'So, did you want to see the pitch, or...?'

'I'd really like to be taken to wherever the public broadcasts are made,' the man replied. 'Some sort of... television hub?'

'Well, that would be the Media Centre, but...'

'Media Centre. Yes, that's the badger.'

The young steward looked to his colleagues, but they offered no help. 'Uh,' he said, 'unfortunately we've been told that it's strictly out of bounds today. They're getting ready to make this announcement everyone's been talking about. It's all over Twitter?'

The elderly man's blank face revealed the extent of his social media knowledge.

'Well, in any case,' the steward persevered, 'you might find it more comfortable and more interesting to—'

'Let's make haste, gentlemen,' the white-haired man in the striking outfit ordered. 'I may be older than all your years combined, but I can still move when I need to. I really must insist that you take me to the Media Centre. Immediately.'

In a suburban home just down the road from the English national football stadium, a 13-year-old boy was sitting cross-legged on the living room floor watching TV. Like millions of others, he was tuned in to the day's events at Wembley.

'Sweetheart, do you want a sandwich?' his mother called from the kitchen.

'No, thank you,' the boy replied. He was too excited to be hungry. He had just witnessed his own father take charge of a charity football match and coach a team of celebrities – including a Premier League footballer with whom he was personally acquainted – to victory against another team of all-stars.

'Can you believe it, Mum? Wasn't Dad great?' the boy called out.

'He was certainly something,' his mother replied.

The youngster smiled. Minutes ago, his mum had responded to his urgent cries and had joined him in front of the TV. When she'd seen her estranged husband at work, expressing himself on a touchline once more, the boy had seen it in her eyes.

She *did* still love him.

Now the boy watched the footage switch from the post-match analysis to a room that he had visited this very morning, albeit briefly. The much-hyped FA announcement was finally about to be broadcasted from Wembley's Media Centre. Apparently, the presenter said, a footballer was going to read it out any minute now.

The young lad kept watching. It had been such an exciting day – surely there couldn't be any further twists?

25

PETE HARRINGTON was going to be rich.

That wasn't entirely accurate – Pete Harrington was *already* rich. Since hanging up his goalie gloves 15 years ago he'd made an extremely comfortable living, taking full advantage of his standing as England's most-capped player. He had captured the public's imagination throughout his career, not only for his world-class saves and contributions to penalty shootout wins, but for his personality – or rather lack of. Harrington hadn't been an eccentric keeper, with elaborate hairdos or red-faced shouting. Instead, he was known as The Wall, both for how he filled the whole goal and for his unreadable face, in both defeat and victory. After years of emotionally charged failure from the

England men's team, Harrington represented the kind of stoic professionalism more usually associated with the Germans, and he captained his country from the back during its most successful post-1966 period.

Now as he stood in Wembley's largest boardroom and surveyed the dozen wealthy businesspeople who were partnered with his company Research Creating Excellence, each of them with a ten-figure personal net-worth, Harrington reflected on how he had got here.

In truth, he had never much cared for football. Harrington was an extremely unpopular child – distant, introspective, thought of as 'weird'. The other boys shunned him completely at school, until someone had the brainwave that Pete's height (he reached six foot eight as an adult) might make him useful between the sticks during their lunchtime games. And he turned out to be a natural, athletic and with sharp reflexes. Goalkeeper was the one position that no one volunteered to play; every young lad wanted to be the hero, to score and to enjoy the camaraderie out on the pitch. Not Pete Harrington. He preferred isolation, and he began to relish being the last line of defence, the one who had the final say between a goal being scored or not. It began to feel to young Pete like power. But despite his heroic lunchtime performances, the other children still never accepted him, and he remained a loner.

One day, less than a year after his father had died of leukaemia, Pete was playing football in the garden at his Uncle Charlie's 40th birthday BBQ. The man of the hour sat deep in a patio chair with his sixth Famous Grouse and lemonade and watched closely as Pete made save after save from much bigger boys and grown men. Then and there Charlie declared himself his nephew's agent-slash-manager; he soon became a regular fixture in Pete's home, even staying overnight with Pete's mum. Uncle Charlie touted his nephew around the professional clubs and the boy was soon snapped up by Leeds United.

Focusing on the game didn't harm young Pete Harrington academically; he was intelligent and blessed with a cast-iron memory, making his remember-by-rote secondary school education a formality. He dedicated far more energy to observing the world around him, and this helped take his goalkeeping to another level – his growing body certainly contributed, but his main asset was his almost superhuman level of perception. He noticed everything: the player on the ball's intentions, the player's teammates' movement for possible passes, the shape of his own defence; and always he watched the ref, for when he could 'accidentally' punch someone in the face during a corner or whether he could get away with tackling a striker and making it look like the man had dived.

He saw everything coming because he observed and analysed – and this was not just on the pitch. He took note of how his Uncle Charlie latched onto people and exploited them – the depressed widow of his deceased brother, his nephew's talent. Charlie Harrington managed Pete's lucrative career entirely for his own benefit. He used his nephew's first professional paycheque to start a property portfolio and continued to funnel Pete's earnings into investments throughout his career. He had long ago retired to Saint Lucia at age 50, only three years younger than Pete was today.

Observing how wealthy his uncle was getting from the game, the young goalkeeper looked for ways he could maximise his own earning potential. He lapped up every sponsorship going: personalised gloves, razors, sports drinks, boots, even a brand of cement mixture ('Your *only* choice when building *The Wall*'). After he hung up his gloves there was the after-dinner speaking and media work, including a regular pundit slot on *Match of the Day* and as a team captain on *A Question of Sport* (where he was mercilessly mocked as 'the boring one'), as well as ambassador roles at his old clubs.

But within these ventures he was still just a tool for someone else. What Pete Harrington craved (beyond, of course, money) was control. He wanted to be more than just rich; he wanted to leave a legacy, to really change the game. The knuckle-dragging plebs who lurched into stadiums up and down the country, the nauseating families and the groups of beer-swilling mates with their stupid grinning faces and braying laughter; he wanted those reprobates to come to know football as having pre- and post-Pete Harrington eras. So he rebranded himself as a 'sport development consultant,' founded RCE, built up an eye-wateringly lucrative package of sponsors under the promise of making football the world's most internationally marketable sporting product, and then with his top marketing minds at RCE came up with a set of changes to the game's rules that would make that product a reality, along with developing methods to ensure that implementing the changes would cause minimal friction. The easy part was persuading the FA: they were so broke after the Wembley rebuild overspend that they practically snapped Harrington's hand off.

All this had led up to him standing here right now, with the sponsors sitting before him, waiting for him to speak. Within minutes, the deal would be complete, and football would finally be reshaped in Harrington's own image. Plus, he would become rich beyond his wildest dreams.

'Ladies and gentlemen,' Harrington began, slowly pacing around Conference Room One. 'Thank you for coming today. You have completed your tour of this historic stadium and have met many esteemed members of the FA, including the chairman and the chief executive. This morning you watched our exciting summary presentation in this very room. Now, myself as RCE founder and CEO, and the FA's director of communications and partnerships, Ms Susan Clyne,' – he gestured to Susan, standing in the corner – 'bring you to the climax of your day.

'Your investment into this scheme and the administration necessary to carry it out has been much appreciated, and today our hard work finally reaches its apex.'

Pete paused and looked at Susan. The FA had promoted her on the strength of this deal and seconded her to him as its official representative. He knew that he was lucky to have her to gauge the public's mood; Harrington himself wasn't exactly a man of the people, despite his high profile and big social media presence. It had been Susan's idea to make the announcement minutes before the season's first round of fixtures, leaving the fans with no time to figure out what was really going on before the kick of a ball made it official under the ancient footballing laws. And Harrington had agreed with her that gestures were needed to soften the masses into passivity, hence the refunded tickets – a drop in the ocean compared to the coming profits – and the preposterous carnival that was going on outside. Of course, when they'd initially discussed the matter at the first of their weekly lunch meetings, Susan hadn't been privy to the full extent of Harrington's ambitions for the game, and when he had finally revealed them at *Undici a Lato* restaurant yesterday, he had been anxious about her buckling under the weight of some pesky moral imperative. But he needn't have worried about her loyalty: it had been Susan's quick action, after all, that had stopped the tablet fiasco today from putting the whole deal in jeopardy. And most importantly it was a deal that, once formally concluded in a matter of minutes, was going to net her a life-changing bonus.

Harrington turned back to his audience.

'Yes, this is the day,' he told them. 'And we waited until today to make our announcement so we could be sure to control any reaction from *the fans*.' He made it sound like a dirty word, jerking a thumb in the direction of the Wembley pitch. 'We know how upset *those* imbeciles can get.'

Laughter from the dignitaries, none of whom had actually ever attended a football match.

'Because isn't that what this deal is really about? Why should football remain the domain of the "average fan" – the great unwashed, as we say in my country? The drunken chanting – so aggressive and unpleasant. The crowds of boorish, ignorant Neanderthals, devoted to just one team, often some outfit unknown beyond the British Isles. What, I ask, is the point of that? This is the 21st Century, football is an *international* game. Clubs with a rich heritage, who are supported in all corners of the globe, *they* are the future. And when today's deal is finalised,' – he glanced at the wall clock – 'we will finally tip the power over to the elite, where it belongs. Forever.'

Applause from the floor. Harrington looked to Susan for one of her reassuring smiles but found her face a blank canvas.

Focused on the task until the end, Harrington thought. *My kind of woman.*

It was a pity about the husband and kids, but with the amount of work Pete had planned for Susan, that marriage would soon crumble. And who was going to be there to pick up the pieces?

For good, this time.

'And now,' said Harrington when the clapping had died down, 'without further ado—'

'Let us in, ya bastards.'

Harrington's head jerked to face Conference Room One's glass wall.

Three figures stood at the Media Centre's entrance, a woman and two men. The man who was shouting was an England midfielder, whose national team debut had happened to have been in the same game where Harrington made his final appearance.

'Excuse me,' Susan said as she hurried from the room.

The dignitaries looked at each other and at Harrington.

'Looks like some minions have found their way to the top of the ivory tower,' their host said, trying for joviality but unable to hide his anxiety.

He followed Susan and waved his hand to send half a dozen yellow polo shirt-wearing men and women to the Media Centre's entrance.

Now Harrington's guests were approaching Conference Centre One's glass wall to get a better look at the commotion.

'Security will deal with this,' Harrington called back to his VIPs.

'Hey,' said the dignitary from a Malaysian gambling website, 'is that not Mr Kevin Maxwell?'

'It sure is,' said the CEO of an American sportswear manufacturer.

Harrington cursed under his breath.

Harrington was wrong: security *wasn't* dealing with the intruders.

'Mate, you know who I am,' Kevin was saying to the men blocking Frank, Claire and him from entering the Media Centre. 'So, you know you've gotta get out the way.'

Susan arrived from within. 'Let them in,' she said.

The guards fell back, and the trio entered.

Claire was straight onto Susan. 'What the hell is firing me all about, then? I can't believe after all these years—'

'Claire, please, we don't have time to—'

Frank chipped in. 'And what's the big idea luring my boy here? And you think you're gonna get away with ripping the soul out of football?'

Frank noticed Gary in the corner, trying to remain out of sight. Still addressing Susan, Frank pointed at him.

'And what about using this melt as a bloody spy and leading your goons right to us all day?'

From his safe distance, Gary spat, 'You'll never be as good a coach as me, Tuttle. *Never.*'

Frank just glared at the younger man.

'How could you, Gary?' Claire asked.

'Smart people always support the winning team, Claire,' he replied.

She sneered at him and hissed, 'Glory hunter.'

Gary withered back towards where Fullarton was standing, as if expecting him to offer protection. Fullarton, meanwhile, ignored Gary and just stood on the periphery, watching the scene unfold.

The six RCE employees now loomed over the intruders.

'Oh, great,' said Claire. 'More of these idiots.'

Harrington had now reached the commotion.

'Why have these trespassers been allowed inside?' he asked Susan. To his dismay, the dignitaries were spilling out of Conference Room One into the main Media Centre and were heading over.

'Pete Harrington?' said Kevin.

'*You're* behind all this?' asked Frank.

'But you're a national hero,' exclaimed Claire.

Harrington ignored them and faced the guards. 'Security, remove these individuals right away. My RCE people will assist.'

'Wait,' said Susan, halting the guards with her hand.

'Susan, what are you *doing?*' Harrington spluttered.

Just as Susan was about to speak, the Media Centre's doors opened again.

'Ah, bollocks,' said Kevin.

It was Stu Donaldson, dressed to the nines.

Kevin rushed over to the space marked BROADCAST CORNER.

'Oi, Maxwell,' yelled Donno. 'Get away from that camera. You're not even wearing a suit – this is a Tom Ford.'

'Still looking better than you, Stuart,' Kevin called back as he approached the TV director, who cautiously handed him a cordless microphone.

'I thought that other footballer was doing it?' the director asked Kevin.

'I'm a bloody footballer, in't I? Now start the flipping camera.'

The director shrugged and told his team to get set up.

Harrington now felt a measure of relief. 'Well then, I'm sure Mr Donaldson must be disappointed,' he said, addressing the group while placing a hand on Donno's shoulder to both console him and hold him back, 'but whichever footballer reads out the announcement is all the same really, isn't it?'

Claire, meanwhile, was staring at Kevin with disappointment.

Why? she mouthed to him.

Kevin shot her a wink.

And to her relief – and Harrington's horror – the footballer held out the microphone to Frank, who snatched it and swapped places with him.

Harrington gestured the guards and his RCE goons towards Frank. 'Security, remove this man from the premises *this instant—*'

'No,' said Susan.

Harrington was shocked. 'Susan? What has got into you?'

'Pete,' she said to her boss calmly, 'we're going to let Frank do it.'

'This is impossible,' Harrington blustered. 'Susan, I've trusted your instincts so far, but now I'm beginning to question whether—'

'Come on, Harrington,' interrupted the American dignitary. 'They've hauled ass all the way up here, let *this* fella read out the announcement.'

'Yes, why can it not be him?' asked the woman from a Swiss bank.

Harrington felt powerless; he couldn't lose face in front of his VIPs.

Reluctantly, he motioned to the TV director and the man fired up the autocue.

Harrington turned on his megawatt smile and approached Frank. 'Well, Mr Tuttle, it looks like you're privileged to give the most important announcement in football history. You *will* do a good job, won't you?' His question carried distinct menace.

Frank nodded curtly and stepped up onto a podium as indicated by the director. He was now isolated. He looked to Claire, who smiled. He looked to Kevin, who saluted him. Harrington was now standing with his dignitaries, keeping up appearances but looking nervous. Susan was next to Kevin and Claire, urgency in her eyes. Stu Donaldson stood further back, angry but impotent. Further back still, Frank saw Gary and Fullarton watching intently from the sidelines. In addition, the room was full of FA employees, all staring right at him, not to mention the security guards and Harrington's yellow-shirts.

And as if this wasn't audience enough, there were the thousands watching the Wembley screen outside and the ones transfixed by screens in other football stadiums across the country. Oh, and not forgetting the millions glued to their televisions or watching online.

Frank swallowed hard.

The camera was now pointing at his face, as were the studio lights that were so bright they were making his eyes water. The director got Frank's attention and pointed to the autocue, then he held out his hand and counted down fingers from five. After 'one', the red light on the camera came on.

Frank was live.

Outside the Fun Day was silent. The Media Centre was the same. Everyone was waiting for Frank Tuttle to speak.

Bloody hell, he thought.

FRANK was frozen under the spotlights.

Now that his eyes had adjusted to the glare, he could see out the huge window down onto the Wembley pitch, where everyone was staring up at his face, gigantic on the stadium screens. The caption FRANK TUTTLE – A FAN was displayed under him.

Frank studied them, the members of the public. The ones whose weeks crawled by in anticipation of the football at the end, the ones who renewed their season ticket each year without worrying about the rising price, the ones who chose their club and stuck with them through thick and thin, the ones who checked football websites every day, the ones who recorded every TV highlights show and paid extra to watch live games at home.

Frank found the courage to open his mouth. For them.

'Good afternoon, um, ladies and, er, gentlemen,' he stammered.

Then it seemed like he was losing his nerve again. But he was actually deciding something.

'You know what, the stuff I've got to say isn't for you lot out there. It's for some people I've got with me in here, in this Media Centre place in Wembley.'

Frank turned to the VIP sponsors.

'I've got some things to say to you lot in here – you business people who wanted to get some football rules changed today that would make you even richer, but what would ruin the game for the rest of us.'

The director tilted the camera to show the dignitaries, and then put it back on Frank.

Despite the live camera, Harrington went for Frank. But in a flash, Fullarton grabbed the ex-England captain and held him back, gesturing for the door guards to help. Harrington appealed to his RCE staff, but they backed away sheepishly.

Susan leaned in and whispered to the director, 'Whatever happens, do not stop broadcasting.'

Frank was starting up again.

'So, yeah, good afternoon. I don't know who any of you lot are, but my name's Frank Tuttle. I'm... well, I'm just an ordinary fan. Sorry to come barging in like this, but I've got something you need to hear.

'Football's brilliant, isn't it? I dunno if it's just a business opportunity to you lot, or whether you actually love the game. Sometimes, some of us fans' passion goes too far, and we lash out.' Frank directed this next part straight down the camera. 'It's happened to me and it was wrong, and I just wanted to say, I'm sorry.'

He addressed the VIPs again. 'But I guess you lot *can't* genuinely love the game, otherwise you wouldn't be trying to push through these horrible new rules. I've seen what the FA's really up to, what you've got planned, stuff that you didn't want to come out today. It didn't make for pleasant reading; in fact, it made me feel sick.

'There isn't gonna be a sport left to sponsor if you push these new rules through. People won't stand for it; they'll go and watch something else. You'll kill the professional game and will have wasted millions of pounds.

'I've been chasing around London all day with my pals, trying to stop this from happening. And along the way I've realised the true meaning of football.'

Frank held up the Wembley ticket stub he drew on earlier. He rotated it slowly to give everyone in the room and the camera a good look.

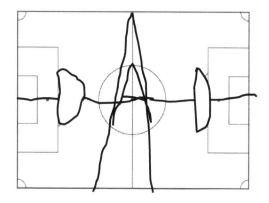

'When those men nearly 160 years ago wrote down football's rules,' Frank said, 'they made the game fair. And they put stuff in place to stop things like today from happening – to *keep* it fair.

'Football isn't about your TV rights and your international viewing figures; it's not about who has the most trophies in the cabinet or the highest attendances. Football is about togetherness. Dads – and mums – taking their kids to games. Bringing them into their club like a second family, one they'll stick with for the rest of their lives. Carrying on the tradition, keeping the game alive.

'Yeah, it's *people* who keep the game alive, not money. You put all the cameras down and take away the sponsors and everything and what you have left is generation after generation enjoying something together. You can broadcast it, you can sponsor it, you can sell it around the world. Go for it. But if you rip its heart out, then you're killing not just the game, but the people. Because people *are* the game.'

Frank lowered the mic. Each and every person in the Media Centre was staring at him in stunned silence.

He looked out onto the pitch again. There too, every man, woman and child was dumbfounded.

Not sure what else to do, Frank raised the microphone once more. 'Um, so yeah, that's it.'

This awkward postscript broke the tension. There was a smattering of laughter. Then the laughter grew and was joined by clapping, which escalated into full-blown applause and cheering – a wild, joyful uproar.

The dignitaries in the Media Centre were pounding their hands together too, as were the FA's comms team and everyone else present – except for Harrington and Gary, who both looked like they were going to throw up, and the RCE staff, who were starting to think that they might be unemployed.

Frank struggled to take it all in. Terrace-style chants came from outside:

'People are the game! People are the game!'

'There's only one Frankie Tuttle! One Frankie Tuttle...!'

'Leave the rules, leave the rules!'

The TV director looked to Susan, who was clapping and grinning at Frank. After basking in the atmosphere for a few more seconds, she gave the man the nod and he cut the transmission.

The director took the mic back from Frank. The noise carried on outside, but the Media Centre had fallen silent again.

Harrington wrestled one arm free and pointed at Frank. 'You are in big trouble, mate. How dare you come in here and... and disrupt what is the most... most monumental—'

'Harrington,' snapped the head of a Chinese brewer. 'Shut up please. This man is making the correct point.'

'How could we miss this in our market research?' asked a German woman, the CEO of a major automobile manufacturer.

All 12 dignitaries glared at Harrington, who shrank where he stood.

'Mr Tuttle,' the Chinese VIP said, 'you have made our eyes see. We will need to think again about our strategy for marketing in football.'

'So, the rules change, the deal,' asked Claire tentatively. 'It's all off?'

'Dead as Dillinger,' confirmed the American, who then turned to Harrington and said definitively, '*No deal.*'

The man now turned to Frank. 'Son, I think I speak for all of us when I say that you sure opened our eyes today. Taught us a little something.'

Frank looked away bashfully.

'So now we're gonna completely rethink our sponsorship strategy. It's gonna revolve around a new word: *family.*'

The other 11 VIPs all murmured their agreement.

'All our commercials, billboards, slogans... family, family, family. So thanks a bunch for your help.' He shook Frank's hand then turned to his business partners. 'We best get moving, you guys. We got work to do.'

With that, and with no further word to their host Harrington, the 12 dignitaries headed for the Media Centre's exit.

Frank and Claire looked at each other.

'Well,' said Claire. 'That's... better.'

Frank tilted his head. 'Guess so.'

Harrington, stunned to see his VIPs leaving, turned his fury onto Susan. 'This is *your* fault. You let Tuttle and these lunatics in here. How could you—'

'Oh, put a sock in it, Harrington,' snapped Susan. 'Haven't you worked it out yet?'

Harrington's eyes widened. 'No... Surely not, Susan.'

'Yes. I set it all up.'

Harrington was trembling with anger. 'You are done, Susan Clyne. The FA won't stand for this – you are finished with them.'

'Good. It'll save me the trouble of resigning.'

Exasperated, Harrington tried to salvage something from the situation by chasing after his VIPs.

'Please,' the former England goalkeeper and captain cried. 'Don't leave, we can fix this. We can still do business together.'

But the last of them exited without looking back.

Undeterred, Harrington carried on into the corridor after them, launching into a humiliating display of posturing and begging.

Meanwhile, Gary had approached Susan.

'So, I'm still on for Monday, right?' he asked nervously.

Susan fixed Gary with a cold stare. 'Gareth, would you like to know why you've never been able to get onto our coaching scheme?'

Gary gulped. 'Why?'

'You couldn't pass the part of the application that covers integrity.'

Gary's jaw dropped. Thinking fast, he bolted from the room. 'Mr Harrington,' he called. 'I can help you, wait.'

Stu Donaldson, denied his chance to address the nation, now felt the need to step forward and comment on the unfurling events.

'This is some messed up shit going on here today,' he said.

No one disagreed with him.

So Frank, Claire, Kevin, Donno and Fullarton were now left with Susan. All were waiting for answers from her.

Susan looked anxiously towards the FA comms team, weighing up what she could say in front of them.

While she was still deliberating, one of her team said, 'Hi again, Frank.'

Startled, Frank peered across the room. A young woman was waving at him from an end-desk. It was Cassandra, the hen from last night, much more conservatively dressed now. He recognised some of her friends, too.

Frank waved back. He tried to get his head around it. 'You know,' he said to Susan, 'I *thought* I couldn't remember there being any VIP bar prize for that fantasy football game.'

'That's because the prize doesn't exist,' Susan said. 'But you *do* exist, Frank. The only one who could save football.'

'*Me*?' asked Frank.

'Why Frank?' asked Claire.

'Yeah, what makes old Franko so special?' asked Kevin.

'I think I can shed some light on that,' said a voice from the doorway.

They all turned to see Albert Tuttle entering. He was dressed in his full Chelsea Pensioner splendour: black gold-trimmed tricorne hat, long scarlet-red coat with gold buttons, black military trousers and shoes, medals pinned to his chest.

Everyone took a respectful step back, except for Fullarton and Susan, who approached Albert and bowed, both saying, 'Your Excellency, it is an honour.'

The others all shared a bemused look.

Frank said, 'Dad...?'

Albert approached his son. 'You've done a good job today, Francis.'

Frank was embarrassed and pleased at the same time. 'Aw, Dad, come on...'

'My boy, I'm afraid I haven't been entirely honest about your heritage.'

THE FIRST thing Susan did upon re-entering Conference Room One was to turn off the screen that was still showing Pete Harrington's rule changes presentation. The mere sight of it made her feel nauseous.

She, Frank, Kevin, Claire, Fullarton and Albert were all now sitting at one end of the long table, munching on what remained of the fruit and sipping still-warm coffee. Donno had been asked to wait outside, but when the ex-footballer had realised that the FA's communications team was mostly young women, he had been only too happy to comply.

'Well, it's been quite a day for all of us, hasn't it?' smiled Albert. He turned to Kevin. 'Mr Maxwell, it is an honour to share your company. Don't listen to the small-minded who focus on irrelevancies – you are undoubtedly the finest footballing talent of your generation.'

Kevin was overwhelmed into a flattered silence.

'And Miss Butterfield, I can't thank you enough for your help today. From what I've heard, the game is eternally in your debt.'

Claire blushed away from such commendation. But she was also puzzled. 'Heard, Mr Tuttle? From who?'

'Not *Gary?*' asked Frank.

'No no. From Sister Susan.'

'What you mean, "sister"?' asked Kevin. 'Are you lot, like, related?'

Albert, Susan and Fullarton all chuckled. 'Not by blood,' Fullarton said.

'What then?' asked Claire.

Albert shuffled in his seat, readying himself. 'I am The Captain, the highest member of The Custodians,' he declared.

'You *are?*' blurted Frank.

'Yes, Francis.'

'So, these "Custodians" really do exist?' asked Claire.

'Yes. We have done since the dawn of association football. Our membership has grown over the years and we are not only in football-related institutions like the FA, but in all manner of private and public organisations. And I, in fact, am descended from the original Captain, who led that first team of 11 men in making the game's rules official, all those years ago in the Freemasons Tavern.'

Claire and Kevin looked at Frank.

'So, Franko,' Kevin chuckled, 'this means you're like football royalty. No wonder you've got all those bonkers-but-brilliant tactics.'

Frank was flabbergasted. He went to open his mouth, but Albert raised a finger. 'In a moment, Francis.'

Albert continued. 'As you've seen, as well as drawing up the basic rules, the founding Custodians took precautions to protect the game. They were concerned – rightly, as it turns out – that one day football's power would start to shift to those who only see it as a money-making enterprise. That it would become unbalanced and tip too far over from a sport into a business.'

Frank and Claire nodded in recognition.

'So they constructed two safeguards designed to combat such an occurrence and hid them in London, then wrote a set of challenges for whoever was worthy enough to follow them and find the safeguards, which the Custodians named Halves. They concluded The Campaign with an insight into the true meaning of football, to be used as an additional weapon.'

The others nodded again.

Albert shifted his weight and continued. 'The original Campaign was written on a parchment and held in the Football Association's headquarters. It has been held here ever since and The Custodians' scribes have updated it several times, to align it to football's changes and to match current technology.

'The Campaign could only be activated when two things happened. First, a senior Custodian,' he indicated Susan, 'must deem that the game is under sufficient threat. Then The Custodians must identify a worthy subject to embark on The Campaign.' He nodded at his bemused son.

Susan took over. 'Pete Harrington knew that The Campaign could jeopardise his plan. He isn't a Custodian – thank God – but he was well aware of the rumours and was cautious enough to take them seriously. So, he insisted that all FA hardware that could conceivably contain The Campaign be magnetically erased. He gave me that order yesterday over lunch, when he finally revealed to me the full extent of his plot – and I knew I had to step in. That's when I got a call made to Frank luring him to a bar, where I know the owners and so could set up the prizes, and I arranged for the tablet and some members of my comms team to be there to make sure that Frank not only found the tablet, but didn't get a chance to hand it in to the staff – not that they ever knew the full story, of course.'

Claire had been itching to speak.

'But why did you sack me?' She failed to keep the hurt from her voice. 'Because of my *blog*?'

'I'm sorry, Claire,' Susan said with genuine feeling. 'It was never a real sacking. I didn't even know you had a blog.'

Claire scowled.

'I saw you as the ideal person to help Frank complete The Campaign,' Susan continued, 'so I needed to get you outside and together with him. And I knew that if you thought you'd been fired it would spur you on.'

'You couldn't have just *told* me? Or Frank, for that matter?'

'The Custodians' decrees forbid any members from helping those who are embarking on The Campaign or even letting them know that we know that they're doing it – it would undermine The Campaign's intention of only being solved by someone worthy. I'm afraid my hands were tied.'

Susan smiled weakly. Claire remained stony-faced.

Susan cleared her throat and carried on. 'I was relying on you and Frank crossing paths and once I had Gary on board I planned to use him to push you together, but in the end you all found each other anyway.'

'Wait, so what was the deal with Gary?' asked a confused Kevin. Susan explained that when Harrington found out that the tablet was missing (and had gone missing only by accident, Susan managed to convince him), and that it had landed in a member of the public's hands, Harrington insisted that Susan find someone she could use to get it back. Her hasty search led her to Gary.

'But while I gave Harrington the impression I was using Gary to get the tablet back, or at least stall you guys until the announcement was already made...'

'You were actually texting him instructions to help us,' Claire finished.

Susan nodded. 'And keeping tabs on your progress. Although it was still up to the three of you to solve it – I don't know the content of The Campaign, only The Captain and the Custodian scribes do. Plus, I had to keep the RCE people on you – they report back to Harrington, not me, and I couldn't let him suspect anything. At one point I thought all was lost, I didn't know that Brother William had found out through his own sources that the tablet was missing and was following his protocol to get it back.

'So, when Gary told me that Brother Will had recovered the tablet, I thought the game was up. But then he updated me that you'd switched it – and that was great work, Claire, by the way.' Susan smiled at her former employee again, but Claire still had no warmth to return.

Susan sighed. She had said her piece.

Now Frank wanted answers.

'So, it was you who called my mobile, wasn't it?' he asked Susan.

'Yes, using the FA's voice scrambling technology. I'm so sorry about what happened with Ian. As you know, he wasn't harmed, he was having a great time. Like I said, I had to show Harrington that I was doing *something* so he wouldn't get suspicious, and I also needed to give you your own motivation to take The Campaign seriously. I... I'm sorry.'

Frank had nothing to say to this.

Then he asked, 'But why didn't you just sabotage the deal yourself? Why did you need me at all?'

Susan glanced at Fullarton and Albert. 'Because after all the recent football scandals and underachievement, people needed their faith in the game renewed. Months of build-up to an announcement and then nothing would only fuel their cynicism. They needed a hero, someone to remind them about the good in the game. They needed you, Frank, and *your* announcement. People are susceptible to going along with the crowd, and that can be a bad thing – but they *can* be herded towards the good, if they have the right shepherd.'

Claire asked, 'But why the need for the big brainwashing cover-up with the footballers? Did you really think they might rebel against the rule changes? Because from what Stu Donno told us they were pretty much unfazed as long as their wages didn't go down.'

'It wasn't so much that,' said Susan. 'It was more the chance of them spilling the beans on social media; the conditioning repressed what is, for a lot of footballers, a very strong urge to broadcast every aspect of their lives to anyone who will pay attention.'

They all looked at Kevin, who was tapping away at his phone.

'Eh?' The footballer looked up. 'Oh, don't worry, I in't saying owt about this. Just sharing a YouTube clip of a cat scoring a free kick.'

Claire smirked at Kevin then said to Susan, 'But the Boy Wonder here being in Wembley today and being immune to the hypnotism...?'

'Just a quirk of fate – what we Custodians call "things evening out over the season." Although he *was* useful when I found out you had nearly given up and I needed a way for you to grasp the extent of the danger – I knew that as soon as he read the PowerPoint slides he would send you photos of them. And as for his immunity to the hypnotism, Kevin is simply the exception that proves the rule.'

'Better believe I'm exceptional.' Kevin said, putting his phone down. 'Did you *see* me out there on the pitch?'

No one deemed a response to this necessary. Claire had more to get off her chest. 'There's just one more thing I don't understand. Why did The Custodians not just make the two Halves part of the regular rules? Why the need and... and the *risk* for a convoluted quest like The Campaign in the first place?'

'Two reasons,' Albert said. 'One is as we've been trying to illustrate: the purity of the game depends on those who are devoted to it possessing the integrity to understand the need for fairness *without* it being made an explicit law. That faith is what gives the game its power. The two Halves represent the game's soul: everyone should receive the same treatment, and all concerned should agree on what that treatment is. Together, these form the essence of fairness. And like any soul, their power comes from being kept safely inside. Under the earth in the nation's capital and inside every person who loves football.

'The other reason for hiding the Halves, and for the existence of The Campaign, has to do with something I must now tell my son.'

Frank looked imploringly at his father.

'You deserve an explanation, Francis,' Albert said. 'You see, when Sister Susan called me yesterday afternoon, I had no doubts about who to recommend to take The Campaign. You have many special attributes, my boy, and together they mean you fit the criteria.'

'Eh?' said Frank. 'What criteria?'

'You're the son of a high-level Custodian,' said Albert, reeling a list off his fingers. 'You have a unique football coaching ability, you were dismissed from a coaching role by the governing body when they needed you the most, your offspring plays the game and, perhaps most importantly of all, you love football and would do anything to protect it. In short, everything The Prophecy foretells about The Chosen One.'

'Er, hold on a minute,' said Kevin. 'Prophecy? *Chosen One?*'

'Yes,' said Albert. 'The one who would complete The Campaign and bring balance to football.'

'Prophesised by the game's founding fathers,' added Fullarton, backed up by a nodding Susan.

Frank, Claire and Kevin shared a bewildered look.

'I don't know about you lot,' said Frank finally, 'but I could murder a pint.'

The whole gang – Frank, Claire, Kevin, Susan, Fullarton and Albert, with Donno in tow – were making their way through the labyrinth of Wembley corridors towards a back exit.

Kevin and Donno led, followed by Albert and Frank, with Susan, Claire and Fullarton bringing up the rear.

Susan was sheepish around Claire. 'I'm going to make sure that the FA reverses your sacking first thing Monday. Sorry again that I had to do that.'

285

'Forget it, Susan.'

Susan was relieved. 'Great, I'm glad we can put this behind us.'

'No, I mean forget the job. I don't want it anymore.'

'What?' Susan hadn't expected that.

Claire held up her thumb and forefinger a short distance apart. 'You came this close to destroying football.'

'Yes, but in the end I—'

'I'm sorry, but I can't work for someone who would take that risk.'

Claire walked on ahead.

Fullarton glanced pityingly at his saddened Custodian Sister, then caught up with Claire.

'Miss Butterfield – Claire,' he said. 'That was quite a move you pulled outside the Freemasons Arms, swapping the tablets.'

'It was necessary,' she replied bluntly, treating Fullarton with the same contempt she had for Susan – lumping them together as Custodian co-conspirators.

'You must understand,' he said, responding to her tone, 'that I've been just as much in the dark about all this as you have.'

Claire studied him. When she concluded that he was telling the truth, she softened.

'I'd heard stories about The Custodians, everyone at the FA has.'

'Naturally.'

'But I didn't realise they were actually real.'

'Very real. And as today's events have proved, very necessary.'

Claire hesitated. 'How does someone... I mean, could I join?'

Fullarton smiled. 'First, you must be recommended by an existing member.'

'Oh yeah?' It was Claire's turn to smile.

'But aren't you more concerned about being out of work?'

How could Claire forget? 'Oh yeah, *that*.'

'Why don't you send me your CV? My email address is on my card.'

'Really? Switch to the Department of Fair Play?'

'I think you're just what we need – in fact, I think that *you* could have a crucial role to play in the future of football.'

'*Me?*'

Fullarton looked at her pointedly.

'But Fullarton – William, I'm not very, I'm not the most... how do I put this...'

'By-the-book?'

'Yes.'

'Claire, I'm beginning to think that that is exactly what we need.'

Claire reflected. And smiled again.

Meanwhile, Frank was speaking to his father.

'I can't believe it was Pete Harrington all along. Probably the biggest England legend ever.'

Albert was troubled. 'It's unfortunate how greed can corrupt. And to think, when you came to see me earlier today, I had been arguing passionately that he was England's greatest ever captain...' He shook his head. 'But as you've seen, so long as there are people who love football it will rise above impure forces. Just like in the game's early days, when local pubs organised the matches and would provide their grounds to play on and their taverns for drinking in afterwards. When these breweries started to have too much influence over the running of the game, shaping it to serve their own profits, a group of men fought back.'

'The Custodians,' said Frank.

'Yes. So, you see, this is all just a case of history repeating itself.'

After a few more steps, Frank asked, 'So you never thought to tell me about any of this?'

'Francis, it's not that I didn't want to. I suspected from a young age that you might turn out to be The Chosen One. And the way the game has been heading, The Custodians knew that it was only a matter of time before The

Campaign would be needed – if it hadn't been the events of today, it would have been something else.'

'But Dad, me? *Really*? Come on, I'm just a regular bloke.'

'But *being* regular, one of the people – that's part of it.'

It was all too much for Frank. He rubbed his temples.

'So why didn't you say anything when we saw you earlier today? Why didn't you help us more directly? I thought that you... that you were...'

'Just a senile old man spouting gibberish?'

Frank hung his head in shame.

'Don't worry, son. I *was* being intentionally ambiguous. I had to be, for the same reason I couldn't ever tell you about The Custodians and my suspicions about your importance to football. It's the same reason that Sister Susan couldn't be more upfront with Claire. You had to prove yourself on your own without any assurances, with only your own belief and devotion to guide you – the most we could do was to place things in your path and then trust that you would do what was necessary. You needed faith, the faith that every fan must cling to so that they keep supporting their team through thick and thin, turning up again and again despite past heartaches and the inevitability of more heartache to come.'

Frank was sheepish. 'But it wasn't really *me*, was it? I mean, I didn't exactly work alone...'

Albert laughed. 'What manager does? Francis, you were the one who convinced others to follow you, and you were the one who made the speech that convinced those unscrupulous billionaires to leave football alone. I'm proud of you.'

That made Frank feel better.

'So now that I *do* know about these Custodians and how I fit in... what happens next?'

'Next... well, next we have a lot to talk about.'

His father winked mischievously.

288

Susan had caught up with the two Tuttle men. 'Sorry to interrupt,' she said.

'Quite alright, my dear,' said Albert. 'So sad that you have to leave your job. The FA is a fine organisation, despite the odd bad egg getting into the basket.'

Susan waved dismissively. 'It's fine. I'll find another comms role, one that doesn't make me work Saturdays. I want to start going to football matches with my family again – enjoy the game, like I used to, before it became just a job.'

Albert nodded.

Susan now turned to Frank. 'You know, we could use you on that coaching scheme, the one Gary was so keen to get onto.'

Frank was startled. 'Um, thanks, but isn't it a "young" coaches course? Hardly *young*, am I? I'm the wrong side of 40.'

Susan smiled. 'I'm talking about you being one of the ones *coaching* the coaches. Frank, with your ingenious tactical brain, I'm even going to put you in touch with the head of UEFA's licencing committee. I'm sure he'd be very interested in having a chat.'

Frank was so overwhelmed he could only stammer incoherently.

'I think what Frank's trying to say is, "thank you,"' grinned Albert.

At the front of the pack, Donno and Kevin were having a rare conversation that didn't involve bants.

'Whoa,' Kevin was saying, scanning his phone. 'Every Premier League manager I know has texted me.'

Donno grinned. 'Better dust off those football boots, Mini.'

'I were good out there, weren't I?'

'Yeah, you were alright. What you want, a medal?'

Kevin beamed, knowing that the understatement and sarcasm were just masking genuine approval from a fellow professional.

'It'll be sound to get back in the dressing room, among the lads again.'

'Blatantly,' agreed Donno. 'Take my advice, Min: carry on playing as long as you can, 'cause when you stop, you proper miss it. This media lark's not the same.'

'But I suppose you're vexed about not getting on camera back there?'

'Nah,' said Donno. 'I still got paid. And your boy gave it the best bants ever. It was, like, *meaningful* bants.' He turned around to face Frank. 'Nice one.'

Frank caught up with the two footballers. 'Right chaps, pub then, is it?'

'Great idea,' said Claire. She was looking at Kevin.

The group had reached the back exit to the outside world. Donno grasped its handle and turned to Frank.

'Forget the pub – I know somewhere much better.'

28

MEMBERS of the public are never usually invited to a footballer's party. The guests tend to be players, the odd young manager and a host of assorted celebrities along with their hangers-on – agents, publicists, stylists.

But that Saturday was an exception. That Saturday, recently retired striker Stuart Donaldson flung the doors of his luxury home open to those who had spent the day fighting so hard to save the game. On that day, and late into the night, they and their guests were taken into football's inner circle and treated as equals.

Frank Tuttle – showered, shaved and in fresh jeans and shirt – was standing in the garden beside Donno's swimming pool, sipping a bottle of lager. The mansion was bursting with guests and waiting staff; a full bar stood across from a DJ booth where a famous young man wearing Ray-Bans manned a laptop.

Frank was smiling while watching his friends Joel and Andy in the pool. Each had a lingerie model on his shoulders and the two girls were grappling with each other. Frank shook his head and glanced across the water at Claire and Kevin, who were cuddled up on a sun lounger, laughing about something. Frank caught Claire's eye and she waved. Kevin raised his glass of vodka and called out, 'Gaffer.'

Frank grinned and raised his own drink.

He looked to the patio and saw Fullarton and Susan sharing a bottle of wine and speaking in hushed, scheming tones – they seemed to be arguing, and glanced between Frank and Claire as they spoke. Not far from those two, Claire and Kevin's fathers were getting to know each other, reminiscing about going to football games in the 1970s.

Further afield, sitting at a table on the decking, Frank's dad Albert was regaling a group of footballers about how brutal the game was in his day. Frank chuckled to himself as the players winced at Albert's graphic stories.

Frank finished his panoramic by glancing idly back inside. He drained the last of his lager and wondered whether to go get another or walk over to the sun loungers. While he was staring back into the house, someone familiar came into view.

Bethan.

Their eyes met and Frank raised his hand to slowly wave.

'Dad!' Ian came rushing out from behind his mother and straight through into the garden. His father hugged the boy on impact.

'What's all this?' asked Frank. 'Bit underage for a do like this aren't you, young man?'

'Kevin invited me, he tweeted me.' Now out of his oversized football kit, Ian looked so grown up, with his smart polo shirt buttoned up and way too much gel in his hair.

Frank looked over at the footballer. 'Oh, Kevin invited you, did he?' he asked loudly.

'Hey, I thought it was about time the kid had his first bevvy.'

Claire hit Kevin on the arm.

'Hi, Ian,' she called over.

Ian stuck shyly to his dad and waved.

Bethan had caught up. She was looking pretty in a summer dress.

'Hi,' Frank said. 'Glad you came.'

'Yes, well, after that speech on TV... Besides, what girl could turn down a celebrity party? I saw three soap stars just taking off my coat.'

'*You're* a celebrity now, Dad,' declared Ian. 'Your speech has gone viral.'

'Oh,' said Frank, unsure how to feel. 'That's... great?'

Ian nodded vigorously. 'Is it true you were mobbed trying to leave Wembley by people asking for selfies?'

Bethan laughed gently at Frank's embarrassment.

Instead of answering Ian, Frank moved the conversation on by turning to Kevin and Claire. 'This is Bethan,' he called out. Then he looked straight at her. 'My wife.'

Bethan smiled slowly. She exchanged waves with her husband's two new friends.

'So,' said Frank.

'Yes,' said Bethan.

'Go on you two, get a drink or something,' said Ian impatiently. 'I wanna see if Donno's got a Playstation so I can give Kevin a rematch on *Ultima Soc.*'

With that, their son left them and made his way around the pool, staring at Joel and Andy's antics in the water along the way.

'I guess a drink is a good idea,' Bethan said to Frank.

'Yeah,' Frank agreed, 'I reckon it is.' He smiled. 'Come on, I'll escort you to the bar.'

He led her away. As they went, Frank tentatively reached for Bethan's hand.

At his touch, she took his hand in hers.

So that was the first day of the new football season. In the end, it was much the same as it always is. Some fans were pleased with their team's result, others were disappointed. Many of the favourites won, but there were upsets. Arguments broke out over refereeing decisions. There was controversy, debate. But through it all everyone was together; everyone was equal, and everyone was happy.

It was good.

It was right.

It was beautiful.

29

D AWN.

At the same time that Donno's party was entering the karaoke, conga, make-your own-cocktail-from-what's-left phase, Pete Harrington was standing alone, sipping from a glass of 16-year-old single malt Cragganmore.

He stood on his penthouse's roof terrace, admiring the spectacular view across London. Wembley was visible in the distance, the first hint of daylight rising behind the stadium.

Staring at the clear summer's morning, Harrington let himself sink into a calm optimism. It was partly fuelled by the hope that a new day brings, partly by the nearly empty bottle sitting on his desk back inside.

But mostly it was an internet search that had perked him up.

He had been angry. Furious! He had badly wanted today to go ahead and struggled to accept that the rewards were no longer forthcoming. His legacy would have to wait, but he found that what really riled him was that he would no longer be able to buy a new Learjet. What if the one he already owned broke down?

But now Harrington was smiling again. He stumbled back inside to his laptop, nearly tripping on the way.

He unlocked the screen. Yes, he had come to realise that there were so many more options out there.

One was covered with green felt.

One was hard and red.

Another, white with two red strips stitched around it.

Another wasn't even round, but egg-shaped.

So many alternatives. So many possibilities.

Harrington took another sip and his smile vanished.

THE END

Coming soon from Jonathan Last

Diary of a
Young Filmmaker

It's 1995, and 16-year-old social misfit Stephen Ricketts is determined to be a movie director. He's made enough no-budget splatter shorts now and has decided to just go for it and make his first feature film.

But it isn't going to be easy. Not only does he have few resources beyond a Hi8 camcorder, some equally inept friends and a bucket of fake blood, he also has to contend with raging hormones, peer pressure, trying to get into pubs, winging his A Levels, and coming up with ways to raise funds for the movie – no matter how humiliating.

Diary of a Young Filmmaker is a heartfelt coming of age comedy about always chasing your dream, even when you trip up at every step.

Printed in Great Britain
by Amazon

51565953R00180